Redemption

Where Darkness Reigns

Book 4

Josie's Story

By: Mary Reason Theriot

Dedication

Without the love and support of my family and friends, I would not have pursued this new path in life. I would especially like to thank those that have proofread copy after copy, to give me their honest opinion of the books.

Theresa, thank you so much for your continued encouragement. Without you, some of the characters would not have "come to life."

To my wonderful husband, Malwen, your continued love and support mean the world to me.   I don't know what I would do without you in my life. These books wouldn't be what they are without you pushing me forward.

To my fans, I would like to offer a special thank you for your continued support.

Dear Reader,

There are some characters that I loved so much that they had to be brought back. *Where Darkness Reigns* contains some of my favorite characters who had to meet and join forces with other characters.

Bianca Honore's story begins in <u>A Deadly Combination</u>, but when she partners with Joshua Savoie in <u>Seduced by Voodoo</u> you learn that her heart and soul are just as black as the voodoo she practices.

Joshua Savoie's story begins in <u>CarnEvil of Souls</u>, but, as in life, true evil never dies but remains hidden until the opportune moment. Joshua comes back in <u>Seduced by Voodoo</u> to see his diabolical plan come to fruition.

Rayne Simoneaud is betrayed by her lover, Dominic St Germaine, in <u>A Deadly Combination</u>, but seeks out her revenge in <u>Seduced by Voodoo</u>.

Josie Bellows is a young vamp from <u>CarnEvil of Souls</u> who searches for the vampire who turned her so that she can find <u>Redemption</u>.

Detective Grace Hutcherson has fought vampires in <u>CarnEvil of Souls</u>, survived the battle of good versus evil in <u>Seduced by Voodoo</u> and now finds herself plagued by <u>Haunted Visions</u>.

***

CarnEvil of Souls – Joshua's Story
A Deadly Combination – Bianca's Story
Seduced by Voodoo – Lovers Unite
Redemption – Josie's Story
Haunted Visions – Detective Grace Hutcherson's Story

ISBN-10: 1-945393-46-7
ISBN-13: 978-1-945393-46-4

Also Available by Mary Reason Theriot:

The Hideaway
The Traveler
Dr. Frankenstein
Above Suspicion
Horror in the Night
Deadly Seduction
Echoes on the Bayou
Seven Deadly Sins
A Deadly Combination
Seduced by Voodoo
CarnEvil of Souls
Haunted Visions
Unrequited Love
No One Left
Love's Embrace

www.maryreasontheriot.com

Chapter 1
New Orleans, Louisiana 1867

As the master vampire looked over at his mistress, he asked, "Did you have success this time, mon cher?"

Ezrielle observed the man who had become her most recent lover and replied, "Soon, mon cher, soon. This little experiment of mine was not as successful as I hoped."

Ezrielle snapped her fingers and a creature walked from the shadows. "I will call this one Grunch."

He looked at the creature and was taken aback by its grotesque features. "It is but a goat in the body of a man!"

"Ah, but this particular one is unique. At one time, he was a vampire. And this creature craves human blood."

Pulling her into his arms, he whispered, "I am beginning to lose faith in your abilities, mon cher. This creature you created took no imagination at all."

Furious, Ezrielle pushed him away, "You dare question my powers!" Tsking him, she added, "That is not wise."

The creature's eyes turned red, and his true form took shape. She could see the outline of the evil lurking beneath him, daring to break free from its human constraints. "It is not wise to threaten me, my pet. The Dukes of Hell may have granted you immortality, but with one bite, I can send you back to your maker."

Ezrielle attempted to placate him, "These are nothing but simple experiments." She quickly said, "I still have other creatures that I am working on. My Rougarou is more than enough to protect your children."

The master nodded in approval, "My Joshua needs some for his own purposes. I will pay handsomely for his and mine as well."

"As you wish. Come tonight and claim your Rougarou. I will make sure that the packs for each of you will obey your commands."

The master looked over at the creatures Ezrielle had created in disgust, "You know, cher, I do believe the civilized world would frown upon what you do here."

"Ah, but the civilized world will have a hard time finding me. The only way you can find me is if I allow it. Just remember, if I truly wanted to, I could keep you from finding me as well."

Chapter 2
New Orleans - 1870

Tyler immediately spotted the woman across the street. She was the fairest maiden he had ever seen. Her beauty had him mesmerized; she beguiled him with her bewitching eyes and long flowing hair twisting in the wind.

When she beckoned him to her, he went willingly. The distance between them closed fast as her beauty pulled him to her. He dared not utter a word as she slipped her hand in his. She looked up at him with such sweet innocence; it took his breath away.

Unable to stop himself, his mouth seized hers in a kiss that rocked him to the core. Her deep, ruby lips were succulent, beyond anything he'd ever known. He tasted their sweetness, and they made him crave even more.

He entwined his fingers in her hair to bring her closer to him. She smiled up at him as the energy around them turned frenetic. Being young and inexperienced with women, he was clumsy and unsure how to handle himself in the presence of such a beautiful woman.

He was drawn to her, wanting to grant her every wish. She pulled away from him and walked ahead, leading him away like a puppy dog deep into the swamps and away from the town.

As her long cloak flowed in the wind, he saw a glimpse of her body. His breath caught at the mere sight of a bare ankle.

When they entered a clearing in the swamp, she pulled him back into her arms. He moaned in sheer ecstasy as her body pressed against his. Kissing him fervently, she took everything he had to give. Desire took over all conscious thought.

Without warning, her passionate kisses turned cold. Torches broke the tree line and bathed them both in the flickering light. Chants filled the air. He looked at her beseechingly, unsure of what was happening.

Tyler was confused as she ran her finger along his strong jaw line and said, "I was ruined by a man much like you once, mon cher. He soon learned the cost of betraying me." Kissing him once more, she added, "I decided then and there to teach all men a lesson. I would no longer allow them to use women, ruin their lives, and toss them aside like an old tattered rag."

The homunculi, evil little creatures created by an alchemist, appeared out of nowhere and formed a tight circle around them. The creatures were barely four feet tall and all bone, muscle, and sinew. Pure terror paralyzed Tyler.

From the darkness, a vile creature, standing just over five feet tall and covered with fine hair, appeared. It had cloven hooves for feet and the short tail of a goat.

Even the head of the creature resembled more of a goat than a man, complete with a small pair of horns protruding from the top of its head. A large pair of red eyes glowed in the dark as it moved closer to him. He bit back a scream as the vile creature opened its mouth and saw it was full of long, sharp fangs dripping with blood, to let out an ear piercing scream.

The woman greeted the creature, "Welcome my pet." She turned to Tyler and said, "This is one of my latest creations. It is a Grunch, half-man and half-goat. He and a few of his brothers protect the perimeters of my land." She ran a finger along Tyler's strong jaw line and added, "But you, cher, will be something so much more." From the darkness, even more creatures arrived. These creatures had the shape of half-wolf and half-man. With a sinister smile, she taunted Tyler, "These are my Rougarou. They will be your brothers." She looked over at the Rougarou forming a circle around them. "Welcome your new brother, my loves."

As if sensing his discomfort, the voodoo priestess ran her hands over his well-defined body. "You have the Dukes of Hell and alchemists to thank for my powers and pets." As she stretched languidly in the moonlight, she explained, "The Dukes of Hell gave me what I desired most you see – immortality." Reaching behind her, he watched as she pulled a raven out of a cage. He was disgusted as he watched her cut open its chest and remove its still beating heart with a long nail. She ran the bloody muscle along Tyler's lips as he tried to avoid the ghastly thing. "For you see, when a woman stays young and beautiful forever; the world will be hers."

Tyler watched in horror as she swallowed the beating heart in one gulp. Once more, he tried to free himself, unsure how he'd landed in this nightmare. As the torches were extinguished, and the darkness enveloped the area, he felt the icy grasp of death near him. Looking up to the full moon, he questioned what he'd done to deserve this.

He turned his gaze to the woman. This time, he didn't see her for the beautiful woman she portrayed, but instead, the woman she truly was. His eyes were no longer clouded with desire and infatuation.

As the chanting continued, a piercing cold spread throughout him. Before long, the cold turned into a burning fire. The blood inside of his veins felt as if it were literally boiling. As the chanting increased, rising in tempo, his skin began to melt off and was replaced with fur. He screamed in agony as his body was transformed into the hideous Rougarou.

Chapter 3

New Orleans – Present Day

Josie felt as if Tyler and she were alone among the living, finding no solace. All they had in this world was each other. Neither had been given a choice when their lives were cursed.

She rolled over and stared at his sleeping form. The sunlight quickly faded from the boards that barely covered the windows. This was the life they were forced to live now; they had to hide in abandoned buildings until they could find a place to call their own. She was ready to settle down and move onto the next phase of their plan. With the world finally rid of Joshua, it was time to find their makers and end their lives as well.

She watched as the shadows began to lengthen as the sun set. Soon, the moonlight would erase all evidence of the sun, and then, it would be their time.

Sitting up, she struggled to brush out the tangles in her hair and longed for a hot bath. It was so easy to miss the simple things in life when you no longer had them.

Josie stretched languidly as Tyler smiled over at her. He brought her close to kiss her. "I don't know about you, but I am famished," he whispered in her ear.

"Do you have a preference on what you eat tonight?" Unlike her, Tyler refused to feed on human flesh. She fed with him, but when the hunger for human blood became too much for her, she only sought out those who deserved to die, the dregs of humanity. And there was an unending supply in New Orleans.

Tyler said, "There are a few cattle not far from here." They must be careful on how many they fed on this close to the city, though. In these parts, there were few wolves or larger animals that could bring down the number of cattle needed to satisfy their hunger. Even the coyotes here didn't kill the number Josie and Tyler needed to survive. Just for him to transform, it took a great deal of energy.

Even when Josie belonged with the CarnEvil of Souls, a carnival of traveling vampires, she wouldn't kill a human, unless, of course, they deserved to die. She could partially drain a person without them remembering anything. That was the master vampire of the CarnEvil's, Joshua, first mistake - he left behind too many unanswered questions. Families came searching for their missing loved ones. Although they did not leave corpses behind, families still sought closure.

Some nights, Josie wondered if her family mourned over her disappearance. Did they go to the ends of the earth looking for her?

After the sun set, they prepared to hunt. Josie exclaimed, "Maybe tonight we can take a dip in the river."

Tyler gave her a smirk and said, "We are a mess aren't we? I think enough time has passed where I can start looking at houses."

***

With the decision being made to search for a house, Tyler began perusing the classifieds. He found a few near where he believed Ezrielle hid; still, there was a chance that after all this time she had moved on. He prayed that she was somewhere in New Orleans though. This was her home; she had her followers here, and he couldn't see her leaving this town where she was worshiped.

Tyler hoped that moving back to New Orleans would help him remember his past, the time before Ezrielle entered his life. Before her, his life was a distant, faded dream. He had no recollection of anything before she cursed him. She erased all memories he'd had before he lived with her. She wanted his world to revolve around her, but she didn't count on his strong persona, or his refusal to abide by her wishes.

He knew that she was still alive. Experience had taught him that evil did not die; instead, it just lay dormant, waiting for the perfect moment to strike. He must be prepared, however. Her powers of darkness were strong, and right now, she was beyond his reach. He would be a fool to challenge her wrath at present.

Tyler watched as Josie walked to him in the moonlight. Her beautiful face, bathed in the glow of the full moon, smiled at him as she neared. He kept the shadow of fear that lived deep inside of him hidden from her. They were foolish to contemplate searching for those who'd cursed them. It could not come to a good end.

Chapter 4

Cold, a bone chilling cold, settled deep in Jenny's body.

Her head throbbed as a vile stench filled the room. Images floated through her mind as she tried to remember what happened.

In the distance, she heard the whine of a motor. She tried to make out her surroundings, but she was enveloped in an all-consuming darkness.

Just blinking her eyes caused her severe agony. She reached up to touch her face and gasped. The simple movement of her arms wracked her body with extreme pain.

Cold, clammy sweat began to cover her body. She shuddered in fear as she reached out to feel what could be around her. Panic gripped her heart at what she found.

She was trapped, caught in a cage, just like an animal. The bars of the cage were cold against her fingers.

She breathed in the air once more and gagged on the stench. What was that smell? It smelled like something was rotten or possibly decaying, as if something had died in here.

A rustling sound caught her attention. Was someone else held captive in this room? No, the noise was moving closer to her.

Her stomach was in knots as the sound moved even closer. She tried to scoot further away from the sound, but the cage was too small. She winced in pain from the attempt to move. How could she be in so much pain, yet still be alive?

An image invaded her mind. Hands were grabbing at her, and alligator skin boots were kicking at her body. Who did this? Who brought her to this place?

She remembered seeing the man's face in the bar. He looked so handsome and mysterious, dressed in black. She should know better than to fall for such a handsome man. Why would someone that good-looking even be interested in someone as plain as her?

The whining of an engine came closer. A truck's motor rumbled somewhere in the distance as maniacal laughter filled the air. She swallowed back a scream as a pair of red eyes glowed in the dark. Suddenly, even more glowing red eyes surrounded her cage. Fear had her paralyzed as the creatures moved in closer.

Terror snaked down her body as she closed her eyes tightly. Her mind begged to shut out the images in front of her, to reject what was happening. She quickly began to pray. As she prayed, she held the tiny crucifix firmly in her palm.

She could hear as the vampires hissed at the prayers. She just knew that God would be her savior. Surely, she wasn't meant to die this way? As the vampires continued to hiss at her, she continued to pray the Lord's Prayer.

The vampires parted as another man in his forties appeared before her. He looked her over before nodding his head. "She will do fine." He turned to a man near the doorway and ordered, "I expect her to be delivered to the mansion before sunrise."

Tears flowed down her cheeks as she listened to the orders given. She prayed her death would be quick.

Chapter 5

The weather in New Orleans was hot with patches of sweltering heat. Then again, Detective John Newman was used to the cooler climate of New York. In New York, summer was a welcome change of the season, a reprieve from the long winter. But here people looked forward to winter so that they could finally have a break from the oppressive heat that plagued the city.

After ten years of working for the New York City Police Department, he had wanted a change. One restless night, he searched for jobs available elsewhere. At the time, it didn't help that New York was having the worst snow storm of the century. He had grown tired of the countless acts of violence and the bone chilling cold.

He never expected to get the job, however. It took him by surprise when the Human Resources Department responded and requested a phone interview. At first, he found it strange when the HR director questioned his beliefs regarding the supernatural and paranormal. But, he simply shrugged it off. He'd heard Louisiana, especially the residents of New Orleans, had more than a few believers in the supernatural. From what research he'd done on the city, some there practiced Voodoo. Newman was astonished when the HR director told him that he was hired and that they would pay for his relocation down there.

When Newman first arrived in New Orleans, he was astonished at how different the architecture here was than in New York. Here, there were no tall skyscrapers, and the most prominent building was the Superdome. However, there was a unique aura that hovered over the city. Even Hurricane Katrina could not destroy the instilled pride that was deeply rooted in this city. In South Louisiana, it wasn't just a way of life, but their heritage and pride.

He found a reasonably priced apartment that was a few blocks from the station. The only luxury in the small apartment was central air conditioning, which was a necessity down here. The neighborhood was not prestigious, but it did have several art galleries, boutiques, and coffee shops nearby.

He fell in love with the French Quarter at first sight. The French Quarter was a party twelve months out of the year. The area consisted of various clubs, restaurants, and stores. Although it was French in name, the architectural style leaned more towards Spanish influences. There were flat tiled roofs, elaborate ironwork balconies, stuccos, and pastel paints.

Visitors to the French Quarter came to lose themselves in the ambiance here. Unfortunately, the area also appealed to the underbelly of New Orleans; those who preyed on the innocent. These very individuals kept the New Orleans Police Department working.

***

After working for a few short months, Newman was unexpectedly called into the Captain's office. "Take a seat and get comfortable," Captain Grant Benoit said in his heavy Louisiana accent, which somehow became thicker when he needed something. "Ya are doing well here, mon ami. Everyone is impressed with how well ya are catching on to dings. Your detective skills are better dan expected for a Yankee."

"It's just good police work, sir."

Captain Benoit shook his head and said, "Mais non, son. Ya have good instincts, very good instincts. An opening in one of our more unique departments has become available. However, it may not be to yar envie."

Newman looked at his new Captain and wondered what he wanted. Thankfully, he'd caught on to some of the phrases said around here. At first, he was completely lost with all the Cajun terms thrown around the station, but he soon realized that *mon ami* meant my friend. And *envie* meant heart's desire.

Captain Benoit looked over his new detective once more. "Dere is an opening in de supernatural department here."

"I'm sorry, sir, but did you say supernatural?"

"Mais oui, I did. Three of my top detectives decided to enter the civilian world once again. Damn shame too, dey were good at what dey did. Ya will be a good fit dere. Dis department handles special investigations where ya have to keep yar mind open and tink outside of de box."

Newman ran his hand through his hair as he looked at the Captain in disbelief. "I still don't understand; why do we have a supernatural department, sir?"

"Mais, dere are certain cases here dat even de local detectives refuse to investigate."

"How many are in the department, sir?"

"Currently, dere are three other detectives dedicated to de cases, but dey have noticed a change in the air so to speak. Their case load is increasing. But Detectives Guy Mayon, Mike Bailey, and Grace Hutcherson did agree to be available if anyone needed help."

New Orleans was filled with mystery and intrigue so he shouldn't be surprised that there was a supernatural department here. As they say down here – Laissez les bon temps roule! Let the good times roll!

Chapter 6

As beauties go, his Josie was the loveliest of all. Tyler was spellbound when he watched her. When she smiled at him, his breath caught in his throat, and in her presence, his heart raced. When their gazes met, it seemed as if all their problems melted away.

He loved the way her hair glimmered in the pale moonlight, how her clothes molded against her curves and complimented her fair skin.

When she talked, her voice was a solace to his crazy life. Even when she was away from him, she was constantly on his mind. She haunted his dreams until he finally managed to fall asleep.

He could not keep his hands off of her. Her skin was so soft, reminiscent of rose petals. She was so perfect in his eyes; small, elegant, and strong.

He glowed with happiness when she was around him. If only he could keep her all to himself. The beast inside of him demanded that he carry her off and hide her away.

Josie never once feared him, and he did not fear her. He found her bravery in the face of the dangers she confronted simply amazing. He was the luckiest being on this earth to have her in his life.

Lately, they never seemed to have enough time together. Every moment he spent in her company was bittersweet. One day soon, he planned on never letting her leave his side, not for a single moment. They would abandon this quest for redemption, and only live for each other. Though for now, he must let Josie do what she felt she must.

Today, he was busy looking for items to fill their house and possible older silver items they could melt down to help with their quest for redemption. Josie could not walk in daylight and search the flea market rejects with him. She was sitting safely at home, out of the sun's deadly rays and told Tyler just what she liked.

He had no desire to be here, but for his beloved Josie, he would do anything. Even if that meant walking through this bustling flea market. He carefully made his way down the aisle of vendors, dodging several elderly ladies on scooters, avoiding distracted mothers pushing strollers with screaming children and laughing at wives dragging their ever so bored husbands behind them.

As he looked at the various trinkets and items proudly on display by the vendors, he saw a lifespan reflected here in the items that were so easily discarded. There was a range of items from cribs and car seats to clear leftovers from estate sales.

As he surveyed the crowd, he easily picked out the young lovers looking to furnish their first home, young college kids looking for something inexpensive for their new dorm, and young women looking for just the right antique for their new apartments.

Tyler wondered just how his, or even Josie's, life would have turned out had they been allowed to live a normal, human life. Would his items be displayed here for the masses to rummage over after his death?

Most of the items here were not worth buying. Stalls were piled high with torn and tattered clothes, broken kitchen gadgets, and a few vendors had old vinyl records. The desire to leave was overly tempting, but he pressed on. Surely, he could find a treasure buried here among this junk.

As he moved on to the next vendor, a flicker of excitement washed over him. The remnants of an estate sale were proudly laid out on an antique dining room table. There were a few mismatched pieces of china and glittering crystal, but there also were a few pieces of antique silverware. If correct in his assumptions, this could be a veritable gold mine for him.

The young lady working the stall clearly didn't care about what she was selling. Popping gum loudly she said, "If you want the whole lot, I will sell it to you for $10."

Knowing that the silver was worth way more than that, Tyler gladly handed over a $10 bill. He didn't even bother to say anything as she dropped the silver into a box for him. It wouldn't matter if she scratched the silver; he intended on melting it down for bullets as soon as he got home.

Chapter 7

Many years ago, Ezrielle made a pact with the Dukes of Hell for immortal life and power. She wanted to become a powerful voodoo priestess, and turn the man who betrayed her love into a Rougarou. Her wish was granted, and behind her estate, she created a world of her own. If anyone looked through the veil shrouding the area, they would shudder in fear of what lurked here.

As she prepared for tonight's ceremony, she stepped into the waters of the bayou for her ritual bath. She scrubbed her skin thoroughly with soap lathered moss until her skin tingled. Then, she walked back to her small cabin naked, not wanting her body to be defiled by any garment other than her white robe she wore on this most sacred of nights.

She caught a fisherman staring in disbelief at her bathing in the water. As his hungry eyes feasted upon her body, Ezrielle paid him no attention. If he knew who she was, he wouldn't lust after her the way he did; instead, he would fear her.

Those who had no choice but to live here with their families in the small, old shacks that lined the bank knew to turn a deaf ear to the strange rituals being practiced. As hard as they may try, it was impossible to tune out the incessant beating of drums.

The deep throbbing of the drums began just after sundown. The rhythm filled the darkness on this truly sacred night of All Hallow's Eve. It was the one night of the year where the spirits of the dead walked the earth to take their rightful place among the living.

As Ezrielle donned her white robe, she wrapped her long, dark hair in white linen. While she checked her image in the mirror to make sure that all of her hair was hidden beneath the soft fabric, she frowned at the smallest sign of a wrinkle that marred her perfect skin. She would have to consume the youth of an innocent soon.

As Ezrielle entered the clearing, a loud cry erupted from the waiting crowd. The tempo of the beating drums changed to announce her arrival. When she stepped into the large circle, the night became silent. The drums ceased in anticipation of what was to come.

Her followers' dark eyes anxiously watched her. She felt their growing need; each hoped to be the one chosen by her.

Her breathtaking beauty had yet to fade even after all these years. Her powers didn't falter as she aged; they only grew stronger with each passing year. No other voodoo priestess had powers that could rival the powers of the spirit housed within Ezrielle.

Ezrielle searched the crowd until she found the one she was looking for. She beckoned him to her as her followers watched in anticipation. As he made his way to her, the homunculi manning the drums stood up; their white saggy pants showed no signs of dirt from the ground. They patiently waited for Ezrielle to acknowledge that she was ready to begin the ceremony.

With the young man standing before her, she began to chant from deep within her throat. Even though her followers did not understand the words that came out of her, they listened intently. The words became more disjointed as the chanting progressed. Ezrielle's high pitched voice dipped extremely low only to resemble a moan. As she continued her chant, her body swayed back and forth.

Her hands reached out to the young man and hovered near his body, but did not touch it. The young man began to dance and chant the same strange, hypnotizing words that passed from her lips.

Cheers erupted from the lips of the creatures surrounding them as the transformation took place. Fur burst from his flesh, claws sprang from his hands and feet, and his body reshaped.

The rhythm of the drums slowed as the transformation ended. The others shifted to join their new brother.

Once this part of the ceremony was complete, an elderly woman stepped forth. Ezrielle had looked her over before she asked, "Whom do you desire to speak with?"

The elderly woman pulled her thin, white shawl tight over her sagging shoulders and answered, "My garcon."

"A tall, thin young man is standing to the right of you. He has deep set eyes the color of warm honey."

The words brought a smile to the withered face of the elderly woman as she answered, "Dat is my Samuel."

"He said to stop your worrying; he is fine. He crossed over, and his soul does not wander this earth lost. He watches over you from up above."

The old woman wiped the tears from her eyes and smiled at the voodoo priestess with everlasting gratitude. She placed a basket of homemade pralines on the ground as an offering. One by one, more loved ones wished to hear an endearing message from those who'd passed on. Ezrielle watched as tears fell, and offerings were placed at her feet. No one in front of her questioned as spirits recounted through her a fond memory that no one else could know.

****

As he watched from the shadows, he knew that she was aware of his presence. So many times he'd entertained the idea of having them live together; he could have her whenever he desired.

If only that were possible, but he could not have strangers on the estate. There were too many secrets there. As a voodoo high priestess, Ezrielle had too many that came to call on her. Instead, they kept their relationship hidden.

Chapter 8

The full moon cast a pale light over the dense foliage as he made his way to his destination. He paid no attention to the briars and branches that reached out across the path. A strong stench of rotting flora hung heavy in the night air. He stayed alert to any sounds that came from approaching danger. He paid no mind to the sharp fangs of the water moccasins that swam in the murky water of the bayou as he pushed forward. On and on he ran until at last he reached his destination. No sound greeted him; even the night creatures knew of his arrival.

Viewed from afar, the tiny little house nestled here on the bayou gave the appearance of true southern charm. It appeared serene and calm. The dark energy that lived nearby kept to the shadows and never provided a glimpse of its sinister portrayal until it was too late. This house and its surroundings harbored a dark secret; a secret that reached back for decades, almost a century to be exact. For centuries now, stories were told of a creature that lived in the swamps of Louisiana. A creature that killed young children and those who ventured too close to its lair.

From generation to generation, the bayou people in these parts passed on folktales of the Rougarou. Those residing here knew far better than most that the story

was not merely a fable. Danger lurked in these waters.
They kept their children close to their hearts.

As he watched from the shadows, loud grunts from the
alligators echoed along the bank and broke the silence
of the night. Storm clouds rushed in and hid the full
moon. In the distance, he heard the low rumblings of
thunder.

When the clouds moved away from the moon, nature
called to release him from the confines of his human
body. Taking a deep breath to relax, he shut out the
world around him for a brief moment in time. He
concentrated on the sounds surrounding him; the wind
blowing through the trees, the water lapping against
the banks, and the frogs calling for their mates.

He closed his eyes as his human body manifested into
something nightmares were made of. Once again, he
found himself wandering the grounds of his former
home. His heart picked up speed as he caught
movement. His amber eyes were alert as a sharp odor
filled his senses. Just a simple scent brought forth vivid
images he wished to forget. Images flashed like a
nightmare in his mind; the sound of tearing flesh and
loud feeding noises of a fiendish hunger being satisfied
while another innocent soul was ripped from this earth
filled his mind.

With the passing of each year, he watched from afar as
his family and friends moved on to their eternal resting

places, all except for him. He was cursed to live this half-life of his. He would never be granted eternal rest.

Tension washed over him as he observed the young couple. Someone was moving into HIS house, and from the fetid smell that surrounded them, they were not of the mortal world.

This putrid odor transported him back to the blood-drenched walls and the smell of bodies left to lie in the sweltering Louisiana heat after the pulse of their life faded. He forced those memories from his mind. A long, deep-throated howl escaped him and it combined with the peals of thunder.

It had been a long time since anyone dared to live in the house. He couldn't bear the fact that someone had moved in once again, especially the likes of these two. No, evil was born in this house. This house was HIS, and he refused to let anyone live in it. He should have burned it down years ago, but he could never bring himself to do it.

Chapter 9

Josie returned home after all these years of traveling in an attempt to forget her death sentence. She returned to the place of her birth, and death. Tears welled up inside of her as she looked around this city she once called home. She came back each year with the carnival, but this time was different. There was no carnival; there was no Joshua. It was just her and Tyler.

So much had changed here. New Orleans had become a popular tourist destination; even Hurricane Katrina could not keep people away from this beloved city. Josie wondered if the craziness that happened on Bourbon Street was what also lured the vampires. They could fit in, blend into the crowds while they preyed on the innocent.

Evil lurked just beneath the darkness of the night. She could feel the terror the vampires brought to their victims' lives. She'd committed those same acts, but now, it was time for retribution. She must try to make right all the wrongs she'd done.

Pure hatred boiled within her at the thought of her maker. The hatred was so great that all other emotions paled in comparison. She had returned home, but now it was time for what she craved most of all – revenge.

He'd turned her without ever asking if this was the life she wanted. No one could change her past, but she had the power to change the future of others. She must be the protector of the weak and defenseless. These humans didn't have the ability to overcome their oppressors, but she did. She desperately wanted to wash away her sins by ridding this world of the pure carnal evil that walked this earth.

She often wondered what the humans here would do if they found out about their existence. In the past, vampires were hunted down with little mercy shown to them. She'd heard the stories of good vampires being killed just because of what they were. Over the years, stories were told and retold about the myths of vampires and shape shifters. Some facts were mixed into the fantasy stories, but more often than not, the stories were pure fiction. The stories embellished and distorted the truths of their kind. Most vampires treated the shape shifters as their servants.

In Josie's mind, shape shifters were the superior being. They were not forced to walk only in the darkness of the night. They wouldn't burst into ash at the slightest touch of sunlight.

There were times in the past when she wished she could transform herself into another being. How she envied Tyler's ability to alter his form and free himself from his human confines.

When Josie first started traveling with the carnival, she noticed all of the attention she received from men. They were not only attracted to her beauty, but also her mystique. Her hair was the color of rich chocolate, and her eyes were the color of a full-bodied coffee.

She politely turned them away, not wanting to complicate her life with the pain of love. However, Tyler refused to give up on winning her love. Even though their love was forbidden, they managed to keep it hidden from the others in the carnival. Over the years, they grew tired of running and wanted to stay in one place.

It took them several months to establish themselves here in New Orleans. Decades ago, they'd started to tuck money away. While traveling with the carnival, neither needed money since Joshua made sure that all of their needs were met. Josie needed to have a sense of security if something ever went awry. She wanted to ensure that she had money to help her get back on her feet. Well that time was now.

Josie was surprised at how well her investments paid off over the years. Between them, they had more than enough money to purchase a nice little house tucked away from the city. The real estate agent said that the house had been vacant for a few years now, so it was a steal. The rumors of the house being haunted discouraged prospective buyers, but she laughed at the possibility. She had seen what went bump in the night, and a ghost would not scare her, or Tyler, away.

Thinking about the past caused her heart to pound fiercely in her chest. For a moment, she struggled to catch her breath as her chest grew tighter with each passing moment. She wanted to bury herself under the blankets and cover her ears in an attempt to drown out her pounding heartbeat. Even if she could drown out the sound, it would not stop the bombardment of the memories that flooded her mind. She prayed they would stop before she was forced to relive the horrors of the carnival again.

Why didn't she die back then? Why must she be forced to endure this life? Sometimes she wished she had the courage to end it all. However, she would then be forced to leave Tyler. He was the one constant that made her life worth living. Without him, she would be nothing. What would her life be if she had never met Joshua or her master? Would she have lived a happy, normal life? Was this what fate had in store for her? Was this her destiny, to search out unknown dangers that lurked in the darkness of the night?

She anxiously waited for the moon to come out and the darkness to envelop her so that she could walk outside. As she waited, her phone rang. It was Tyler calling her from work to tell her, "Be careful tonight, my love. I am with you in spirit, if not in body. You are always in my heart." The deep melody of his voice filled her mind with the warm chorus of words. She felt the tingle of his words all the way to the tips of her toes. She wished he was here with her, but he would be home soon. The burning ache of resentment ebbed from her body as his loving words calmed her.

Sensing that she still wasn't fully relaxed, he continued, "Josie, my love, soon I will be there to kiss your worries away. For now let my words caress your body and ease your troubled mind."

His voice and loving words eased the tumultuous feelings that ran through her mind. His soft words allowed her to prepare for the night ahead. Josie and Tyler lived in two worlds right now; one was the world that humans called reality, and the other was their real life, the one involving the paranormal and supernatural. They lived in a parallel dimension where mythical creatures and humans both created chaos.

She could easily tune into the evil that lived in both and locate their negative energy in the air. While working in the carnival, she'd learned how to read minds and fed off those humans that deserved to die.

She walked outside to a black sky. The darkness was shattered only by brief bursts of lightning flashing across the sky. All around her, the night life on the bayou was alive and made their presence known. Bullfrogs sang out for their mates, alligators slipped into the bayou in search of food, insects buzzed about in search of fresh blood, and coyotes called out to the moon. As a guttural howling pierced the air, Josie thought back to her visions where she saw a creature roaming these woods like Tyler. She'd heard the myths that a Rougarou lived in the bayous. However, if another Rougarou were nearby, surely Tyler would have picked up on the scent.

What if the baying and howling at the moon were not a pack of coyotes? What if there were more Rougarou living on the bayou? She had yet to tell Tyler of her fears, but did he possibly fear the same thing?

She stepped carefully as she made her way to the water's edge. She hoped that one of these days she had time to work on the grounds. The terrain here was uneven, riddled with ruts and erosion as well as protruding tree roots. One misstep could cause her to stumble into the murky water.

As she looked over the water, she enjoyed the scenery. Twilight was here. The world was cast into the shadows as the certainty of what was around her became lost.

There was something magical about looking over the water at night. She could sit here all night and watch the waves as the stars reflected off the water. As the soft murmur of the water lapped against the bank, she lost herself in its steady rhythm. Her thoughts drifted in and out with the ebb and flow of the tide.

Tyler chose this place because of the nearby woods. From the back door, he could run free without detection by a curious neighbor. There was a genuine peacefulness to this area that she'd never experienced before. He was right; this was the perfect place for them to live.

Out of instinct, she pulled her jacket closer to her body. Tyler mentioned winter should be mild this year, but that didn't concern her. Ever since she was turned, she was always cold. Even being exposed to the mild elements of winter tortured her.

As she walked through the darkness of the night, raindrops pelted her. She looked up at the sky to find the moon. She craved to feel the sun's rays once more on her skin, but daylight would turn her body to ashes. No, she was forced to live in the darkness with the other creatures of the night. She bitterly laughed at herself. She was no longer alive; she ceased living a long time ago. Now, all she did was exist. In the distance, she heard the deep hoot of an owl. A feeling of nervousness surged through her as she was reminded of old superstitions. It was said the call of an owl was a bad omen.

Soon, it would be time for her to hunt. When they bought this house, they'd splurged and bought them each a car. Tyler chose a fully loaded GMC Denali truck, to fit his massive frame. Josie, on the other hand, wanted something sleek yet fast and chose an Audi R8.

Before getting into the car, she ran her hands along its sleek curves. This car was built for speed; that was just what she needed to help her run away from her past.

Revving the engine, she drove to the French Quarter to find her supper. Even at this hour finding a parking spot in New Orleans was almost impossible. Once her car was safely secured, she blended into the crowd. In the distance, she spotted an excellent lookout point and slipped into an alleyway. Scaling the wall, she made herself comfortable on the roof, staying in the shadows. The success of her work depended on her going unnoticed.

From the shadows, she watched intently as a woman, clearly drunk and stumbling, made her way deeper into the alley. This poor woman should know better than to walk into the shadows alone.

Josie's attention shifted to a shadow thicker than the others. When she noticed a man wearing dark tattered clothes curled up against the dumpster, her senses went on full alert. She saw the pulse beating in his jugular, but when she tried to read his mind, it was too cloudy from the effects of the recent alcohol he'd drunk. She had no idea if he planned to hurt the approaching woman or not.

As the woman moved closer to him, he held out a gnarled hand, dirty from the streets and said, "Spare some change miss."

Josie was thankful to see that the young woman had enough common sense to move away from the man. "I'm sorry; I don't have any change on me," the woman answered.

Josie took a stance and readied herself to act on a moment's notice as the man stood up. Staggering to his feet, he had a difficult time finding his ground. "Please miss. It's been so long since I ate," he pleaded.

A shadow masked the man's face even though he was under a street light now. Josie watched as the shadow seemed to envelop the man.

The night breeze carried a heady scent in the air. The smell of copper was easy to recognize--blood.

Suddenly, the shadow moved in. Josie hollered out to the young girl as she took action, "Look out."

A vampire stepped out of the darkness as he slammed the woman against the brick wall. In one swift movement, he had the woman off of her feet while the homeless man dropped to the ground and curled into a tight ball.

The young girl kicked and screamed as she tried to pummel the attacker with her hands while using her feet to kick any part of his body she could make contact with. Unfazed by her struggles, he tipped her head back, ready to bite as two more figures emerged from the shadows. One easily picked up the man curled on the ground and held him high in the air while the other stood by watching. Almost as though he was keeping watch over the others.

These vampires had to be freshly turned; they looked mean and hungry. Their cheeks and eyes were sunken in, and their pale skin was scored with dark veins.

When the vampire saw the crucifix on the young woman's neck, he hissed and cringed at the sight. The cross on her neck wasn't that large, but it was enough to irritate the vampire. It gave Josie sufficient time to step in as the vampire swatted to free the crucifix from her neck. The other two tossed the homeless man back and forth, intent on playing with their food before drinking his blood.

Without warning, the vampire threw the young woman hard against the wall. She sailed into the air and crumpled to the ground after hitting the wall with great force.

Josie moved into action, throwing a silver dagger into the vampire's heart. The dagger smoldered the skin as it entered its body. As the knife plunged into the vampire's heart, Josie was surprised when she caught a glimpse of what the woman was like before her soul was condemned. The vampire let out a terrible hiss and a feral scream as it burst into tiny particles.

This vampire was recently turned. She had a look of utter surprise as she died; she had no idea that a silver dagger could hurt so much.

Josie watched intently as another vampire dropped the homeless man and prepared to attack. Taking out another silver dagger, she saw his glowing red eyes instantly focus on the sharp knife. He looked at Josie and laughed, "I am much quicker than my friend."

As his sneer turned into a ferocious hiss, Josie prepared herself for his attack. He lunged forward as Josie prepared to throw. The silver dagger missed its mark, slicing the vampire in the face instead. But it still smoldered the skin when it sliced through the decaying flesh. He let out a feral hiss while he swiped at the fiery pain ravaging his face. His inhuman screams echoed through the night. The vampire looked at Josie as if he didn't understand. "I am surprised that your master didn't warn you about the dangers of silver," Josie taunted.

Josie took her gun and fired. She made sure not to miss her mark this time.

Before the dust of the vampire settled, the third vampire lunged for Josie. She caught him as he was

careening through the air. Throwing him into a brick
wall, the brick and mortar came crumbling down. The
vampire bounced back quickly from the impact and
found his feet faster than Josie liked.

Without giving him a second chance to make a move,
Josie fired her gun once again. She hit his heart dead
on. Once satisfied that no more vampires were waiting
to attack, she bent down to retrieve her daggers.

Before leaving the area, she checked on both victims
and erased their memories.

***

The intrusion into the Rougarou's mind took the
creature by complete surprise. The voodoo priestess
had left him alone for all these years, why now? Over
the years, it survived on urges and instinct, not
thought.

Now, as it crouched in the shadows of the pine trees,
his mind was in a state of total confusion. When the
voice reached out and entered his mind, he was
hunting food. He stayed far away from the humans
and preferred his solitary life, feeding on small animals
living in the swamps for many years now.

He was fortunate that very few hunters dared to
venture out into this particular area of the swamp.
The rumors of Rougarou kept most humans far away.

Most humans didn't even understand the truth about the world they lived in. Humans were led to believe these stories were told merely to scare children to keep them from wandering around in the darkness of the night. If only that was the truth.

As he took on his Rougarou body, its pelt glimmered in the moonlight. He ventured closer, keeping his instincts sharp. There had been an aura about the place since their arrival. When the creature attempted to get closer to the house, his head began to ache more. Had a spell been put on this area, such as Ezrielle kept on her own house? Did these two work for her?

The closer he came to the dwelling, the stronger the probing into his mind became. It was reminiscent to a burning sensation. Trying to resist the probing, the creature rolled onto the ground and swatted at the air with its massive paws.

Ezrielle's voice called out to him, "You will not continue to block me. You are still mine even though I let you hide from the fold. If you want to be left alone, you will tell me about these newcomers. One dared to kill a vampire."

Fear surged through his body at that point. Ezrielle probed his mind once more. Fearing detection from the creature in the house more than Ezrielle, he quickly headed to his lair.

He was sure a vampire lived in his house. Surely one of
his own kind did not live with this vile creature. Yet,
why was Ezrielle so interested in her?

Chapter 10

Detective Newman slowly stepped out of his SUV. The smell of death hung heavy in the air. Even after all these years, he had not become used to the dank odor.

In his short time working here in New Orleans, he felt more like a watch dog rather than a police detective. Working these supernatural deaths took some very skilled detective work on his part.

Straightening his shoulders, he walked towards the dead body in the ditch. The responding officer believed the death was vampire related, but Newman wasn't convinced.

Newman told the responding officer, "We need backup here ASAP." Pointing to the woods, he added, "Watch the forensics team closely in case whatever did this is still nearby."

Just looking at the body made him gag, this kill was especially brutal. He stopped himself from recoiling at the dead eyes staring up at him. The poor victim's mouth was frozen as if he died trying to scream once more. A look of pure terror was etched on his face.

The killer ripped out the victim's throat. Blood soaked the ground beneath his body.   Newman noticed deep scratches all over his body. The poor guy tried to fight back, but his efforts were futile. Death did not come easy for him.

Up above, the rising sun resembled a ball of fire over the trees. Brilliant red streaks skated along the sky. You knew the damn work was getting old when even the sky appeared to be streaked with blood. With jaws clenched, he walked the crime scene as he searched for the killer's footprints.

Why couldn't these vampires make his life easier by feeding on those willing to donate their blood? He had only worked here a few months but already had grown tired of witnessing all the deaths caused by vampires.

His partner, Detective Roy Dupre, let out a long sigh as he looked at the body. "This isn't good, neg." Newman shook his head at Dupre's term of endearment for a man. In all honesty, he wasn't sure if he would ever get used to all the slang used by most of the department.

Newman looked over at him and said, "There was a lot of carnage."

Dupre shook his head and added, "It's not just the carnage. This fellow here worked for The Gazette. Something tells me he was snooping around where he shouldn't have been as usual."

Newman looked at the body and shuddered involuntarily. "What exactly did he do for the paper?"

"This man here is Kevin Broussard. He is, or was, one of the best investigative reporters they have," Dupre explained.

"So, you think he more than likely asked questions for the wrong story?"

Dupre nodded his head in agreement. "Yeah, this guy was a real piece of work. He had a way of ruffling feathers just with a look. He never did heed warnings."

A twig snapped in the distance, and out of instinct, his hand curled around the butt of his gun. Newman had yet to meet a vampire or any other supernatural creature that may lurk in New Orleans, but he was warned they move at superhuman speed. When it came to monsters that kill using fangs, it involved a whole new set of rules. Silver bullets had to be used in his gun, and the handcuffs had to be made of silver.

Dupre shook his head and pointed to a fellow officer surveying the woods, "Easy. That is just Officer Tyler LeBlanc."

Tyler called out to the detectives, "We have a blood trail here in the woods."

Walking towards the woods, Dupre said grimly, "It's a good thing that the sun is out. At least we don't have to worry about being attacked by a vampire."

Newman responded, "I'm still not sure we are dealing with a vampire. That sure in the hell looks like claw marks to me."

In the distance, the wail of sirens was heard. At least their backup arrived before they ventured into the swamplands. While vampires and sunlight may not mix, who knew what other supernatural creatures may lurk about?

***

As they moved deeper into the swamp, Tyler used his supernatural powers to his advantage. Unlike some of the other Rougarou, he'd learned how to control the change. He released only parts of the beast when he needed to.

Thanks to his wolf-like senses, he caught a whiff of the rogue Rougarou's trail. When he first saw the body, he knew that those were claw marks on the body. Now, he needed to find out if this Rougarou killed on his own terms or under the control of Ezrielle.

The wolf inside of him begged to be let out and hunt this creature down. He wanted to end these needless killings, but with the humans' right behind him, he wasn't able to.

Chapter 11

As blood ran down Josie's throat, the warm metallic scent filled her senses. She looked down to see the floor and bed stained with the color of death. Beneath her was a young man, barely twenty. Her eyes were still wild with a raging hunger that she couldn't contain. A maniacal laugh echoed through her mind as her eyes darted around the room.

At the sight in front of her, she wept as her cries of anguish broke through the silence of the night. She collapsed on the bed and sobbed tears of crimson, for what she had become and what she had done once more.

Waking with a start, Josie bolted straight up in bed as she gasped for air. The memories would always haunt her, torture her dreams. Every time she remembered, she felt tormented and horrified at what she was. It took her a few moments to realize that she was no longer a part of the carnival. No matter how many souls she may save, she would never shake the memories of what she had done.

If Josie had known what was in store for her on that fateful night, she would have plunged a knife deep into her heart then. What happened that night condemned her to hell and cost her her very soul. She paid for that curse every day she walked this earth. She despised what she had become, but in order for her to survive, she was forced to adapt.

Over the years, she had watched the sun rise in different cities and lived through wars and famine. She learned the hard way that in this world good and evil co-mingled. Most humans didn't even realize that evil walked amongst them in the form of vampires. Some humans have discovered the truth of their existence, but most died at the hands of the blood thirsty creatures.

Most vampires preferred to hide during the daylight hours in abandoned warehouses and buildings. Some burrowed deep underground at old cemeteries, while others pretended to be human and lived amongst the mortals. These vampires survived on blood obtained from blood banks or volunteer donors.

While most vampires preferred to keep their existence hidden, Josie had noticed a change lately. Some vampires had become brazen, feeding in the city and leaving the bodies to be found. Josie knew from personal experience that once a vampire became addicted to feeding on fear, the addiction was never ending. The creature craved that fear and had to satiate their immense thirst. It lost all intelligence and control as the need for the taste of fear filled blood on its tongue increased. Fear intensified the tantalizing taste of blood like no other emotion.

A shiver ran through her as she thought of Joshua. He paid for his crimes, but what about the one who made her? He was from New Orleans and Joshua said he never left, but kept hidden in the confines of his home, only leaving to feed. She vowed to find him and make him pay for turning her.

As she stared out into the night, Tyler walked up behind her and pulled her into his warm embrace. "What are you thinking of my love?"

"He is somewhere in this city, and I will find him."

Tyler turned her to him and kissed her. "If he hadn't turned you, then we wouldn't have met," he whispered.

She placed her head on his chest, she sighed and said, "This is true, but I cannot forgive him for condemning my soul to hell." Josie looked up into Tyler's eyes and said, "You do know that I love you more than anything, don't you? Before you came into my life, there was nothing but cold darkness. You changed me; you taught me what love is. No matter what happens, I will always love you. You showed me that there is more to this world than the darkness that surrounds me."

As Tyler brushed back the blood stained tears that fell from her eyes, she added, "I know that Joshua would have never allowed our love if we stayed."

"Joshua is gone from our lives. He is in hell, where he belongs my love." Tilting Josie's face up to his, he looked deeply into her eyes. "I do understand the need to find your master. I want to banish the woman that cursed my life from this world. But, I couldn't bear it if something happened to you."

Josie looked around their peaceful little home as she contemplated her life. She'd believed true love would never be a part of her future once she was turned into this monster. She didn't think she would ever experience that particular emotion, but she was wrong.

Strangely, falling in love was a lot like death. It chose the perfect moment and the chain of events that intersected your life in which it was to occur. You were nothing more than a ball of clay in its warm hands. Neither love nor death asked if you wanted or needed it. Instead, love came in and filled that gaping hole of destiny's design.

For the first time, Josie's life bloomed with love's beautiful never-ending ache. To keep that feeling, she would forsake her entire being. Now that she'd found love, she couldn't live without it.

Wanting to take her mind off her troubles and fears, Tyler brought Josie closer to his body. He nuzzled and nibbled on her neck. "I am under your spell. You intoxicate me. As soon as I saw you, I knew I had to be named your guardian. It was so easy to convince Joshua to let me have you under my charge," he explained.

Josie listened to Tyler talk. His voice was as smooth as whiskey as the words brushed over her skin and created tiny sparks of awareness. He ran his hands over her body and said, "I love the exquisite lines of your body. The sexy tumble of curls that cascade down your back and the way your hair contrasts against your ivory skin." There was a low rumble to his voice that sent chills down her spine.

Tyler turned Josie to face him and took her mouth in his. Even through his thick clothing, Josie felt the searing heat radiating from his body. It seeped deep into her body as she melted into his.

She looked up and saw that his eyes looked golden. The deeper he looked into Josie's eyes, the brighter they glowed with a fire burning deep inside of them for her and her only.

Josie breathed in his enticing scent; it clouded her mind and made it impossible to think. She treasured their time together when they were a simple couple. Maybe, they could go for a run tonight.

Out of instinct, Josie licked her lips as his gaze dropped to her mouth once more. He crushed her hard against his chest, and she felt the muscles ripple beneath her.

Liquid pools of fire stared down at her and left her in danger of getting lost in their depths.

The night air was heavy and damp, making it hard to breath. Just having him close made her dizzy. He took her lips in his; the taste of him sent desire rippling throughout her body.

She felt his racing heartbeat and heard the blood course through his veins. It called out to her. Something low and deep inside of her growled and called forth the creature in her. She saw his pulse beat as he drew her closer.

Heavy emotion surged through her and overwhelmed her senses. She ran her hands along his well-corded muscles and relished the feel of him. The heady mix of his scent and desire came together in a deadly combination.

"I love you so much Tyler. You are my whole life."

***

Josie and Tyler tenderly held hands as they watched the moon slowly rise over the tops of the oaks that graced their yard. There was a time when they'd both cursed the full moon; they despised the way it taunted them mercilessly with each painful ascent. Now, they had come to love it.

Electrical charges danced in the air around them. A silvery mist formed around Tyler, nearly disguising the sight of his twisted and elongated limbs. She could not tear her gaze away from his when he turned from human to a Rougarou.

It was a truly poignantly moving moment to watch Tyler transform before her eyes. She loved being able to witness this magic. As the mist dissipated, it left behind only his most basic form. Tonight, they would both enjoy the call of the moon.

In human form, Tyler was a magnificent specimen. He had a broad, chiseled chest, with powerful shoulders, washboard abs and long, muscular legs. Even now in his true form, she could see his true power; it was as if he was ready to pounce at any moment.

From their first meeting, there was a sense of connection. She felt it as soon as she laid eyes on him. From the very beginning, he made her feel cherished. Only under Tyler's gaze did she feel beautiful.

At times, Tyler's alpha personality was almost too much for Josie to handle. At first, she relished in his fierce protectiveness, but, eventually, it rode roughshod over her. She took a stand and informed him that she didn't always need him there. They soon learned how to coexist well together.

***

Tyler looked up at Josie before taking off. She believed that they were going strictly for a night run; however, he was on the lookout. He sensed another presence near and needed to be sure. He would never allow anything to happen to her, not now, not ever.

As they headed deeper into the swamp, Tyler kept his attention trained on the ever changing landscape. In the bayous of Louisiana, the very ground could change beneath your feet without a moment's notice. There were no roads or permanent trails of any kind here. Even the lily-clogged canals deep in the swamps could be there one day and gone the next.

Yes, this was the perfect place for monsters to hide. Thankfully, he was the most dangerous beast around.

***

Josie watched as Tyler walked into the room after finishing his shower. His body was bathed in the soft light of the moonlight that shone through the window. Just the sight of him fed her hunger.

She held out her arms to welcome him and, without hesitation, he wrapped her in his strong arms and devoured her with his hot mouth.

With a deep, seductive growl, he slid his ravenous mouth over her skin until he sought what he most hungered for. As the first rays of dawn filled the morning sky, they fell asleep, sated.

Chapter 12

Tonight, Newman saw more of New Orleans than he cared to and wanted to drink the rest of the night away. They still weren't sure exactly what killed the victim, but it practically tore the poor guy's throat out.

He walked into a jazz club and found a table in the back. He sat and listened to the aging jazz pianist with a wrinkled, caramel face play a tune and allowed the music to wash over him.

As the dawn threatened to shed unwanted daylight in a few hours, customers left the bar. Only a few remained as the night slowly moved on.

Newman sipped his tenth whiskey of the night and felt his body relax. He still couldn't get over what he'd witnessed. Jesus H. Christ, what would do that to someone? He'd hoped drinking would erase some of the memory, but unfortunately it hadn't.

When the piano player left, another man took his place. This bald man with skin the color of rich milk chocolate wore a shiny blue sharkskin suit with a pale blue shirt. The rather large man made the small, unimpressive stage appear even smaller somehow. As the man began to sing, his rich baritone voice filled the room.

He sang as if he was singing to a long lost lover. The man's style immediately caught Newman's attention. He put down his drink and listened intently as he lost himself to the mournful nature of the song.

Where others seemed to sing to impress an audience, this man sang from his soul. A woman's voice purred softly in his ear, "His singing is mesmerizing, mais oui?"

Newman looked up to find himself enthralled by a young sensuous woman. The dress she wore appeared to be painted on her. Her skin was the color of coffee and her eyes as silver as the moonlight outside. Her raven black hair cascaded down her back in lustrous waves. For a moment, he found himself under a trance as he stared deeply into her eyes.

"Do you mind if I sit down, mon cher?" Her New Orleans accent was seductive to his ears.

"I would be honored."

The young woman slid gracefully into a chair across from him and continued to stare at him. His body immediately reacted to her. Her scent seemed to fill the air around them, and, with little effort, she had him completely enchanted.

She called the bartender over. He arranged a tray with two glasses, a silver slotted absinthe spoon, a small dish containing sugar cubes, a glass pitcher of cold water, and a bottle of absinthe. He placed the tray on the table, and she asked, "Would you care to partake in a little of the green fairy with me?"

"Isn't that absinthe?"

With a sultry smile, she purred, "Mais oui, mon cher."

Newman shook his head. He dared not try anything that new to him. Absinthe was illegal, and he did not need to be caught with it in his system.   "I need to keep my mind clear for work."

"Hmm... that line sounds as if you have a story to tell. I love to listen to people's stories."

He let out a laugh as he replied, "I have no story to tell. Besides, I would rather learn more about you."

With a twinkle in her eyes, she asked, "Did you know that there is a ritual involved in preparing absinthe?"

Intrigued, he said, "No, I did not. To be honest, I am a virgin to absinthe." He found himself infatuated with this woman in front of him and couldn't take his eyes off her for even a moment.

"Hmm, it's been a long time since I had a virgin before me. First, you see, you must pour the absinthe in a glass made from the finest crystal." She carefully picked up the green absinthe and filled her glass a third of the way full. "Next, gently place the slotted spoon over the glass and place a sugar cube on it. Lastly, you slowly pour cold water over the sugar cube, drop by drop."

Newman watched in fascination as the drink transformed into a milky green liquid. She continued to explain to him, "This result is called the louche. The ritual is very important. This is what helps the flavors blossom. The flavors of the star anise, the fennel, and other herbs rise above the less appealing ingredients such as the wormwood. Some believers swear the ritual dilutes the absinthe, but I assure you, it does not. It makes the drink sweeter, better in my opinion."

He watched as she sampled her absinthe. "You never told me your name," he said.

"Ah, cher, what is in a name?"

Newman took another drink of his whiskey while never taking his eyes off the woman. "So what do I owe the pleasure of your company tonight," he asked.

"I like to welcome all the strangers who grace this establishment." Her voice was almost as hypnotic as her eyes. "Besides, I am a very lustful woman, and I believe you would please me." A sly smile formed across her face and showed off her full bottom lip.

For a moment, he thought he saw something else in her eyes, something a bit frightening. A shiver of trepidation snaked down his spine. "You are a lucky man tonight. I am drawn to you. I like you."

Before he could respond, his cell phone rang. "Sorry, duty calls."

***

As she watched the young man leave, she wondered if he knew just how lucky he really was. She would make sure that their paths crossed again. There was something intriguing about this one.

***

Newman found himself at St. Louis Cemetery #1, right in front of the famous Voodoo Queen, Marie Laveau's, tomb. Her final resting place was a dirty white vault built in Greek revival style. There was a long line of buried dead here, including some of the most famous and infamous citizens of New Orleans. Death played no favorites when it came to your social status. In the end, everyone was the same, ashes to ashes and dust to dust.

He noticed a few small differences in Marie Laveau's vault. A small bronze plaque identified her, many small x's in sets of three adorned her vault and then, of course, the dead body by the front of her vault.

The sky up above lost the darkness of night as sunrise colored the sky with hues of pink, purple and orange.

Newman pointed to the x's and asked, "What is with all the x's on the tomb?"

One of the medical examiner's technicians shared with him, "People like to make requests to Marie Laveau. They believe even in death she will grant them their wish if she is asked properly. Now, if she feels slighted or disrespected by their wish or actions, she curses them. People around here are careful of her juju."

Newman looked at the dead body and said, "Well, somebody wasn't scared of her juju since they left this body here."

"Mais non, someone wants to send a word of warning to the Voodoo community is my guess."

Even in the early morning hours, the humidity was heavy in the air, wrapping itself around his body. Newman swore the sweat sticking to his clothes weighed him down.

It appeared that whatever creature ripped these bodies apart wanted to send a clear message.

***

Watching from the shadows, the Rougarou took on human form for now. He hoped Ezrielle found that it was best to leave him alone and allow him to live this cursed existence in peace. Tonight, he easily killed one of her prized creatures to prove his point.

Chapter 13

Julie Hargrave called out as she left the restaurant, "See you tomorrow!" Her feet ached from her long shift, and she couldn't wait to get home to soak them. Normally, she was home by now, but one of the other waitresses failed to show up, so the manager asked Julie to please cover. Needing all the money she could earn before school resumed, she quickly accepted the offer.

Darkness surrounded her as she walked home the four blocks to her tiny apartment. The moon hid behind the growing storm clouds. Only a thin ribbon of light bled through. The low lying fog had an eerie glow to it.

Julie was one block from her apartment when a noise from behind caught her attention. It sounded like laughing. Unsure of what the person found amusing, she picked up her speed. The clacking of her heels echoed in the stillness of the night. Her eyes darted every which way, and her ponytail bounced as she tried to shorten the distance between her and her home. Julie's body trembled in fear as the sound of laughter reached her ears once more.

She told herself that it was the wind. Only, there wasn't any wind, and, as far as she knew, the wind never sounded like laughter.

A low whistle sounded behind her and made her jump. Fear consumed her as a scream formed at the base of her throat. A tall man with piercing silver eyes suddenly stepped out of the darkness. Even in this heat, he wore a black leather jacket that only added to his massive, muscular frame. Not wanting to slow down, she sidestepped his hulking figure when he called out. "It is late for a beautiful girl such as you to be walking all alone."

A husky edge to his voice caused her blood to turn to ice. She froze in fear when he reached out and grabbed her shoulder. She scanned the area, hoping to see if someone else was around who might help if this turned out bad for her.

Something was not right about th s man; he screamed danger. Julie glanced nervously up at him, and a chill rushed through her. She swore those piercing silver eyes turned red as he cocked his head to the side much like a curious cat. When he smiled down at her with a wicked smirk, her eyes widened in horror. He revealed a set of long, white fangs.

Before she could run for her life, his arm snaked out and grabbed her by the waist to pull her close to him. His large hands held her easily in place. She could not get away from his bruising grasp, no matter how hard she struggled.

She screamed and kicked wildly hoping to free herself from the man's firm grasp. Carrying her off, he clamped one hand hard over her mouth to silence her. Sheer terror pulsed through her veins as she realized his hand was cold as ice.

Within seconds, he'd brought her into a dark alleyway. "Hello, mon douce, my sweet."

***

Josie watched the young girl from the shadows. Her image wavered not more than three feet from her. She sensed the vampire hiding somewhere in the shadows and waited as she watched for potential danger. She could smell its decay; there was no mistaking this putrid odor. It swirled heavy in the air and filled her nose, similar to a heavy, oppressive perfume. Generally, only very old vampires carried this putrid odor.

The girl didn't know it yet, but she was walking straight into the path of her death. Leaping to the next rooftop, Josie watched and waited to protect this young girl from imminent death.

Just as the creature went to satisfy his hunger, Josie called out, "Let her go!"

Josie pulled out her gun and pointed it directly at him. As the click of the safety was released, the sound echoed through the alley. A low growl emitted from deep within his chest as his lips curled into a sinister smirk. "It's a shame to let a tasty morsel like this go. Are you sure you wouldn't rather join me instead?" The vampire sniffed the young woman's neck seductively. "Her blood is perfectly aged," he added. Motioning for Josie to come closer he said, "You hear her fresh blood rushing through her veins? The fear heightens the taste."

Without a word, Josie fired the gun and watched as the vampire was carried away with the wind.

Chapter 14

He scanned the darkness that surrounded him. Tonight, he was searching for the one who was hunting him. He could smell her vile scent. At first, her scent was enchanting; muskiness with a crisp, fruity base quality. The smell was so tantalizing that one couldn't help but enter the world of the forbidden. It wasn't until you were in her world that you truly knew the hell she meant for you. Now, just the smell of fruit turned his stomach.

Tonight, the stench became so heavy in the air it was overpowering. He had no doubt that was her plan. She wanted to feel his fear, and let him know she was tracking him to his demise. He should have known she would seek out retaliation for killing one of her beloved.

As he pushed through the fog, he felt his doom closing in on him as he continued on.

Ezrielle called out to him for the mere pleasure of taunting him, "Run for your pathetic life."

As he continued to run, her laughter pierced through the night. Her sickly sweet voice continued to taunt him, but he refused to look back. He trudged through the knee deep muck of the marshland, back to his lair.

He knew better. Why did he venture this far from the safety of his lair?

"What's wrong, cher? Are you afraid you won't make it back to your pitiful home?" Her heinous laughter snaked down his spine and wrapped itself around him.

Pushing through the sludge, he refused to slow down. When something brushed up against his fur, he tensed as fear gripped him. Had she finally found him?

He had never ventured to this part of her land, and fear prevented him from seeing what was near him. He slowly cleared the sludge away from his eyes and gasped in horror. All around him were skeletons of different sizes. He desperately tried to free himself from the sludge he traveled in. The dead eyes of the trapped souls watched him and silently pleaded for his help.

Ezrielle must have realized where he was because she taunted, "What's wrong, cher? You don't like seeing what has become of those poor victims you killed all in my name? Surely, death doesn't bother you? After all, some of those trapped here were done by you."

She laughed to mock and wickedly taunt him. He feared that she was close now as he desperately scrambled away from the floating corpses. He must get out of the water before they could drag him to his murky death.

As the bodies reached out for him, they wailed, "Don't go. Join us." He continued to struggle and escape this watery grave. He shook off the corpses as he emerged from the water.

"I'm so sorry for causing you this pain," he cried out. He'd never felt as helpless as he did right then. Once again, her laughter echoed through the night air.

"Don't you want to stay with those you sent here?" Her voice slithered down his body as she choked him with her laughter. He swore that if she continued to laugh, he would suffocate.

He ran into the darkness once more. He must escape this place; he must escape her. There was no other choice. His lungs burned as he took off in a fast run. It had been a mistake to venture this close to her land.

He heard footsteps quickly approaching him from behind. Suddenly, she seemed to whisper in his ear, "You are mine now." He looked down at his feet and saw bodies reach up from the ground in an effort to slow him down. Their dead eyes focused on him. He became their prey as they were once his.

He found an extra burst of energy as he rushed to leave the area. Even now, she still had a hold on him. He realized he must break these invisible bonds that held him to her.

As she materialized behind him, he felt the energy around him change. "You should not have left me. We were good for each other."

He looked down at his body and sneered, "You did this to me. I never asked for this."

Walking towards him, she kicked the crawling corpses out of her way as if they were tattered rag dolls. "You have already destroyed my life. Leave me be woman."

The corpses dug their skeletal hands deep into his body. They tore into him as he prepared to make a run for it. He refused to die in this horrific way. He was not willing to surrender just yet. As if Ezrielle had read his mind, her face turned into an ugly mask of hate and anger. There was nothing but evil left in her heart.

With renewed energy, he fled the area, far away from Ezrielle. This time he managed to escape, but what about next time?

Chapter 15

Josie woke with a determined purpose tonight. The cosmic balance of the world had shifted. Impending doom hung over the city. And she had to find out why.

She was grateful that Antoinette LaRue and she had become such close friends. When it came to spells and psychic readings, she relied on Antoinette. Antoinette graciously offered to protect their home with some magical safeguards to ward off any unwelcome visitors. So far, the spells she'd cast seemed to be working.

Antoinette also used magic on their weapons and bullets. Her spells helped to kill the supernatural faster. Older vampires could typically be harder to kill, but not with the spelled weapons they now carried. They died with the same ease as the recently turned.

She had been a creature of the night for almost a century now. In the past, she'd killed without remorse. She knew what pure evil was; had looked it directly in the eyes. She never asked for this life; it was forced upon her. She finally came to terms with this fact. However, if she could prevent others from having this life thrust upon them, then so be it. While out, she fed off of the cesspool of criminals that seemed to congregate in this humid city. She made sure her victims would be found, but the cause of death would be labeled uncertain. The victims were completely drained of blood, and she left no bite marks. She could simply drop the bodies deep in the bayous for the alligators, but she wanted the police to know that they didn't have to worry about this particular criminal anymore. It would be a waste of tax dollars if they thought the criminal bolted instead of having justice served. It was a perfect plan; Josie satisfied her hunger while saving the judicial system countless amounts of money.

The thirst was her biggest problem. If she must feed on human blood, then it may as well be from those who deserved to die. When the moon was full, she had to hunt; she could not resist the urge.

After a quick snack, she went for a walk. She left a note for Tyler in case he worried about where she was. He had been restless lately and was more than likely on the prowl. Their plan so far was working perfectly. Tyler was now a member of the New Orleans Police Department, and he helped her find criminals that deserved a fast and swift punishment.

As soon as she walked outside, a white, stagnant cloud enveloped her. The thick fog made the world look ethereal. If only that were true - but evil lurked under the cover of these low clouds rolling in off the water.

When she rounded the corner, she found the person she was searching for. He went into a local pool hall where a motley crew of oil field workers, shrimp boat captains, and the dark shadows of the swamp came to blow off steam. This guy came to find out which house would be ripe for the picking tonight.

Tyler mentioned that the cops could not find any concrete evidence that this man lured young boys away from their home with the promise of candy and video games, but they knew it was him. They had him under constant watch, but he had yet to slip up.

As soon as she walked into the pool hall, she could tell the air was thick with aggression. Tourists avoided this pool hall, leaving the locals that patronized here alone. Most times, this place was a cesspit of danger. As she smelled the air, she caught the scent of evil that emitted from this man and used her senses to intrude his mind. What she saw lurking in the deep recesses of his mind sickened her. She had no qualms about expunging his existence from this earth.

The feeling to end his life right here became overwhelming. She could already taste the coppery blood as she sat next to him at the bar. It took all her self-control not to tilt his neck back right then and there. Her mouth watered as her fangs grew. She concentrated on the moody blues ballad that reverberated off the walls and seemed to soak into her bones. The band's lead singer strummed the guitar and sang from his very soul – about loss, hopelessness, and utter loneliness. Josie related this song to her life before she had Tyler. . As the band started to play another song, a mellow jazz tune filled the room; Josie knew that it was time.

With her urge under control, she smiled over at the man, "Can I buy you a drink?"

He looked over at her and said, "Beat it lady. You aren't my type."

She looked him deep in the eyes and waited until he was under her spell before she spoke, "I think I am your type. What do you say we leave this joint and find some place nice and private? I have something you and I can share."

Josie dropped a twenty dollar bill as he stood and followed her out the door.

Even in the middle of the night, the streets of New Orleans were bathed in heat and humidity. The humid air swirled with a mixture of smells that ranged from stale beer to night blooming jasmine and all of the different foods cooked in the area. Josie's ears still rang from the bass beats that thumped inside of the club. Even outside of the club, she received no relief. Music filled the night air from the various clubs on Bourbon Street.

As they made their way down Bourbon Street, they had to avoid the people carrying plastic cups that sloshed alcohol onto the ground and anyone who happened to be in the vicinity. Here, the party never ended. Most of these people would never remember what they did in these early morning hours.

Josie found a deserted alley not far from Pirate's Alley. As they made their way deeper inside, the smell of human body odor, urine, and alcohol mingled together in a combination that is distinctively the smell of the French Quarter. A loud rumble of thunder sounded overhead as they continued.

***

As Josie left the body, a humid breeze swept through the alleyway. It tugged at her ponytail and caressed her pale ivory skin. Something in the breeze caught her attention, and her dark eyes narrowed up at the midnight sky.

Something beyond the stale beer and body odor that seemed to cling to the alleyway was drawing her attention. The tantalizing smell had a rich, intoxicating musky aroma. The scent was familiar to her, taunted her memory. The hairs on the back of her neck tingled in warning. Someone was watching her.

She kept to the shadows; her pace decidedly laggard. Ever since moving here, it amazed her how alive this city was even after dark. No one seemed to care about the dangers that lurked around every corner. The bars stayed open until dawn, and party goers danced in the streets all night.

As she continued down the street, she ducked into another alley. When the wind picked up once more, she lifted her face to the sky and smelled the night air once again. The rain was not far away, and she hoped to make it home before the heavens opened up.

As she looked up, she missed seeing the stars in the city; the city lights blocked out the stars. She could barely make out the moon as the clouds danced through the sky.

Almost as if taunting, a large raindrop hit her shoulder. Then slowly more raindrops fell from the sky. People ran for cover before the rain turned into a downpour. Quickening her pace, she made her way home.

When she crossed yet another of the cobblestone lined streets, a stealthy figure caught her attention. The figure kept to the shadows, but she saw the creature's red eyes glowing in the night. This creature had a familiarity to it and as she tried to read its mind, she realized that it blocked her from intruding into its thoughts.

Her body tightened, going on full alert. She crept forward and let her senses take over. She smelled the air, hoping to catch a familiar scent emanating off this creature. The only smell hanging heavy in the air was the freshness of the rain.

Were her eyes playing tricks on her? Maybe, she didn't even see a creature lurking in the shadows.

Suddenly, emerging from the shadows of the night, Josie found herself surrounded by two deadly vampires. The first hissed at her, "You have upset our master."

Josie hissed back, "Your master started this, but I will finish it."

The second vampire sneered at her while hissing, "It won't be tonight, vamp."

Josie smiled wickedly at the two while saying, "So, Master sent two of you to finish me off. It's really too bad that I will send two of his children back to the fires of hell at the same time."

"Foolish, vamp, do you honestly think that you can kill me? I am much older than you. You fool; a pitiful vamp set on revenge cannot kill me."

Josie discreetly removed the silver dagger from her waistband as the two vampires continued circling her, hissing and taunting. She let them continue as to keep them distracted. "You upset Master terribly. He can't believe one of his own children is killing our own."

One of them pounced on Josie and sent her flying into a brick wall. While they believed Josie was down, she made her move. She threw the silver dagger at the vamp that pounced her. It hit directly in the heart; the loud searing sound echoed through the night as it screamed out in pain as it burst into ash.

The second vampire laughed at Josie, "I won't be so easy to kill, vamp." Josie took out her small crossbow and prepared to fire. Hissing, it lunged at her as she aimed and sent the arrow directly into its heart.

***

The master vampire stopped feeding on the young morsel in front of him and screamed out in pain, "My children!"

Mournfully, he asked his flock, "Why must she seek us out to kill? Why can't she just leave us in peace? Did I not stress to my two beloveds how important it was not to toy with her, but kill their sister before she destroyed our family?"

Chapter 16

Jamie Romero slowly walked home, enjoying the night air on her skin when she felt herself being lifted in mid-air by strong hands. Suddenly, she went soaring through the air. Before she could scream, a gag was wrapped around her mouth while a blindfold was placed over her eyes.

The silvery moonlight that she'd just enjoyed was taken away from her and replaced with darkness. She felt herself being dropped to the ground and asphalt cut into her skin. A knee dug into the small of her back while she was effortlessly restrained.

Once again, she was picked up and went soaring through the air before landing unceremoniously on the ground. As the engine roared to life, she realized that she was in a boat. As her captor sped off, she tried to figure out if there was a way to escape. There wasn't time to react or contemplate how to escape until now.

Jamie tried to loosen the restraints on her wrists, but any movement caused them to bite into her flesh. She realized that her abductor had no plans of allowing her to escape.

She had no family or friends here in New Orleans; no one would notice her missing. The manager of the hotel would assume she'd bailed - not wanting to pay for another night.

As the engine died on the boat, muffled noises came from above. She was heaved out of the boat and slung over the shoulder of a man, or a very large woman. She bounced along the captor's shoulder before being dropped onto a cement floor. She heard laughter in the background and keys jingling. Muffled voices were all around her, and a whimper came from somewhere in the room.

A man hollered out, "Quiet!"

A loud banging noise filled the air, and she jumped back instinctively. It sounded like a bat being struck against a metal pipe. As she was shoved in a cage, someone removed her blindfold. The man told her, "If you are good, then I will take off the restraints."

She looked around and noticed at least a dozen other women in cages as well. Several were still restrained while others were simply held inside theirs.

Jamie feared that she had been abducted for a human trafficking ring and shuddered at the very thought of what she may endure.

The hushed whispers silenced as the hollow sound of footsteps grew near. As a figure appeared out of the darkness, the hair on the back of her neck stood up, and goosebumps crawled up her skin.

A growling voice asked in disappointment, "Is this all you have for me?"

A cowering voice answered from a corner, "Yes, Master. This is all we could round up tonight."

The man they called Master replied, "Well, let me see what you have, but next time I expect better."

"Yes, Master."

The man standing in the center of the cages explained to the captives, "Do not speak to the master unless spoken to. No one here will help you so don't bother asking. If you disobey the master's commands, then I promise, you will not like the consequences."

The master walked along the first row of cages. He stopped by each one and inspected the women. One of the women cried hysterically, pleading with anyone to let her go.

When the master shook his head, his voice was low and threatening. "No, this one will not do. She is only good for food." With that simple command, two men carted off the woman's cage. Jamie didn't know what to think about this. These men must have superhuman strength to lift the cage and woman so easily with no exertion.

The master continued to walk down the line of cages, inspecting each woman. Jamie wondered how such a handsome man could be this evil. Women dreamed of meeting this kind of man. He had high cheekbones, lips that begged to be kissed, and eyes that mesmerized you. His eyes were as dark as night; the kind of eyes that looked directly into your soul. Even standing here in this filthy warehouse, there was an air of authority to him.

Though, when he smiled at her, terror gripped her body. Amongst the perfect straight white teeth were a pair of fangs. The master announced to the men, "The rest will do fine. I expect them to be delivered by sunrise."

Without another word, the master left. The man who'd addressed them earlier shared his expectations, "You were all chosen to be slaves. As long as you do what your master commands, you will find the living arrangements quite agreeable. However, you will find that disobeying your master will be very detrimental."

Chapter 17

Tyler looked down at the cup of coffee with utter disgust. Josie spoiled him with the rich blend she made for him at home. The late nights with her and working all day had forced him to drink the swill that the police station here tried to pass off as coffee.

He forced it down, knowing that beggars couldn't be choosers. He desperately needed caffeine as he looked at the clock once again. The hands barely moved today, and it was nothing but pure torture. He swore that for the last hour it felt like the time stayed at three o'clock in the afternoon. He was ready for his shift to end so he could get home to Josie, so they had a few hours to snuggle before she went off to hunt.

The sudden bustle of the police station and the appearance of a young woman at the front desk caught his attention. The woman reminded him of a china doll with her fair skin and the tiny demeanor. If it hadn't been daylight, he would swear she was a vampire. As if sensing that he was watching her, she turned her eyes on him. His breath caught as the most intriguing pair of violet eyes stared straight at him.

She looked as if she was made of porcelain, but looks could be deceiving. Josie was one of the most alluring creatures he'd ever met; yet, at first glance, you would not guess what she was.

As the mystery woman continued to stare at him, he
realized there was something off about her, way off.

Suddenly, the woman left the police station before
talking with whomever she came here to see. He
looked at the clock hoping it was time to punch out,
but there were still another twenty minutes before he
could leave. However, he doubted that this would be
the last time he saw the mysterious woman.

Chapter 18

When would this nightmare end for them? They were treated worse than cattle on their way to slaughter.

Jamie lost count of how much time had passed since her abduction. They were loaded onto trucks the same night of the inspection and brought to a dank barn and held there.

Once again, they were moved but this time by foot. They were led by chains to what appeared to be a large antebellum plantation. From the sounds echoing through the night, she could hear the water lapping up to the bank.

She wasn't sure, but she believed they were still near New Orleans. She suspected the truck driver kept driving in circles for a bit to keep them from guessing their exact location. Even though it felt as if they'd driven for hours, some of the noises stayed consistent.

They were brought in through the kitchen and led directly into the adjacent dining room. A large table running the entire length of the room appeared to be the center of attention.

Jamie and the other captives were lined up against one wall overlooking the table as men and women filled the room. She watched in horror as the men and women chose a captive and brought them to the table.

Something inside of her told her that they were not here as dinner guests.

Screams filled the air as they fed on the captives. Jamie froze in fear as a vampire wrapped his hand around her neck and bit into it. One by one the vampires finished their meals and relinquished their victims. On shaky legs, the captives were once again returned to the dank barn.

"You will be brought food and drink. You WILL eat so that you can keep up your health. The master will be unhappy with poorly fed slaves."

As each day passed living the same hell, Jamie wondered what she'd done to deserve this punishment.

Chapter 19

The scent of fear, mingled with blood, was heavy in the air and stopped Josie in her tracks. Instinctively, her fangs slid out. This one simple occurrence had her feeling like the monster she was.

She smelled the air once more. The scent of blood was still there, tempting her. Taking a deep breath in, she forced herself not to think about the blood and its tantalizing taste. Instead, she reminded herself that it was her destiny to protect this human. As her breathing slowed, the raw intensity of her thirst subsided, and she concentrated on what she needed to do.

Sniffing the air once again, she solidified her fears. Someone was in trouble and, from the smell of it, it was a human.

Closing her eyes, she allowed her other senses to take over. All around her was darkness except for the rapid beating of a heart. In her mind, she sensed, rather than saw, her surroundings. She heard the injured person calling out for help in an alleyway nearby. There was another presence in there with him, though. This tormentor was playing with his prey as a cat would with a mouse. This creature was a dead, soulless shell of a human – just like her.

The guilt of her past hit her hard. She may be a vampire, but she refused to be like this one. She found a way to overcome the thirst, and tonight, she would save another soul. She had a new purpose in life, to protect these humans from prowling vampires.

Adrenaline coursed through her body at the thought of confronting a vampire toying with a human. She must calm her nerves, or the vampire would sense her presence. She used her speed and agility to keep her movements stealthy to keep him from hearing her approach.

When she stepped into the alley, a cloud chose that moment to move in front of the moon, and helped to keep her bathed in the shadows. The frantic heartbeat of the human directed her to the destination better than using her night vision.

She had caught the vampire by surprise before he made a meal of the human he'd cornered. His oily hair hid most of the creature's face, but she felt his eyes on her. He hoped to intimidate her, but instead she met his harsh stare with the same intensity. He still hadn't noticed that she was a vampire, and she planned to keep it that way. Josie taunted the vampire, "Hasn't anyone taught you not to play with your food?"

Not answering right away, the vampire slowly licked away the blood from his lips with careful and deliberate movements. The vampire had yet to let the human go; keeping him in a firm grasp. Josie watched this creature's every movement, knowing he would strike at any moment. "Beat it. I don't share," the vampire growled out.

"Neither do I! He's mine," Josie yelled out. Confused, the vampire just stared at her.

Josie showed the vampire her wrist and explained, "This is my tattoo, and I assure you this one bears my mark as well."

Josie hoped that this distracted him long enough for her to free the human without too much resistance.

She looked over at the human and curled her finger to instruct him, "Come here." Without further hesitation, he freed himself from the vampire's grasp and walked her way.

The vampire reached out for the human once again, but Josie was quicker. Her eyes glowed red to show him that she meant business tonight. The vampire sensed that he wouldn't be feeding off this human and turned to leave. Before he could flee, Josie took out her gun and shot him straight through the heart.

Thankfully, the human was still under her trance, and it never even registered that a vampire just blew into a million tiny little dust particles right before his eyes.

***

Josie made it home in the early morning hours to find Tyler waiting for her on the front porch. "I was worried about you," he said as he held out his arms.

She moved into his welcoming arms.

As he wrapped them around her even tighter, she melted into his warm body. They stood next to each other, gazing out into the night.

In the glimmering moonlight, she felt his eyes on her. "You are so beautiful," he said. Tyler nibbled on the curve of her neck. "So unbelievably beautiful."

He turned her around taking her lips in his. The kiss started off gentle, but neither of them could keep it that way. As the kiss deepened, he carried her into the house. All thoughts about what she'd done earlier left her mind as her breathing became ragged. Tyler traced his fingers down her body as he slipped the clothes off her. Not wanting to wait any longer before she felt his touch on her bare skin, she ripped the remainder of them off.

As he continued to touch her, she closed her eyes and melted into him. She ran her fingers down his muscular back, exploring his body even further. He trailed kisses from her ear to her neck, and she gave herself to him completely.

Chapter 20

He made sure his wife was asleep. With her sleeping, he could pursue what he yearned for all day. Walking across the room, he pulled open the heavy curtains. The full moon caressed his body, and he reveled in its seductive touch.

Walking out into the night, he allowed the moonlight to shower over him; bringing forth the changes his body needed to be made whole. The ground beneath his feet felt like heaven as he covered the miles between his house and his quest for food. It had been a while since his last feeding, and he couldn't wait any longer. Tonight, he wanted to enjoy himself at his leisure, not a rush feeding.

He sniffed the air and found a tantalizing morsel a few short feet in front of him. As he neared, he smiled wickedly at the discovery of a lone jogger. The young man's body rippled with taut muscles as he moved with little effort.

In one quick pounce, he was on top of him. The man's fear pulsed through the night, adding to the richness of his blood. Fear got the adrenaline rushing and helped give the raw flesh a wild taste that he craved.

Before the man could draw a scream, his throat was sliced open and warm, red blood rushed into the waiting mouth. A low growl of contentment escaped his throat as he relished in the warm, sweet taste he craved. Once his needs were fulfilled, he hurried back home. Dawn was fast approaching, and it would be time to return to his human life.

He wondered what the world would think if they knew his true self. Would they continue to put their trust in him?

Chapter 21

As Josie leapt from rooftop to rooftop, she caught sight of strange shadows. Her body tensed in anticipation as she realized the movements were too fast to be human.

Moonlight washed over the area as she made out the vampire carrying the human to the alley. She eased her gun out of its holster as she moved in closer.

The vampire snarled and hissed as Josie approached it. It still had not released the human from its firm grasp. As she moved closer to the creature, it forgot about his meal in order to fight for his life.

He took off with lightning speed with Josie fast on his trail. Running with astounding speed, she could not get a clear shot at him.

Without warning, he stopped and leapt toward Josie. She found herself looking directly into his face. As she brought her gun up to shoot, the creature reached out and knocked it out of her hand. The gun soared through the air and landed several feet away from her. Before she could react, the vampire shoved her into a brick wall. She winced from the pain, but recovered quickly. She bared her fangs at the vampire and hissed.

Another vampire stepped out of the shadows. Everything became a blur as two more vampires immediately descended on Josie. One of the vampires looked familiar to her. He must have sensed the recognition in her eyes as he said, "What is wrong Josie? You don't recognize me?" His voice was familiar. She stared at him wide-eyed. His thick, wavy, dark hair barely touched his shoulders. He still had a tall and well-defined muscled body with the most mesmerizing almond-shaped eyes as well as a strong jaw line. There was a hard edged raspiness to his voice when he asked, "Did you think I was killed along with the others?"

Josie shook her head in disbelief. "James? James is that really you?" she asked.

That small amount of time used for shock and hesitation should have cost her her life, but instead, James smiled mischievously at her. However, James's partner kept her pinned against the wall. Josie looked around to make sure that the human at least escaped unharmed. "You needn't worry about the human. He was merely a ploy to get you here," James explained.

Josie looked into his scarlet eyes and asked, "What do you want with me James?"

Josie was surprised that James had escaped and stayed here in New Orleans. James sneered at her saying, "A few of us managed to escape that night. Some had high hopes that they could relocate the carnival and keep on going, but some of us knew the risk was too great. A few moved on, but most of us stayed here in New Orleans. We found the city intoxicating. It got under our skin, and we didn't want to leave. Besides, we seem to fit in here." Laughing out loud with hatred in his voice, he added, "I actually thought our master would come for us. Instead, he left us to fend for ourselves."

It didn't surprise Josie that they stayed. Tourists often commented on how they would love to live here. As much as she hated to admit it, New Orleans was her home, and she had indeed missed it. If only there weren't just as many bad memories as good here. "Joshua had his own plans, and I am afraid that those plans did not include us."

James laughed at her statement, his fangs glinting in the moonlight. "Yes, and now, you are helping these innocent humans. Have you forgotten what you are?"

Hissing, she said, "I have forgotten nothing."

"You turned your back on your kind, cher. I know you still have bloodlust in your veins. We all do, why must you deny it?"

She stared at him in silence, refusing to answer. He could not entice her into his fold. That life was in her past, and she wouldn't let this sweet reunion continue. Sensing her uneasiness, he said, "Relax Josie, we didn't lure you here to kill you; we only want to have you come to an understanding."

She asked with a voice mixed with curiosity and anger, "What kind of understanding?"

The wind picked up, taking fragments of paper and whirling dust from the cracked ground. Shimmers of heat danced across the road. Even at this hour, the oppressive heat was stifling.

In the distance, sirens pierced the night air, and they sounded as if they were getting closer. What happened to have so many sirens at this hour? Even without the vampires, there was an abundance of crime in this city recently. She saw many changes in her lifetime, and she had a feeling that the violence would continue to rise.

Shaking the other vampire off of her, she stepped forward. She was determined to find out what James wanted. "What do you want James? You have my attention."

"Some vampires do not deserve to be hunted down Josie. We are not all the heartless, black souls you think of us."

She looked at him and saw in his features that he was sincere and honest. Still, she couldn't push her nagging troubles away. Yet, he was taking a risk in seeking her out. "You know that I am right. We are like you, just wanting to survive on the bane of the earth. We only seek out those that deserve to be removed from this earth, and none of us would dare turn another individual into a vampire."

She shook her head in disbelief. "I know that not all vampires hunt just for the fun of it, but lately, there has been an increase in feedings, more than there should be. Whoever is doing this has no qualms about leaving the bodies to be discovered."

"Please be aware that some of us only feed on those as you do." He turned his wrist over to show her his tattoo and explained, "Those who belong to our coven have this tattoo."

Josie moved to inspect his wrist closer. He took the brand that Joshua used for their family and turned it into something to be used for their coven. "I will try to distinguish if the vampire feeding is from your coven, but I cannot promise that it will be something accomplished every time. If they come charging at me, I will have no choice but to kill them," she promised.

"I can understand that. I will let the members of my coven know."

She furrowed her brows. "And how do I know that you are only feeding on those that deserve to die?"

"I know that you have your connections. I have been following you closely."

Josie narrowed her eyes and let her mind access his thoughts. Images and voices swirled together as she watched him stake her out, along with some of the same criminals she stalked. Unlike her though, they tended to leave their victims in abandoned buildings. "The sun will be up soon. I am sure you have someone who will be worried about you if you don't show up."

"I don't understand. How did you know about me?" she asked.

He let out a sigh and said, "I saw you late one night. You were busy saving the young woman, but I watched and was intrigued. It was surprisingly easy to keep out of your sight. You are right though; there is a shift in the balance here. Your master may be responsible for some of these vampires. Someone out there has some very nasty plans in store. I don't know all the details yet, but I will keep you up-to-date if I hear anything."

Josie asked, "How will I find you?"

His jaw set and his eyes clouded over. "For now, I will find you. It would be in your best interest if not everyone knew of your existence at this time."

Josie sighed in exasperation. Right now, there was nothing else she could do. There was definitely something unusual going on, and she had every intention of finding out just what it was, no matter what it took. But she wasn't about to pass up help on that front. She looked at James one more time before she turned and left the alley.

Josie sped through downtown New Orleans to get back home before the sun rose. Just the thought of the orange and pink hues of the sunrise chasing her caused her great anxiety. She was foolish to stay out this long. The others must have a hideout nearby if they didn't fear the sunrise.

She reached the safety of her home just as the sun made its way over the horizon. Tonight had been a close call, in more ways than one. Somehow, this coven knew about her and that she had an informant in the police force. Did they know Tyler was more than just an informant? Did they suspect that he was a shape shifter? That could prove dangerous for him. They might use that to their benefit. She intended on finding out just how they knew what they did.

Tyler pulled her into his arms as soon as she walked in the door. "Is everything okay? I was so worried about you. You weren't answering your phone."

She looked down at her phone and explained. "I turned it to silent before I went hunting. Everything is fine; I was held up a little bit longer than I expected."

Tyler looked at her, his brows creasing with worry. "I don't like that you stay out this close to sunrise."

She reached up and kissed him on the lips. "I don't want you to worry, but I ran into some vampires that know about me, and they suspect that I have an informant in the police force."

Tyler let out a long list of curse words. "I don't like this one bit."

She reached up, stroked his cheek, and said, "I know, my love. I promise to be careful, but I want you to be careful as well."

"Maybe, I should look into having them switch me to nights again."

Shaking her head, she said, "No, you are more helpful working the day shift. Vampires will sense your presence if you are with me at night."

"Go and get some rest. Something tells me that you will have another busy night ahead of you. Just promise me that you won't stay out as late next time," he gave her a kiss on the forehead before turning her towards the bedroom.

A soft yawn escaped her mouth as Tyler left for work. In no time, Josie showered and was lying in bed with the lights out; though sleep eluded her. Tonight's conversation kept playing over and over in her mind. Even though James mentioned they'd followed her there, part of her hoped she didn't meet up with him again. Seeing him made her remember more than she was ready to admit to. However, she was relieved that others like her had regrets and wanted to make amends for their past sins.

Still, something bothered her; something wasn't right. Josie found herself drifting off to sleep with her mind once again filled with memories.

James was one of Joshua's pets. Everyone at the carnival knew James was one of the more elite vampires; one you didn't want to cross in a fight. Josie saw James's true nature in the early years, and, unlike the other female vampires, she didn't swoon over the man. She still wasn't sure if she could trust him.

Chapter 22

For a Saturday night, Detective Newman was surprised to find Faux Pas empty. Usually the place was packed with customers drinking and dancing. However, tonight there seemed to be no one frequenting here.

As he walked up to the bar, the bartender nodded his head in acknowledgment. "What can I get for you?"

Newman picked up on the bartender's body signals. He portrayed innocence, but he was hiding something. Newman had heard rumors of the parties this particular establishment held for vampires, and that the bartender found the best humans who would cater to the darker desires of the vampires.

"I hear that you hold parties for certain clientele." The bartender didn't even flinch at the statement. Instead, he continued drying the wine glass in his hand.

He shrugged his shoulders as he said, "I have no idea what you are talking about, mon ami."

Newman stared at him, not believing a word he was saying. "Oh, but I think you do. There must be a reason why there aren't many people in here tonight. Are you expecting some important guests later on?"

"Detective, you can see that the bar is open. I can't help that there are no customers."

Newman glanced around and said, "Something tells me that until I walked in you were telling customers the bar was closed for the night."

The bartender laughed, "Now why would I do that?"

"If you were to have a private party, you wouldn't want just anyone walking in."

As Newman stared at the bartender, his eyes began to shine. A better term for what he saw was glowing. Just what was this bartender?

As he left the bar, he told himself that it would be wise to keep this one under surveillance.

Chapter 23

The taste of blood caused the Rougarou in him to surface. He snarled up into the face of the vampire as he braced for another blow.

He actually welcomed the blow. He didn't care about his orders; he'd sought her out for a fight and to show this vampire who was higher on the food chain.

His bloody lip was quickly forgotten as Josie grabbed the creature by the throat, banging his head against the ground. He anticipated the next blow and blocked it with ease. A loud crunch sounded out as the Rougarou's elbow made contact with Josie's face.

***

Josie laughed at the creature's attempt to hurt her. "You like to play rough don't you, Rougarou?" In one quick move, she sent the Rougarou sailing through the air.

The Rougarou gracefully landed on his feet, preparing for another attack. She hated to end this dance so soon; she was enjoying herself too much.

The creature's psychic abilities were weak, if not non-existent. Josie smiled as the Rougarou advanced. This was pure entertainment to her; everyone needed a good fight now and then - it kept her sharp.

Normally, she preferred to keep the fights fair, but with this poor creature, it was hard to keep it fair. The Rougarou that picked the fight with her had no idea who she truly was. All he cared about was killing a vampire so that he could brag about it.

This one had been on her hit list for a while now. At first, she believed it was another vampire slaughtering the homeless here until she reached into the killer's mind. He was an evil creature who led these poor homeless victims to their death as if they were cattle being led to the slaughterhouse.

Josie knew that Tyler waited for her in the shadows, watching her every move. She thought Tyler would jump in at any minute, but so far, he stayed back, allowing her the chance to prove herself.

Josie rushed the Rougarou, faking a punch while sweeping his legs out from beneath him with a swift kick. Unfortunately, he jumped right back on his feet, recovering fast and coming at her with fangs bared.

Just before he made bodily contact, she threw her weight forward, leaned down low, and tossed him over her shoulder with ease. She didn't allow him a chance to get back on his feet as she quickly unholstered the gun from her back and fired. As he died, he took his human form one last time.

She called out for Tyler, "I know you are back there. You can come out now."

Tyler heard the sirens off in the distance and yelled, "Go. Someone must have called in the altercation."

Josie quickly blew him a kiss. "I will see you at home, my love."

***

Tyler found a safe hiding place and waited. It didn't take long before the New Orleans Police Department was crawling all over the place. Before heading home, he wanted to make sure they didn't find any clues as to this man's true identity.

As another car pulled up, he paid close attention. One of the officers had called in Detective Newman to look into the murder a little deeper.

While Detective Newman looked over the body, he ordered, "Now, explain to me why I was called in."

The young officer working the scene started, "Well, this seemed to be the type of case you guys like, a mysterious death in the middle of the night. The caller swore that a young woman was being attacked by a rabid dog. We heard you were looking for a rabid dog, after all."

Newman looked around. "Well, I don't see a dog lying around anywhere. All I see is a dead, half naked man lying in the street. He did take a beating right before death. But I still don't understand why calling me in at this time was necessary."

Newman worked the scene for a while longer before he informed the young officer, "I will follow up with the coroner, but there isn't anything I can do. You can have forensics work the scene, but I doubt you will find anything helpful. It appears this guy pissed off the wrong person or was just wasted."

Satisfied that the new detective wasn't going to waste time on this particular investigation, Tyler headed home; he just wanted to hold Josie tight in his arms.

Chapter 24

Keith Anderson kept to the shadows in this small neighborhood. With this being a long weekend, there had to be a family somewhere who'd gone on a road trip. All he needed was to slip into the house and steal any prescription drugs they left behind. Most people filled a small travel container with their medicine and left the larger bottles at home. He hit the jackpot last month when he broke into a house and found the owner had a three month supply of oxy on hand.

Just ahead, a movement caught his attention; a figure was hidden up high in the tree. Keith peered into the darkness trying to see what this person was up to. From the shape, it appeared to be a young woman. Was she staking out the neighborhood as well?

Suddenly, the woman jumped down from the tree. When she looked at Keith, her eyes glowed red, and he stepped away from her in surprise. When he scrutinized her the second time, her eyes no longer glowed red; the true color indiscernible in the dark.

Keith found himself drawn to this woman's face. Her radiant, pale skin glimmered in the moonlight. With her hair pulled into a tight ponytail, it brought more attention to her eyes that were mesmerizing this close up. There was a strange iridescence to them that could be noticed even in the dark.

He looked at the woman and warned, "You shouldn't be out here at this time of the night."

The woman smiled at him, a secret lurking behind her eyes. "Something tells me that I am safer than you are, cher."

Her words had him glancing over his shoulder, expecting someone to jump out at him. It wouldn't be the first time a pretty woman helped a man lure victims. Though this time, the area remained empty.

He decided to let the young woman be. "Well, I must be on my way." As Keith walked past the woman, he sighed. He wouldn't be able to break into any of these homes. This woman could easily identify him if a robbery were reported.

As he walked away, he looked back to discover that the woman was no longer there. A shiver raced down his spine. Shaking it off, he headed back to where he'd hidden his car.

As he neared his parked car, he felt someone watching him; felt their gaze focused on his back. However, each time he looked back, no one was there. Then from out of nowhere, someone jumped him from behind, slamming him to the ground. Air burst from his lungs. Before he could take another breath, his attacker pinned him to the ground.

Keith desperately tried to fight his attacker off. He felt a cold breath on his neck as teeth gnashed at his throat. Without warning, he was rolled over. A gasp escaped his lips as he looked at the young woman once more.

As her slim, cold fingers wrapped around his wrists forcing him still, he suddenly realized the insane strength this woman had. He twisted his head from side to side while he desperately tried to buck this crazy woman off of him.

The hair from her ponytail caressed his neck as her teeth lunged for him. Once again, the woman's eyes glowed red. As her vicious teeth sank into the tender flesh of his neck, he wondered what kind of a nightmare he'd landed himself in. His scream of terror and pain pierced the silence of the night.

He became aware of a terrible sucking sensation on his neck as coldness took over his body. A chill started in his fingers and toes and slowly traveled to the core of his body. The coldness consumed him inch by inch.

As the darkness closed in on Keith, his last conscious thought was that no one would miss him.

***

It was a halo of pain and agony that brought Keith out of his unconscious state. A fire burned deep in his body and every nerve in his body felt on fire. Before opening his eyes, he let out a guttural scream.

Writhing in pain, he finally managed to get up on all fours. He desperately tried to escape the pain that seemed to grip his very soul.

A voice called out from the darkness, "Hush now. The pain will soon pass."

A new wave of fear washed over him. As he tried to back away from the location of the voice, pain once again tore at his body. He swore this time it felt as though it would rip him in half.

"What is going on? What did you do to me?" It was hard for him to say each word as his throat burned with every breath.

"Relax, my son. You are turning into something more than a mere human."

He forced the words out with as much strength as he could muster. "I feel as if I am in Hell."

"Only for a moment. Would you like to feel better, my child?"

He groaned out, "Yes, please. Please make this stop."

He looked up and saw a man moved closer to him. There was a slowness to his walk that did not fit his age. It was as if his body had aged before his looks.

When the man raised his own wrist to his mouth, Keith caught a flash of his elongated sharp teeth before they pierced into the man's skin.

As blood flowed from the man's wrist, Keith yelled out, "No, stop. What are you doing?"

Before the man answered, something rose from deep within Keith. It was dark and wicked, a hunger that never existed in him before.

Acting purely out of instinct, with no thoughts or consideration to his actions, Keith grabbed the man's wrist and locked his mouth on the wound. Greedily, he slurped at the blood, gulping down mouthfuls of the thick, cold liquid.

Suddenly, a new pain took over his body. This agonizing pain was directed at the center of his heart. As he scrambled away from the man, a sinister smile formed on his face. The man simply stood over Keith and watched his agony and terror with cold, impassive eyes.

Keith barely croaked out, "What have you done to me?"

Pain took over Keith's every thought, every feeling. It pulsed through him, causing his whole body to begin to spasm. His eyes rolled back in his head as his teeth clamped down harshly, barely missing his tongue.

His heart raced in his body, pounding loudly in his ears. Out of nowhere, his heart suddenly stopped beating, and, along with it, the suffering and agony.

He reached up to touch his face and found his skin smoother and softer than before. His muscles burned with a renewed strength. Even his jaw seemed to be thick and muscular.

Even more surprising was the stillness around him. The sounds that had plagued him his whole life seemed to be quiet. Even that strange whistle that always came from his nose was now gone.

Growling, he asked, "What have you done to me?"

"I've given you a new, better life."

Jumping to his feet with a new agility, he stepped away from the man. "What are you talking about?"

"I told my pet to bring me someone she felt would be a perfect member of our family, and she chose you."

The woman who'd attacked him walked out of the shadows. "He is mine, right poppa? He will stay with me for all eternity?" she asked.

The young woman moved closer to him, lifted his hand, and placed his palm over where her heart would normally be beating. She smiled up at him and explained, "I knew you were perfect for me when I saw you. You are perfect for this family. Just imagine the fun we can have together."

Backing away from the two people he yelled, "You are crazy! I am going home!"

As Keith looked around for an exit, the woman moved swiftly to block his path. She hissed at him, and he stepped back when he noticed her eyes glowed red once more, and she revealed her lethal fangs. "You will not leave me, cher. I am your master."

A ferocious anger rose deep inside of him at her words. "Try and stop me if you must," he snarled as he easily pushed past her.

As soon as he stepped into the night air, he noticed the crisp air and how much sharper the noises were. Desperate to escape the two monsters, he found himself drawn to the beauty of the night. Why had he never noticed how beautiful this was before?

He took off into the night, uncertain of his destination. It was as if he had an internal compass built inside of him, and the moon and stars were calling to him; their points in the sky guided his way.

He ran with a speed he'd never experienced before. Any exhaustion he felt before completely vanished; no sense of fatigue weighed on his body. Instead, he had a new boundless and everlasting energy.

Keith soon found himself near his favorite bar. He was shocked when he found the monstrous woman was suddenly by his side. "I see you are hungry, my pet. Though, you cannot feed in public," she said.

All of a sudden, Keith became aware of the beating all around him. The pulse of the patrons' hearts inside of the bar called out to him. When a young woman walked out of the bar and smiled up at him, he was instantly drawn to her throat. He saw the thump of her heartbeat right in the sweet spot of her neck. It was completely alluring to him. The smell of unshed blood filled his nostrils, perfuming the air like gardenias on this balmy night.

His breathing grew ragged as his fangs elongated. His mouth watered at the thought of sinking his teeth into her neck.

Raising a hand to his mouth, he touched the sharp ends of his teeth. The skin of his finger cut easily by the vicious sharp point of his tooth. He watched in awe as the small cut healed beneath his gaze.

With an overpowering hunger, he leaped in front of the woman, picked her up, and carried her off into a nearby alley. He clamped his hand over her mouth to silence her screams. Unable to control the darkness inside of him, he bit down on the woman's neck and greedily drank the blood from her body. In the distance, he heard his maker laugh at his actions.

Keith now knew that the devil had claimed his soul. The statuesque vampire moved to his side as he began to hate her with a renewed ferociousness. The smell of spilled human blood hung heavy in the air as he looked down at his recent kill.

His maker smiled up at him, "You may hate me at this moment, but my name will forever be on your lips. You will always remember my name. Adrianna. My name will be the one constant that you carry with you for eternity. You are mine forever, cher, and will always remain mine."

Keith looked down at this woman and vowed one day to be free of her. However long it took, he would find retribution for her destroying his life and turning him into this monster.

He would get his revenge.

Chapter 25

Cheryl Granger wanted to curl up in a ball somewhere and die. Today had been one of the worst days of her life. Little did she know, today would also be the day that her world changed.

As she carried her box of personal belongings to her car, she shuddered in fear. Fear of the unknown, and fear of what her husband would do when he found out that she no longer had a job. Heaven forbid he had to find a real job. No, he considered himself a male model and had to sit by the phone and wait for it to ring, needing to be ready at a moment's notice. When she pointed out that that was why there were cell phones, he'd hit her so hard that she passed out for over two hours. Since then, she bit her tongue.

She often wondered how she'd wound up in this predicament. She had a deep sense of foreboding that one of these days he would kill her. She never could find the courage to call and ask her sister for help.

She'd only dated Jason for two months before they eloped to Las Vegas. Now, she was ready to admit that her sister had been right. She didn't know Jason well enough to marry him. Could she swallow her pride and beg her sister for help?

It would be so easy to leave with the meager belongings from her desk and drive straight to her sister's house. But so much time had passed, she may not live there anymore. Jason forced Cheryl to break all ties with her family. She considered using her lunch break to find a public computer since he refused to allow her access to the computer at home and search out her sister. But fear that Jason would somehow find out had prevented her from fulfilling the task. She suspected Jason had placed a tracking device on her since he always knew exactly where she was.

As she pulled up to her house, her heart pounded in fear. Once inside, she was greeted with silence. Silence in her house was never a good thing.

Her heart sank as she walked into the kitchen and found Jason sitting at the kitchen table with his back to her. She swallowed down her fear and forced a smile on her face. She dared not tell him that she'd lost her job. If she did, he would kill her. By the looks of it, he had sat here brooding most of the day. And judging from the number of empty beer bottles on the table, he drank heavily today.

Trying to act cheerful in an attempt to compensate for the dark mood radiating from Jason she asked, "Hi honey, how was your day?"

He snarled up at her, "How the hell do you think my day went? I have been waiting for you to come home and fix supper. Why are you so late?"

She was only a few minutes late, but he was on the verge of igniting his temper. She didn't want to set off any sparks. "Traffic was heavy this evening. I tried to get home as fast as I could."

"What are you planning on fixing for supper? I don't see where you posted the menu like you are supposed to."

Cheryl moaned to herself. She was so tired last night that it slipped her mind. He could smell what she had in the slow cooker or just look inside. At least she remembered to put a meal on before leaving for work. "I am so sorry, honey. I will prepare the menu tonight after we eat."

"No, you will prepare it while I eat. You can eat afterwards."

Ignoring her growling stomach, she replied, "As you wish."

Cheryl hurried over to the slow cooker to ensure that the meat had finished cooking. The aroma of beef roast and gravy tantalized her nose as she checked to see if the roast was tender. At least Jason hadn't turned off the slow cooker as he did once before. He'd blamed her for his oversight that time and punished her severely. She had to call in sick for three days before the bruises faded and could be covered.

As she cooked a pot of rice, Jason called out to her, "Only make enough rice for me tonight. It wouldn't hurt you to cut back on the carbs. Sitting in that chair all day is showing."

A coil of anger stirred inside of her. Biting her tongue, Cheryl cooked Jason a small pot of rice. Now, she second guessed her decision on coming home instead of driving to her sister's home. Why did she let Jason control her life?

She wasn't stupid. Cheryl knew what Jason did to her was wrong. Yet, she took his abuse. No matter how badly he hurt her, she put up with it.

She had a life before Jason and could make it on her own without him. She should be able to live without constantly fearing when a fist would come down on her.

Maybe, what she feared most was what Jason's reaction would be if she did leave him. He had no qualms about giving her a quick punch in the gut if she burned dinner; she could only imagine what he would do if she left him.

Cheryl pulled out another beer from the refrigerator and popped the top off for him. As she handed him a beer, his shoulders relaxed. With a faint smile, she asked him, "Why don't you go into the living room while I finish up supper? I know you worked hard today and would like to put your feet up."

She held her breath as he just sat there sipping his beer. He was still reluctant to leave her alone, which meant that he hadn't decided whether he should punish her or not.

Finally, he admitted, "I am tired. I sat by the phone all day waiting for my agent to call and inform me that I landed the modeling contract I applied for last week. The decision was supposed to be made today."

"I am so sorry, honey. I know how frustrated you must feel."

Instantly, he was on his feet, sending his chair crashing to the floor behind him. He rapidly moved in front of her, putting his face mere inches from hers. She felt his breath hot against her skin as his fingers wrapped around her neck, squeezing tightly. Her breath caught in her throat as his fingers dug in deeper, choking her. "Don't you dare tell me you know how I feel!"

Shoving her backwards, she crashed into the kitchen cabinet. Pain shot up her body as red, hot agony throbbed around her aching ribs and back. Out of instinct, she dropped to the floor and curled up into a fetal position, using her arms to protect her head.

Instead of hitting her again, he grabbed his beer bottle and walked out of the room. It wasn't long before the sound of the television reached her ears. She knew from experience that he was still itching for a fight and could be provoked again at any time. Even if she stayed silent for the rest of the night, he would find a reason to punish her.

Cheryl rolled to her side and pressed her cheek against the cool tiles of the floor. She stayed in this position until the pain subsided. As it dissipated to a familiar ache, she slowly stood up using the cabinets for support.

She didn't deserve to be treated like this. She really should leave him and make a new life for herself; maybe, she would eventually fall in love again. Next time, she would find someone who wanted to love her and not inflict pain.

Suddenly, Jason's voice filled the air once more, "I hope you are finishing up supper. I am getting hungry."

Weakly, she replied, "It's almost ready." Anger burned deep inside of her. Her body may be weak, but the woman inside of her no longer was. She WOULD change her life.

Later that night as Cheryl curled up in bed, Jason's heavy footsteps sounded down the hall. After supper, he had taken a bottle of tequila to the living room and watched television. As he stumbled drunk to the bedroom, her whole body tensed as she waited for him. She forced her body to relax and tried to breath steady hoping he would believe she was fast asleep.

She listened as he finished up in the bathroom and moved into the room with her. As he slid his warm body beside her, she was thankful she'd had the foresight to turn away from his side of the bed. He scooped her up into his arms and pressed her body into his.

As he nuzzled her neck, he whispered into her ear, "I love you so much. Why must you do things to make me angry at you?"

With the smell of alcohol heavy on his breath, Cheryl pretended to be sound asleep and didn't hear a word he said. She didn't even want him to touch her.

Unsatisfied with her silence, he forced her to face him. Out of instinct, Cheryl tensed, causing her body to become hard and unwelcome. Jason ignored the message her body sent out and kissed her face. "You are beautiful, my love," he told her.

She tried to push his body away. "Jason, not tonight, I am really tired."

Putting a finger up to her lips, he whispered, "Hush, my love. You know that I love you. I want to show you just how much."

Trying to push him away once more, she pleaded, "Jason. Please…"

He pinned her to the bed and forced his mouth down on hers. She felt her lips mashing against her teeth. Fear surged through her. Surely, he wouldn't force her to love him.

Suddenly, Jason was freed from her body and flying through the air. Crashing into the far wall, his body made a sickening crunch as he slumped to the floor, groaning. She looked around the room trying to figure out what happened. What caused her husband to go flying through the air?

She carefully approached him as one would a wounded wild animal. "Jason, are you all right?"

As he let out a soft groan, unmoving on the floor, she thought about how much he deserved this. Slowly, Jason's eyes blinked open.

He sat up and told her, "Someone broke into the house. They grabbed me from behind."

Cheryl shook her head. "I didn't see anyone else in the room, Jason."

As she looked down at him, she saw fear in his eyes. She knew that a scared animal could also be a very dangerous one. "No! I am telling you someone is in

here. I felt their hands on me. Their cold hands
grabbed me from behind and threw me off of you."

A chill of fear washed over her as she looked around
the room once more. Jason had a lot to drink tonight,
but surely, he wouldn't have imagined someone
pulling him off of her.

She shook her head when no one suddenly
materialized in the room. Someone couldn't have
entered their bedroom without her seeing them.

Suddenly, Jason's face was full of rage instead of fear.
"Who is he?" Jason demanded. "I know you are
seeing someone. Are you screwing some guy in MY
bed?"

Cheryl's eyes widened with terror as he approached
her. Taking her silence as confirmation, Jason stormed
at her. "You have!" He shouted out incredulously.
"You are seeing someone else behind my back. You
are nothing but a slut!"

The statement hit her hard. Unable to find her voice,
she shook her head as she backed away from her angry
husband. She rasped out, "No... No... I swear to you I
haven't!"

Thankfully, Jason's injuries prevented him from lunging
at her. As if he suddenly remembered he was hurt, he
reached up and touched the back of his head. When

he drew his fingers away from his head, she saw the dark blood on his fingertips.

As soon as he saw the blood, he started to rant, "You need to call an ambulance. I'm bleeding."

She let out a sigh. Leave it to Jason to think that just the mere sight of blood meant that he needed to be carried off to the emergency room.

As she stared at the blood, a sliver of malice ran through her. He gave her far worse injuries without a care for her well-being. Not once was she ever allowed to seek medical attention for any of the injuries he'd caused her, yet, once again, she remained silent.

Taking a deep breath, she looked at him, "Let me put some ice on it and see if the bleeding stops."

Glaring at her, he yelled, "I am telling you I need an ambulance!"

"Jason, you need to think this through. What are you going to say? It's not like you can tell the first responders that an invisible person attacked you. They will ask you if you were drinking, and you won't be able to deny that fact. You can smell the alcohol on your breath. They will more than likely even commit you for some psychological tests and then what? That would hurt your chances of landing any modeling job.

No one wants to hire someone who may have mental issues.”

For once, Jason just stared at her, unable to form a simple reply. Still, Cheryl wondered what really did happen. She saw her husband fly through the air, and there was an actual indentation in the sheetrock from where he'd landed with a powerful force.

Cheryl found her gaze drifting to the window, wondering if someone did manage to slip in and out without their knowing. Suddenly, a woman stepped from the shadows; her pale skin gave her an ethereal glow.

As Jason lunged for the woman, she held out a hand. Jason stopped, frozen in place. The woman looked at Cheryl and asked, “Why do you stay with him?”

Swallowing back her fear, she felt the tears burn in her eyes as she replied, “I have no other place to go.”

Cheryl watched as the woman shook her head. “You are so very wrong, mon cher. Your sister stopped by the police station asking for help. That is why I am here.”

“Are you a cop?”

“Mais non. I am something better. I came to check on you, but I sensed he had ulterior motives tonight. You are lucky I came when I did.” The woman looked back at the man she had under her spell, "You know that he will kill you, don't you?"

"I have feared that."

The woman looked at Cheryl and explained. "No, I saw it in his mind. He planned on doing it tonight. I could have taken care of him earlier, but I wanted you to see just how dangerous he truly was."

Cheryl looked at the woman and asked, "My sister sent you?"

"Yes. Now, I need you to pack and be gone. I must deal with this husband of yours, and you don't want to be here to witness it."

***

Josie had been watching the house intently these last few hours; Tyler came home this afternoon and told her about a worried sister. She had not heard from her sister since she married her husband, Jason Granger, almost three years ago. The sister, Rebecca, feared he beat Cheryl and asked that the police do a wellness check on her.

Tyler had been upset when the local detective brushed the woman off, telling her that there was nothing they could do to help. Tyler had no desire to check in on Cheryl Granger, but he knew that Josie would.

Josie stared into the woman's eyes to make sure that she wouldn't remember seeing her. All this woman needed to remember was seeking out her sister for help. Josie planned on leaving the body near a bar so it appeared as if he died of alcohol poisoning.

Josie saw the true evil that lurked in his soul. He truly intended on killing this woman tonight. He, of course, would have found another woman to scam before killing her as well. No, he deserved to die. She was already growing weak with hunger as the woman scurried out of the house.

As Josie left the body to be found by a passerby, she caught the smell of blood in the air. She lifted her face up to the night sky hoping to find out exactly where the smell came from.

Another vampire was hunting close by. While the vampires were common, it was getting worse since they had started to hunt in packs. They were no longer lone creatures who used their solitary nature to keep them unnoticed. Instead, most learned from Joshua how beneficial a family could be.

Without another thought, Josie leapt into the air. As she soared with outstretched arms, she reveled in the feeling of true weightlessness. She hit the roof of a nearby building with a loud thud. And while the impact jarred her muscles, she felt no pain.

She stealthily leapt from building to building, heading home before sunrise. There wasn't enough time to seek out the other vampire. She must head home, or she would be forced to seek shelter in an abandoned building.

***

Detective Newman shook his head as he continued to look at the dead body. Someone was taking it upon themselves to kill people they believed deserved to die.

This particular vampire killed scumbags and criminals. The murdered victims, upon deeper investigation, were suspected of committing a crime. One victim liked little girls. After his death, several pictures were found of little girls he photographed along with crude notes under each photo. If someone hadn't killed this guy, he would have acted out his fantasy. Some of the other victims were guilty of much worse.

As he looked down at this body, he dreaded finding out what skeletons this man had hidden in his closet. The vampire drained every last drop of blood he had; yet, there was no DNA evidence left behind.

Newman found it strange that a vampire would be worried about forensic evidence. Could it be that they were dealing with a turned cop who spent his nights seeking vengeance on the criminals here in New Orleans?

Hell, even those above him weren't sure if he should waste too many man hours on someone saving them money.

Chapter 26

The beat of the drums disturbed the night. The timbre
of the drums echoed as Ezrielle took her rightful place.
Her hips swayed gently as her white robe parted.

Upon her arrival, the creatures softly chanted,
"Ezrielle." Their whispers carried across the swamp.
As she moved through the swamp, the creatures of the
night went silent. The swamp and crickets stilled in her
presence. Fireflies hovered about unblinking. The only
noise was the beating of the drums; her followers drew
closer in a syncopated rhythm.

"Ezrielle."

She surveyed her followers in the torchlight. The scent
of incense was heavy in the air. Her homunculi beat
down on the drums made of dead cat skin. A bantam
rooster cocked his head and crowed in dismay.

As she entered the circle, her followers dropped to the
ground. Tonight, another man would enter their fold.
Bodies, humid with sweat, swayed in tune with the
beat of the drums. Ezrielle's body moved with the
beat of the drums. Her feet shuffled, and her arms
swung side to side, while her head rolled free. The
power moved through her as the spirits descended on
her. As the power spread throughout her body, her
eyes dilated.

Ezrielle ripped off the head of the rooster in one quick movement. Filling her mouth with its blood, she spat it onto her followers.

The Grunch brought Ezrielle the cage holding the raven. Carefully taking it out, she smoothed its feathers. With one quick slice of the knife, she opened the raven's chest and exposed its heart. She raised the impotent, warm heart to her lips and swallowed the muscle whole.

Her followers called out, "La reine. Glory to our queen."

Ezrielle licked the blood from her mouth as her followers continue to chant. A shiver of excitement ran through her. Before she brought another Rougarou into their fold, she must rejuvenate her youth. She ordered, "Bring me the virgin."

Only a young virgin would do for what she had planned. When the blood of the innocent was spilled, the power of her evil reached its peak. Lately, they had found they must seek out younger girls; they were the only ones with trusting, naïve souls. It was this very innocence that called and tempted the evil to come for them. The young girls meant nothing to her; they were to satisfy The Dukes of Hell.

****

The throbbing of the drums called to Chantelle; it pulled her from her slumber. Throwing the covers over her ears, she tried to go back to sleep, but the pounding drums demanded her to obey.

With a low moan, she slipped out of bed. No longer able to control her movements, she walked out into the night to answer a call she was forbidden to ignore. The full moon cast a pale light over the dense foliage. Her unclad feet did not even feel the briars along the pathway.

The murky scent of the bayou hovered heavy in the night air as a sense of foreboding moved in. She tried to wake herself and attempted to shut out the sounds of the pounding drums calling her to them. The drums continued to summon her, drawing her deeper into the shadowed swamp. She effortlessly walked over the bottomless tombs of quicksand that protected the swamps of the voodoo queen.

Her mind recoiled in fear as the trees seemed to come alive with the sharp claws of their limbs mere inches from her body. As if at any moment, they could snatch her up and swallow her whole. Instead of running in fear, she continued on over the brackish waters, moving deeper into the voodoo queen's swamp.

On and on she walked until at last she saw a clearing. The only sound present was the drums. A group of people gathered in the clearing as the flickering light from the torches bathed the area in an eerie reddish glow. Her throat grew dry as her pulse quickened.

She tried to stop herself from walking into the circle and run back home, but her body refused to obey her commands. A cold chill passed over her as the woman in the center smirked at her.

This woman had a mesmerizing beauty. Chantelle guessed her age to be in the mid-thirties, but the eyes staring back at her showed a depth of living that far surpassed her outward appearance.

***

Ezrielle's powers strengthened with each conjure made, and she was now the strongest of all the voodoo priestesses. When the girl was in her reach, she held out her hand. The deep throbbing of the drums increased in tempo as the chosen one entered the circle.

Ezrielle lifted her arms for silence. On her command, the drums ceased their incessant drumming and the night went quiet.

It was time for the ceremony to begin.

She reached out and lifted the young girl up by the neck and started to breathe in the girl's very soul. She watched as right before her eyes, the young girl aged. It was a sight that Ezrielle had witnessed many times in the past, but she still couldn't get over the amazement she felt each time she did it.

Skin that was once as smooth as a baby's bottom was now shriveled and wrinkled like that of a hundred year old woman. As the last of the girl's spirit left her body, Ezrielle threw the body down. Her group of Rougarou pushed their way to the front of the circle. "Eat my loves. Do not leave any evidence behind."

As the Rougarou sated their hunger, Ezrielle called out for the young man. "It's time that your fellow Rougarou have another family member to welcome into their fold."

The creatures watched in awe as yet another transformation took place in front of their eyes. No matter how many times they watched her commit yet another sin against an unsuspecting soul, they could not stay away.

Chapter 27

The man's pale skin almost looked translucent in the early morning sunlight. His blond hair was matted, heavy with blood. The smooth skin of his neck was left jagged from the bite. The skin on his chest had been gnawed, and white bone gleamed in the fragile light.

Detective Newman watched as Dr. Ortego measured the bite marks on the body with his trusty tape measure. "It looks as if your creature has been busy again. I will know more when I get the DNA results, but I don't think this was a vampire. The bite marks appear to be that of an animal." Shaking his head, Dr. Ortego stated, "He hasn't been dead more than eight hours. Rigor mortis hasn't set in."

Looking at all the blood pooled around the body, Newman stated, "It looks as if he was killed here. Hopefully, we can get some good clues." As he surveyed the area, a fine mist floated over the area, reminiscent of waiting ghosts.

As the low lying mist floated over the body, tiny beads of moisture clung to it, shining like glitter. Newman quickly became concerned. "This mist isn't helping preserve evidence that's for sure."

Dr. Ortego nodded his head in agreement. "I have to move the body to the morgue asap if we want to collect DNA."

Forensic technicians were busy collecting as much evidence as they could before it was all lost to the mist. A crowd built around the crime scene, coming closer to the tape hoping to catch a glimpse of what happened.

As the body was placed in the body bag, Newman caught sight of dark purple bruises settling in over the entire back of his body. Blood always settled at the lowest point of the body. Whoever did this drained most of his blood before death.

Dupre rushed up to the crime scene. "Sorry, I was a little preoccupied when the call came in."

Newman took in the disheveled hair, crumpled T-shirt and jeans. With a grin, Newman said, "Didn't mean to break your rhythm."

"I promised Heather I would make it up to her. I don't think she was too pleased though."

"All right, lover boy, let's get cracking on this case so that we can get you back to your wife. Dr. Ortego is ready to transport the body to the morgue."

Dupre asked, "Who found the body?"

Newman nodded his head towards a patrol car. "The lady in the car. She's taking it pretty hard too."

Rocking on his heels, Dupre said, "I bet. The only dead body she probably ever saw was at a funeral home."

Newman nodded his head in agreement. "That is the best way in my opinion. The poor woman will never forget this."

As they walked towards the car, the woman stepped out. "If I must keep repeating the story, do you think it is possible to get everyone here so that I only have to say this once more?" She asked.

Dupre looked at the poor woman sympathetically. "I am sorry about all of this. I promise, we don't have too many more questions for you and then you can go back home."

"Ha, I need a stiff drink. Every time I close my eyes, I see..." She paused, pointing toward where the dead body had been. "that..."

Chapter 28

The heels of Josie's boots clicked with every step against the cobblestoned walkway of the French Quarter. She easily kept pace with the man she was following. As he rounded the corner, she jumped with well-practiced efficiency onto the roof of the adjacent building. She didn't want him to sense her following him, but at the same time, she wanted to make sure she didn't lose sight of him. She'd learned from Tyler that this man was sly as a fox. Just when the police were ready to move in, he would disappear.

He was searching for his next victim. He preyed strictly on women who worked the streets, but soon, he would seek a victim who presented more of a challenge. She couldn't let him harm another woman, regardless of her reputation.

Her next meal walked down the street with an overconfident stride. He never even bothered to look around to make sure no one had followed him. He honestly believed he was the king of his jungle.

If he only knew how wrong his instincts were. She was about to shatter his sense of security. Just as he moved into the dark alley to take his preferred short cut, she lifted him up into the air.

His eyes looked up at her as horror spread across his face. Too eager for a meal, she shivered in anticipation and quickly bit into his neck. His warm, thick blood filled her throat, melting into her taste buds. As the criminal's life left his body, she dropped him to the ground. When the cops ran his prints, they would thank her for what she'd done. The medics would declare this a heart attack and simply walk away.

Chapter 29

Josie forced her legs to move across the driveway, even though every fiber in her body violently protested against it. Gravel crunched like brittle bones beneath her shoes. It was reminiscent of fingernails scraping against a chalkboard.

Shivers ran down her spine as she moved closer to the plantation home that loomed in front of her. Her steps faltered the closer she got. It was just a house, nothing more, but fear held her feet hostage, not allowing her to move closer.

Sinister shadows danced around the frame of the old plantation home. Panic raced through her veins. Even the subtle wisp of branches scraping along the windows of the house conjured up horrors in her mind, each vision more terrifying than the last.

Bitterness gripped its steely fingers around her heart as fear nearly choked her to death. She struggled to breathe as the hot, humid air seeped into her lungs. Her chest tightened as she forced herself to take in slow, deep breaths.

Josie took a deep breath before stepping onto the porch. She cringed at the mournful creak as the wood moaned beneath her feet. Tears filled her eyes as she stared at the front door.

She shook her head and took a step back. No matter how bad she wanted revenge, she couldn't bring herself to do this. She desperately tried to control her racing thoughts while panic once again took over her body.

She kept telling herself that her Maker would not hurt her. He would welcome her into his house, and then she could exact her revenge. She had the element of surprise here.

A movement from the upstairs window caught her eye. Someone had discovered that she was here. They stared at her morosely as the unforgiving moon shined down on her. She watched as the man in the window let his shoulders slump, almost portraying the demeanor of a broken man. For a moment, her heart began to thaw at the sight. Was he miserable in the confines of his home?

She shook her head to break herself out of her reverie. No, this man was a monster. He'd turned her without asking if she wanted this damned life as he'd done to countless others.

She watched as he stared out the window gazing at the moon before looking down at her again. Icy fear reared its ugly head as goose bumps of awareness formed across her body. She would rather face a pack of bloodthirsty hell hounds right now than confront her maker. She thought she was prepared for this moment, but now, she found herself unsure of what she'd vowed to do.

With a deep, fortifying breath, she walked up to the front door. As she knocked on the door, the sound echoed through the muggy, Louisiana night, traveling deep into the swamp behind the house before eerily bouncing back at her feet. Somewhere near, creatures of the night echoed their sorrowful tune as if predicting what she was here to do. The haunting song sent a wave of panic through her.

She'd heard of the mysteries that surrounded this place and of the horrors that lurked on these grounds. Were they more than myths? Josie took a nervous look around, half expecting to see some terrifying creature emerge from the black, swampy waters nearby.

Without warning, a woman answered the door. Disappointment filled her when she learned that she had the wrong plantation.

As Josie left, she could feel the woman's eyes following her. She was missing something. As she drove away, the plantation disappeared into the night without warning. Her eyes must be playing tricks on her; a house just doesn't vanish.

***

Ezrielle watched as the young vampire left in disappointment. Perhaps, she shouldn't have taunted her or allowed her entry onto the plantation, but she was curious as to what the vampire looked like. So this was the one Tyler had chosen for a mate. He chose the most dangerous creature, one that was strong willed.

Chapter 30

As Lisa's head hit the ATM machine, she wondered if she would die tonight. She felt herself being picked up and thrown against a brick wall. Hitting the ground with a loud thud, the back of her skull cracked as it bounced off the wall. She heard a maniacal laugh in the background as her vision blurred. She lifted her head slowly while trying to stand.

A large alligator skinned boot stomped on her body. She heard, more than felt, something snap as the boot smashed into her face. She was surprised that a couple of her teeth didn't come loose from the kick.

She was about to be killed for a lousy twenty dollars. She was warned of the dangers when stopping by an ATM at night, but she merely brushed them off. Why didn't she just listen to her roommate and grab some cash at the grocery store? She reminded her that a bottle of water was cheaper than an ATM fee. Now, Lisa wished she had listened to her friend's advice. If she had, she wouldn't be here having every bone in her body broken by some maniac.

Why didn't this guy take the money and leave?

Thud! Crack!

The sound of her bones breaking echoed throughout the night air. Why wasn't anyone helping? New

Orleans always seemed to have a night life. Where was a knight in shining armor when you needed one?

Tossed around once more, she noticed there was no longer any pain associated with the attack. She heard that when your body reached a certain level of pain that the nerves stopped sending signals to your brain. Could this be the body's last farewell gift to your soul? Had she finally reached that threshold?

When she was younger, she'd pondered what it would be like to die. She imagined the various ways she could die and always wondered how she would leave this world. She assumed she would fall asleep one night, possibly in her late seventies or early eighties, and never wake up. Not once did she consider the chance of her dying a violent death.

She heard more bones break and watched as her blood was spilled on the sidewalk. Dread filled her when she realized that this was the end. She didn't understand why her tormentor did this. She attempted to give him her money, but instead of taking it, he toyed with her.

She should be thankful that it no longer hurt. She must be stronger and more resilient than she'd given herself credit for in the past. She refused to scream out in the night and plead for help. She refused to give her attacker that satisfaction.

Instead, she came to accept the inevitable; she would not survive this attack. She was ready to die.

Suddenly, a loud thud sounded next to her. It must have been something extremely large since she felt the sidewalk shake from the impact. With a curious detachment, she watched as another figure loomed over her attacker and pierced his heart with a metal stake. Her attacker burst into tiny dust particles carried away by the wind.

Quietness descended over the entire area. The only sound she heard was the wind as it carried away the debris of the street.

Lisa tried to make out the person who'd saved her, but her vision was still too blurred. Her body tensed as the footsteps grew nearer. Without warning, hands reached under her and tenderly picked her up. She was powerless to resist as this person carried her away. With each step, Lisa became aware of the extreme pain raging through her body. She lost consciousness as the lights of the city moved past her.

As she came to once more, the pain became too much and she slipped into unconsciousness again. Unexpectedly, she was surrounded by noise and bright lights that hurt her eyes. She heard voices talking around her, but she couldn't seem to focus on what they said.

***

Josie handed the young woman to Tyler so that he could bring her to the emergency room. Tyler observed the injuries in dismay. He did not expect this much damage. Cradling her limp body in his arms, he realized she was hurt worse than he suspected. She had many bloody gashes on her head, both eyes were bruised heavily, and her lips were cut. She also had several broken and fractured bones, was barely breathing, and her head wound was severe. Even more worrisome was that the cuts on her body appeared not to be clotting.

When Josie looked up at him, he saw the sorrow in her eyes. "I tried to share some of my blood with her to help her heal, but I don't think it was enough. The doctors may be able to help her more than I could."

Tyler nodded his head in understanding and rushed into the emergency room. They both knew that it wasn't safe for Josie to be in there. The smell of blood would be too heavy, and they would ask too many questions when a young woman brought in another badly injured woman. With a cop, they would rush to his side and immediately tend to the injuries.

Tyler gently placed the young woman on the gurney and prayed this poor girl made it through the night. After leaving her in capable hands, he left to check on Josie. She shared her fears that there may have been another man at the scene of the attack who escaped. From what he could understand, the vampires played with the victim, passing her around as if she was a soccer ball.

A chill of apprehension ran down his spine as he thought of Josie fighting those beasts on her own. That could have easily been Josie instead of this poor young woman. Was this merely a trap to lure Josie to them? He rushed to go and check on her when he was suddenly hit with a thought. Was she walking into another trap?

Chapter 31

Josie didn't bother checking the back door to the abandoned warehouse. Taking the heel of her boot, she kicked right beneath the doorknob and the steel door immediately burst open. She watched as the junkies inside went running like cockroaches, but she left them alone. They were not who she wanted.

Not bothering to close the door, she ventured deeper inside the barely lit room. It surprised her that the vampire she was searching for had bothered to hide in here with these addicts.

The whole place was foul with layers of dirt and grime. A heady smell of unwashed bodies and marijuana smoke filled the air.

She found him tucked in a corner feeding on a stoned young man. She doubted any of the junkies noticed someone feeding off one of their own. Most were probably unaware that a vampire was in their midst.

It bothered her that he sought out these sorry individuals to feed on, leaving them behind as if they were trash. As she made her way closer to him, he looked up, snarling and hissing, "Who the hell are you?"

She hissed and snarled back, "I am your worst nightmare." Her voice lowered to a mere whisper as she added, "It is time to pay for your sins."

As the vampire leapt to his feet, Josie reached behind her back to free her guns from the holsters. She saw the beads of sweat pop out on the vampire's forehead as his eyes focused in on the guns she had aimed right at his heart. Her stare never wavered as she cocked them both.

Josie taunted him in her mind. "That's right. Get a good look at what will send you back to hell. I came for you."

He smelled the silver in the air. It was their one true kryptonite. The scent of silver could strike fear in even the coldest of vampire hearts. The smell meant that the death of a vampire was near.

Snarling and hissing even more, he asked, "What are you doing here woman? This is where I feast. Go! Leave me be, vamp."

The vampire in front of her was tall and lanky. The way his eyes darted about showed he had fed on a few too many drug addicts recently. As he raised his sleeves to fight, she noticed he had become addicted to the drugs. There were numerous track marks on the inside of his arms, too many for his body to heal. From the look of his clothes and oily, dirty blond hair hanging lifeless around his face, he hadn't bathed in weeks.

Josie refused to back down, continuing to stare him in the eyes. She prized this moment; the instant they understood that they were about to die. Everything fell into place for the target. It was a thrill to see understanding glaze her prey's eyes; the eyes projected death was imminent. Her breathing quickened as her blood rushed through her veins.

"It is time to return to hell." She told the bloodsucking creature. Her low voice held no sympathy.

She took aim at his heart as he pleaded for his life, "I'm not the one you want. Honestly. You have the wrong person."

Shaking her head, she answered, "No, you are the one I want. You kill these poor victims for their tainted blood. I saw it in your eyes."

His hands flailed wildly in the air as desperation invaded his voice. "There is another vampire in this town that you want. If you spare me, I will tell you who he is. This dude is bad news. He has vamps all over town," he pleaded with her.

The fear exuding from his body mixed with the panicked expressions etched on his face heightened her senses even more. Letting out a small laugh, she said, "I will find him; don't you worry, but first, I need to take care of you."

His eyes bulged until his black as night irises were pin pricks in a sea of white. He knew he was on his way to slaughter. "I know your crimes. I know what you have done. Through your death, I can redeem myself," Josie said.

A tic in his eye showed her he was about to run. Why do they always run as if it would save them? As he shifted to the side hoping to outrun her, she took aim. The silver bullet was encapsulated around a liquid of garlic juice, holy water, and a special ultraviolet liquid. It flew through the air, finding its target with ease. The vampire instantly turned to ash. Another corrupt soul was sent back to hell, where it rightfully belonged.

As Josie watched the dust being carried off into the air, she let out a deep breath. She'd had another successful execution. The vampire also confirmed her fear; another vampire was working the streets of New Orleans. Was her maker starting up a new family?

A noise from the back caught Josie's attention, and the sight instantly repulsed her. In the back of the warehouse was a cage holding a young girl, who couldn't be more than sixteen, captive.

The poor girl hung her head down low in fear; her dirty, tangled mass of hair hid her face. Josie crouched in front of the cage. "It is okay. You are safe now," she whispered to the girl.

The young girl looked at her with fearful green eyes before letting her eyes dance around the room. Josie tried to ease her fears before freeing her from the cage, "I promise. You are safe now. He won't be coming back."

Josie easily ripped off the door of the cage, allowing the young girl her freedom. It was obvious she had been held prisoner for a while now. Bite marks covered her body, and she was unsteady on her feet. Josie gently picked her up to carry her out of the warehouse.

Josie took out her cell phone and called Tyler. "I have a young girl that needs medical attention."

While Josie waited for Tyler behind the emergency room, she thought about what she had learned tonight. She had to tell Tyler, he would know the best way to handle this particular situation.

As Josie handed the girl to Tyler, she said to him, "It appears there is a trafficking ring that we must stop."

"I will let the right people know junkies are hanging out there. If nothing else, they can close this shop down."

Chapter 32

Josie sat on a bench in front of the St. Louis Cathedral and observed her surroundings. Normally she preferred to hide in the shadows or on the rooftops. Those areas helped her stay invisible and unnoticeable to the drug dealers, drunken tourists, punks, and common criminals that frequented the area. Tonight she made herself the prey, hoping to draw out the vilest of criminals – the vampires that preyed on the innocent. By blending in with these humans, she became an easy target. It would be too late when they realized who she was.

As she sat listening to the surrounding noises, she waited for her prey. A fortune teller was giving a tarot card reading to a tourist. The nervous tourist kept shifting from side to side in the chair. Josie could even smell the heady incense the fortune teller had burning and heard the clank of her bangles as she moved the cards on the table. Not far from the fortune teller, a pedestrian staggered off of Decatur and headed towards St. Ann. He slurred his words as he talked to himself while walking towards Bourbon Street and the French Quarter.

Josie pretended to be reading as she continued to listen to the conversations and noises around her, hoping to pick up something useful. Even at this hour, musicians performed and artists displayed their work proudly. On St. Peter, two women were in the middle of a heated argument as they walked toward the church. Josie heard each word clearly as the women made their way towards Josie. The heated conversation changed to their master and his need for more subjects. Josie began to feel anxious; this could be what she needed.

A master vampire had absolute control over the flock, and usually they forbid their children to leave behind bodies. Lately, that had not been happening. Rogue vampires could be roaming the city, a master vampire could be flaunting his coven's kills, or even worse, they didn't care. You didn't stay alive and hidden for centuries unless you were discreet and ruthless.

She eased herself from the bench and followed the women. Despite the oppressive humidity, her clothes stayed crisp and unwrinkled – just as she desired. She was the prime target for a mugger. She looked as if she'd just stepped out of a taxi and portrayed an out of town tourist wanting to experience the nightlife here in New Orleans. As she made her way to the corner of St. Peter, the heels of her shoes rang on the cobblestone sidewalk.

Following the women to Bourbon Street, Josie felt a change in the air. Underneath the oppressive heat was something more tangible. She felt the lust and desire that drew people to this area. Even Josie felt the enchantment of New Orleans and especially the French Quarter.

As the women disappeared into a nearby club, Josie followed, throwing herself into the crowd of people. Somehow, she avoided being splashed by the sloshing mugs of beer and went unnoticed by the men seeking out companionship from the hordes of available women. Josie rolled her eyes at one desperate woman who flashed men in order to find a dance partner on or off the dance floor.

Finding an available seat toward the back of the bar, Josie ordered a drink to blend in and watched the women's every move. To her right, a couple gyrated ferociously. Josie considered telling them to get a room, but she bit her tongue. She didn't need to bring any unwanted attention to herself. If they wanted to make a spectacle of themselves, then so be it. Besides, the couple next to them had the audience's full attention. A young girl slid her hand up and down the man's leg while rubbing her body seductively against his body.

As Josie pretended to sip her drink, she looked around the club. The club seemed to be popular with the younger tourists and college kids. The décor left much to be desired. The chairs and tables were well past their prime. The small café tables were wobbly and cheap. The whole place reeked of stale beer and cigarette smoke mingled with the perfume and cologne the patrons wore. Underneath that heady scent was the smell of lust and another cloying scent that only Josie could pick up, the smell of decay. There were vampires here, very old vampires, who blended in perfectly with these young patrons. She smelled the hunger for blood as they scoped out their prey.

When the waitress passed by, Josie smelled the meth addiction on her. Looking into the waitress's eyes, Josie saw the black hole of emptiness that the drug caused this girl. She shook her head in disgust. If only these young people understood the true dangers of drugs and what it did to their bodies.

Josie took her attention away from the waitress as one of the young women she'd followed moved to the dance floor. She was confident in herself as she made her way to a young man; it looked as if she'd found her prey. The woman bypassed the man and went over to the pole set up on the center stage. The men's eyes followed her, almost as if in a trance, and they couldn't take their eyes off her as she swung her body around the pole.

While dancing, her numerous studs and various piercings on her body caught the stage lights as she slid languidly around the pole. A tattoo on the young woman's lower back caught Josie's attention. The woman had other smaller tattoos, but it was the one on her back that captured Josie's attention. As the muscles under her flesh moved and twitched, the revelation of what Josie was looking at hit her with full force. Without thinking, Josie rubbed the tattoo on her wrist. How could this girl have a tattoo like hers? Joshua branded his children with this particular tattoo. Was it possible that another had elected to use this tattoo from her own master?

The friend came over and whispered something in the woman's ear. The young woman stood up, smoothed her clothes back down, and looked over the room. There were plenty of people to choose from. Several of the conference attendees came up to prove that they were still studs. It was hilarious to watch as they hit on younger women and flung their money around. Typically, vampires avoided this particular group of people as most had loved ones that would miss them.

Bars such as this one were the best places to recruit and pick up food. This coven was similar to a commune with members living together as one big happy family. Besides hunting the clubs and streets for food, they also used their abilities to steal whatever cash these people had on hand. It was easy to entice money from unsuspecting individuals without them ever realizing what they were doing. The person wouldn't remember giving a vampire their cash.   They would wake up thinking they drank and partied more than they intended.

****

Brandi Vidrine always considered herself a simple Louisiana girl. She was raised in St. Francisville, Louisiana but hadn't seen her family since she moved away. Her parents refused to speak to her until she changed her ways. Brandi would not change for them or their strict religious beliefs. They had to accept her for who she was.

Brandi came out of the closet right after entering college. She spent a troubled teenage life trying to fight her true feelings, but became so miserable she contemplated suicide countless times. After she had accepted who she was, life became easier for her. During her senior year of high school, Brandi told her parents that she was hanging out with friends, but, instead, she spent the weekend in Baton Rouge where she could freely be herself. It was during that time, Brandi met her first lover.

If her parents had not surprised her one night at her dorm, they might have never discovered Brandi's new lifestyle. They became upset and spiteful when they found Brandi and her girlfriend in each other's arms. Her dad immediately spewed about fire and brimstone without ever even asking if this was what made her happy. He ordered her to pack and move back home. When she refused, they disowned her.

Brandi worked hard throughout college to pay for her education and to make ends meet. She did it, though, regardless of the hateful letters her parents sent. It came to a point where Brandi refused to open their letters and returned them unopened. They were all the same, how she must seek God's divine intervention and beg for his forgiveness.

After several more tumultuous visits with her parents, Brandi clarified that this was not simply a phase. The stress of their letters and visits became too much for her. Until they accepted her for who she was, she had to separate them from her life. The only form of communication was every year she sent them a Christmas card, letting them know that she was still alive.

As she scanned the crowd in the bar, she wondered once more why she'd let her friends talk her into coming to New Orleans with them. This particular crowd was not for her. However, she found herself drawn to the band and the music they were playing. For a bar band, it surprised her that they had a tuba, trombone, trumpet, as well as the usual drummer and guitarist. Without even meaning to, she moved to the beat of the music. This was simply not the kind of music that let you sit still. She shrugged her shoulders and went with the flow. She walked out onto the dance floor and decided to enjoy herself while here.

A sexy voice whispered in her ear, "I haven't seen you in here before, mon cher."

Brandi turned to find herself looking at a gorgeous woman. As soon as she gazed into her eyes, Brandi was under her spell. "Would you care to dance?"

Brandi just nodded her head, unable to find her voice. After several seductive dances, her dance partner asked, "Would you like to get out of here and go someplace else?"

Brandi leaned in close and answered, "Just let me tell my friends I am going to skip out."

After saying goodbye to her friends, Brandi followed the woman out into the humid night. The lights of the city danced off the water as the colored lights from a nearby building created an eerie glow. So enthralled by the view, she didn't pay attention to where they were going.

As they made their way to the fringe of the Garden District, Brandi noticed that they were no longer where most of the patrons and tourists frequented. The bar was dark and closed in, almost to the point of being vault like in appearance. Upstairs, the rooms were dank, and in the halls people were shooting up. Brandi considered leaving and going back to be with her friends.

However, once in the large room, she relaxed and let the music fill her body. Enjoying herself, she never felt her dance partner bend her head back and pierce the delicate skin of her neck with her sharp fangs. Growing weaker, she held onto the woman while tears filled her eyes as life began to drain from her body.

Somewhere in the midst of this, she found her faith once again and prayed. The prayer flowed from her automatically. She closed her eyes tightly in an effort to block out everything happening around her.

A coldness penetrated deep into her bones as a feeling of total weightlessness engulfed her. Tears stung her eyes as memories flooded her mind. She would never see her parents again. So many regrets plagued her mind as death wrapped her in its cold, cruel embrace.

***

The female vampire licked the blood from her lips as her fellow brothers and sisters continued to feed on the unsuspecting victims. It was so easy to lure these humans here tonight. Their bodies would be found in the halls, giving the appearance that they'd acquired a deadly drug. It was difficult for her not to drain this sweet body quickly of its blood. It had been a long time since the vampire had tasted blood as pure as hers.

Chapter 33

Lisa Grant tapped her foot in annoyance at her friend, Kathryn Pierce. "Loosen up girl. We came here to let our hair down and have some fun. Instead, you have stayed on your phone answering emails and text messages. This is supposed to be a leisure vacation, not a working vacation."

Kathryn sighed as she put her phone back in her purse. "I am sorry, but I can't seem to let my secretary handle anything. I am constantly questioning her when I am gone from the office."

Lisa shook her head. "You really need to learn how to let go of the reins some. Michelle Landry is a good hire and capable of handling anything that comes up," Lisa explained.

"I know, but what if I hired someone who can replace me and my boss finds out just how efficient Michelle really is?"

Lisa rolled her eyes at that remark. "Please. Mark Jameson will never get rid of you. That man believes you walk on water."

"I don't know. When I told him I was taking a vacation, he didn't look too pleased."

Lisa scoffed at that remark, "Of course he didn't like the idea. It meant he had to work."

Kathryn looked at her friend, shocked at the statement, "Mark works hard in the office."

"No, Mark works hard at entertaining prospective clients who will never use your company. You are the one who goes out there and finds real paying clients. Without you, the business would have gone bankrupt, and you know it."

Kathryn let Lisa's ramblings roll off of her back. Even though her friend was right, Kathryn would never admit it. Hopefully, she could at least enjoy herself a little tonight. She did need to forget about work and have some fun.

As they walked through the French Quarter, Kathryn took in the surroundings. The whole atmosphere was surreal. Music spilled out into the streets from the endless bars and clubs. So many people of different ages laughed and partied as if they had not a care in the world.

They were on their second round of drinks when Lisa looked at her. "Okay, my friend, it is time you find a man to dance with. This place is crawling with good looking men."

Kathryn shook her head, laughing. "I don't think I am drunk enough yet for that."

Lisa laughed at her response. "And knowing you, you will never get that drunk. You need to loosen up. When was the last time you went on an actual date or had a man touch you? I mean, it has probably been years." As her best friend said that last remark, Kathryn saw the twinkle of mischief in her eyes.

Kathryn reminded herself that her friend did have her best interest at heart. "Fine, you want me to find someone, I will do it." Kathryn looked around the bar to find someone as miserable as her. What she needed was a non-threatening man who wanted to be left alone.

Lisa shook her head. "No, I will find a man for you. I know what you are doing."

As Lisa scanned the bar, Kathryn inwardly groaned when she saw her friend's eyes light up. With an evil grin, Lisa winked at her friend. "Oh, I do believe I found someone for you. Check out the guy talking to the bartender."

As Kathryn turned to look at the man, her heart caught in her throat. Her jaw dropped to the floor at the sight of him. He was tall, dark, and handsome. Dressed from head to toe in black, he was the epitome of the men Kathryn avoided. She couldn't stop herself from staring at his firm bottom lovingly cupped in the tight jeans. The clothes he wore left nothing to the imagination. With one look at his face, her heart did a flip-flop in her chest.

As he reached for his glass, she caught a glimpse of his rippling muscles. Just that single movement wiped every coherent thought from her mind. This guy radiated danger, raw animal masculinity, and hot seduction. This Adonis dressed in black was the kind of bad boy every girl secretly dreamed of meeting.

She couldn't believe that her friend had picked this bad boy out for her. He would bring only one thing into her life, T-R-O-U-B-L-E. Taking a gulp of her drink for courage, she took a deep breath and headed toward the crowded bar. She felt as if she was walking to her doom.

As she stopped right behind this Adonis in black, she took one more deep breath to steady her nerves. His cologne was sexy and intoxicating. Every inch of him oozed pure animal magnetism.

Just as she considered chickening out, he turned around. One look at his eyes and she was captivated. This man was downright devastatingly, handsome.

"Hello." His deep voice caressed her body with just that one simple word. The urge to flee almost overtook her whole being. As if reading her mind, he took her hand in his. His thumb caressed her inner wrist, sending shivers of delight down her body. If one simple touch sent liquid heat to her very core, she could only imagine what a kiss would do.

She felt the heat radiating on her cheeks. Building up the courage, she asked, "Would you care to dance?"

He kissed her hand. "I can't think of anything more pleasing." As if sensing her trepidation, he asked, "Is this something you want to do, though?" Looking back at her friend, he continued, "Or would you rather I help you get out of it?"

Kathryn closed her eyes and savored the sensation of his breath on her skin as he whispered the question into her ear. This man's endearing question melted her heart, but also shocked her. "No, I want to dance with you," she told him. She wanted his hands on her body, even if only for a dance.

He placed his hand on the small of her back, guiding her to the dance floor. "Then how could I possibly resist?" She shivered from head to toe in anticipation.

She wasn't sure how to handle him. She was fine with a little light teasing, but she was unsure how to handle serious flirting.

As they made their way to the packed dance floor, he asked, "Where do you wish to dance?"

Now, that was a loaded question. Clearing her throat, she answered, "Wherever we can find a spot I guess."

As they danced, Kathryn felt her friend's disbelief radiating across the dance floor. She glanced over to Lisa and gave her a shy smile as the Adonis pulled her deeper into his embrace. She shivered as his hands gripped her waist. It surprised her to find him so cold to the touch.

Kathryn melted into his body as they moved to the music. She noticed a small, unique tattoo on the inside of his wrist; it reminded her of a crucifix or strange sword with barbed wire around it.

As they danced, his muscles quivered against her soft curves. A smile formed on her lips. As he looked down at her, she saw his eyes smoldering. What would it feel like to be kissed by him? It would be so easy to bend his head down to hers. She heard his breath quicken, and it gave her some satisfaction to know he was just as affected as her.

She should stop after this dance, but couldn't bring herself to leave his embrace. Just being near him made it hard for her to think rationally. To avoid looking up into the depths of his gaze, she leaned her head on his chest.

After a few minutes, he tipped her head and gazed into her eyes while everything else faded away. From the heated look he was giving her, she knew he would kiss her, and she had no desire to stop him. As soon as his lips touched hers, sparks of electricity danced through her body.

At first, his lips just touched her lightly, and for a moment, she thought that was it. The chaste kiss soon became deeper as his lips crushed against hers with a greater urgency. His strong arms wrapped around her waist and pulled her tighter against him.

She whispered against his lips, "I don't even know your name."

"Are names important?"

Not knowing why, she shook her head. This guy was light years out of her league. Maybe he was right; she didn't need to know his name. She would be better off walking out the door and forgetting she'd ever met him. Besides, judging from his accent, he was from here, and for her, this was a vacation. She would go back to Chicago, back to her boring life.

With a soft sigh, she whispered against his lips, "Until we meet again."

***

He didn't expect her to walk away. As she slipped through the crowd effortlessly, he couldn't let her get away. This woman intrigued him. She kept her sexiness hidden beneath jeans, a shirt, and hair pulled tight into a ponytail.

Not wanting the desire to fade, he followed her. His hands burned to dive into the rich softness of her hair, pull her close and kiss her again. She felt so right in his arms. He would be crazy to let her walk away. The thought of those soft lips on his again heated his skin. He had never turned a woman just to be with him for eternity, but she had him seriously contemplating just that.

He could already imagine how intoxicating this woman's blood would be. Just having her mouth on his set him ablaze. The crowd grew thick, and it took a moment for him to make his way out of the bar. When he walked outside, she had disappeared. He smelled the air, hoping to find which direction she went. A soft laugh behind him caught his attention. Her friend told him, "We aren't staying far from here. If you hurry, you may catch her."

He took off down the street and as soon as he saw her, he slowed his pace. From this distance, he admired her fine lines. As he approached her, he smiled down at the woman.

"You left before we could dance to another song."

Her eyes widened as if she was a deer caught in the headlights. "I needed to get back to my hotel room. I have some work to catch up on."

Sensing that she was skittish and distrustful, he tried to ease her reluctance, not wanting her to feel pressured.

He had to get her alone just for a taste of her. "You shouldn't work while on vacation, mon cher."

***

Kathryn looked at the man, tempted to walk away from him again. She'd never had a man pursue her with such tenacity. None of the men who came on to her could hold a candle to the one standing in front of her. She found it unbelievable that he was following her. Why would such an attractive man seek her out? This man was a god, and he looked at her like she was a delectable morsel he couldn't wait to sample. She was crazy for turning him down. Maybe, just maybe, she should have a fling while here in New Orleans.

This man was disconcerting, but familiar. A sense of déjà vu came over her when she was next to him. With a twinkle in his eye, he said, "You know a beautiful woman such as yourself shouldn't walk these streets by yourself."

She let out a sultry laugh. A soft breeze blew across the area, bringing little relief to the humid night. She took in a deep breath, savoring the night air. She'd come to love the nights here. "I am sure that it is safe. The concierge at the hotel told us that the police heavily patrol this area so we will be okay."

He lifted her hand to his lips and pressed a gentle kiss on her knuckles. "Mon cher, there are many unseen dangers here in New Orleans."

Smiling up at him, she teased, "Including you, I am sure."

Turning her hand over, he kissed her inner wrist. "Mais oui, I am the most dangerous of them all."

"It is just a few blocks to the hotel. I will be okay. I have my cell phone. If I run into trouble, I can call for help. There is no need to worry."

"Please, let me walk you home. I worry about you on these streets this late at night." He flashed a smile that seemed predatory to her. Her sixth sense told her to run from him and fast.

As if sensing her reluctance, he said, "Look, we can sit here and argue until the sun comes up, or you can give in and let me walk you back."

Shaking her head, she relented. "Oh, all right. You may walk with me, if you insist, but only as far as the hotel. I can see my way to the room."

He handed her his arm while saying, "I am sure that I can persuade you to change your mind before we get there."

On their way back to the hotel, Kathryn thought someone was watching them. She scanned the façade of the buildings to see if she noticed anything. An overwhelming urge came over her to lean in closer to the man next to her.

Before Kathryn could react, this Adonis of a man pulled her into a dark alley. Why didn't she listen to her gut? This man was about to kill her. She was only partly aware of his arms around her. She tried to block out the images rushing through her mind, images of what he might do to her.

Her stomach dropped as an intense feeling of fear overcame her. The wind stung her face as tears built up behind her eyes. There was so much she wanted to do, and now, she never would.

The man's seductive voice reached out to her, ordering her, "Open your eyes." A chill ran through her as all around her; the shadows in the alley looked alive as they slowly danced around. If only she had listened to the warnings that the world was a dangerous place, but now, it was too late.

Against her better judgment, she opened her eyes, and realized the mistake she'd made. The elongated fangs glimmered in the moonlight. As her heart pounded in her chest from fear, she barely noticed her head being tipped back and the fangs piercing her neck. As he drank from her, euphoria overcame her as her life ceased to exist.

Chapter 34

Josie tried to give off the appearance of normalcy as she gripped her coffee. The steam billowed from the slit in the lid; she wished she could enjoy the tantalizing aroma just once more. Before she was turned, she never liked the smell, much less the taste of coffee. Over the years, she'd listened to people around her talk in such exquisite detail of the coffees and foods around her. Now, she wished she could savor these same tastes.

Letting her mind wander for a while, she took in the sights around her as people walked by. For a weekday night, quite a few people still roamed the streets. As the wind blew through her hair, she became aware of a man across the street. Somehow she'd missed him before, but there he was lurking in the shadows, just watching. Josie tried to invade his thoughts only to find that he had blocked her.

Her defenses were suddenly up as she took in his overall appearance. He wasn't a vampire, but he wasn't human either. She breathed in the air deeply to obtain his smell. She looked at the man in surprise. Could this be a Rougarou? She shook her head against that very possibility. They were a private clan, mostly keeping to themselves. Of course, Tyler was an exception to that rule.

She could pick this man out easily on a crowded street. This man would look out of place anywhere he went. He was massive and built like a linebacker. He also looked uncomfortable standing in the dark, watching her. Nothing about him came out and screamed danger, but he made her apprehensive. She didn't pick up any malice from his demeanor, and from his body language, she didn't sense any danger. Not yet at least.

Carefully slipping out her phone, she aimed the small camera and attempted to take a picture of him. As if sensing her plan, the man took off, blending into the shadows. For once, Josie listened to her gut instincts and did not follow. Maybe Tyler could recognize him by her description. They needed to keep a sharp lookout near the house, as well.

Josie threw the now cold coffee in the trash and decided that it would be best for her to move on. She suddenly found it unsettling to be out here in the wide open. Maybe she would be safer watching from the shadows.

Finding a good hiding place on a rooftop several blocks away, Josie surveyed the area for any signs of her mystery man. Satisfied that she wasn't being followed, she observed those wandering the streets.

From her spot, she heard the wind as it whipped through the alleys, carrying with it pieces of trash and debris. Everything about this particular area was at least a familiar comfort to her, and the only sound tonight came from the cars as they passed.

She adored this older district of New Orleans. She felt a strange connection to this area. Perhaps she was being nostalgic since she grew up here and had the opportunity to witness the city expand over the years. The old houses were a reminder of what she had missed out on.

Looking at one of the courtyards, she became envious of the work the older man had put into his landscaping. She never had a green thumb or enjoyed such labors, but the beauty it produced was unquestionable.

Even from here, she could read the thoughts of the people down below. Josie thought she heard her name being called out from the shadows. She turned in the direction of the voice and scanned the area. Shaking her head, she laughed at herself. Too many nights waiting in the dark had caused her imagination to run wild.

As she returned to watch the streets, she heard the whisper again but this time louder. Looking over her shoulder, she caught a glimpse of a man in the shadows. A chill ran down Josie's spine, making the hairs on her neck stand on end. As she tried to read the man's mind, she found that she couldn't read his thoughts. Was he the same man watching her earlier?

As her gaze was transfixed on his image, he stepped out from the shadows. It was the same man from before, but this time he looked even more imposing. He was massive; his broad shoulders stretched the limits of his t-shirt.

Her gut instincts kicked in, warning her to run. Adrenaline rushed through her chest and into her limbs as she picked up her pace.

As she made it closer to her home, she still couldn't shake the feeling of eyes watching her every move in the darkness of the night. A sudden sense of déjà vu overcame her as a chill ran its course through her body. There was a shift in the energy around her, a definite difference in the air. She looked around anxiously and began to feel uneasy.

The closer she was to home, the more uneasy she became. Was she walking into a trap? That very idea was ridiculous, or was it? Her stomach churned as she recalled the other times she'd suspected someone was watching her.

She looked around, waiting for someone to jump out of the shadows. A noise to the left caught her attention. For a fleeting moment, she thought she saw a massive animal run through the shadows. A moment of trepidation encased her as she waited for the attack.

She kept her eyes focused on where she saw the creature.

She slowed her pace when she saw him up ahead. He was leaning against a tree, waiting and watching. She prayed it was close enough to the trees for the spell to help keep her safe.   A chill snaked down her spine as she studied his face. This was no random act; he was following her on purpose, but why?

Even at this distance, she saw the yellow glow of his eyes. She saw the menacing, dangerous glare in his eyes. Out of instinct, she backed away from his massive frame. She looked around and found herself utterly alone, except for this creature.

Her gut instinct was right; he meant to harm her. Adrenaline rushed through her body as she prepared to defend herself. Her eyes quickly surveyed the area, focusing in on her surroundings before taking on this predator. She must make it closer to home. She prayed that she was close enough for the trees and spells to protect her.

She froze when his lips spread into a slow, snarling grin with a faint low growl touching her ears. Goosebumps erupted on her body as adrenaline surged through her veins. Her breathing quickened as the fight or flight response kicked in with a powerful ferocity. She had to let instinct guide her and not second guess herself if she wanted to survive.

With lightning speed, he pounced and knocked her to the ground. She felt the rumble of his growl moving through his body as the sound reached her ears. As he breathed down on her, the repugnant smell of his breath overpowered her.

She tried to buck him off of her body as he snarled down at her. She cringed involuntarily when his eyes glowed in anticipation of something that only she could truly understand. He'd sought her out to kill her.

Tossing her through the air, her body landed violently against the massive oak tree. The impact knocked the wind from her. Gasping for air, she slowly stood up and prepared to fight.

He focused intently on her every movement. Before he had a chance to act, she lurched toward him and tossed him into the air. Massive claws formed on his fingertips that he used to grab at a tree and turn himself with ease. Bark flew through the air from where his claws had cut into the large oak tree. Landing hard on the ground, a ferocious growl burst from his body as he shook his head, "I don't think so, cher."

His growl filled the night air as he made his move. She squirmed to free herself from his crushing grip. Searing pain wracked through her as his claws tore into her delicate skin. The scent of her blood filled the night air.

She drew in a deep breath and summoned all of her energy. She looked him directly in the eyes and met his leer, showing no fear. His eyes rolled back in his head as he howled in anticipation of the attack.

His lips trembled with eagerness. He was larger than she initially suspected, and for once, she was glad to have her supernatural powers. She took her hands and pushed hard against his rigid chest. She used the inexplicable anger that boiled deep inside of her as it flowed through her veins. A feral hiss ripped through her throat as she hurled his body off of her. Her attacker went careening through the air.

Out of nowhere, another Rougarou joined in the fight, helping to fight off her attacker. Josie was relieved to see Tyler. While the attacker remained dazed from the recent ambush, they rushed to their house.

Once safely in the yard, Tyler pulled Josie in his arms. She gratefully fell into his embrace. He let out a low growl as he pulled her even tighter to his body.

She could tell from his body language that he wasn't happy. As her mind processed what had just happened, she looked around for the other Rougarou. Tyler sensed her apprehension, "I guess we will soon discover if the spell keeps out any creatures wanting to kill us."

Josie reached up to kiss Tyler, "I am just lucky that you came when you did."

"Luck had nothing to do with it. I heard you calling for me."

Josie let out a small gasp, "I didn't realize I had even called you."

"Perhaps, we are more in tune than we realized. I heard you calling out just as I was about to roam the woods." Kissing her tenderly, "He meant to kill you."

***

Tyler looked down at Josie and wrapped his arms around her. He would not allow anyone or anything to take her from him. His mouth crushed hers. Her lips parted as his tongue pushed inside of her mouth. He reveled in the very taste of her. Her body pressed against his, and he felt his love for her swathe them.

She was all that ever mattered to him. He held the kiss, savoring her. He couldn't let her go. Tyler lifted his head as Josie's thick lashes rose, neither bothered to speak for a moment. Josie broke the silence, "We are fools. Someone just tried to kill us, and we are standing out here in the moonlight kissing."

Josie's lips trembled as the realization of what just happened rushed through her mind. This was merely a small crack in the strong mask that she presented to the world. Tyler held her close, "When I find who ordered your death, I will kill them." His voice was flat as the words settled over Josie. She had no doubt he would seek out whoever was responsible for the blitz attack.

***

Still restless, but not wanting to venture far from the house, Tyler grabbed an ax from the shed before heading towards the tree that fell in the previous night's storm. Tyler lifted the ax high over his head, and with well-practiced ease, he swung it. The fallen tree split in half with a loud snap.

As Tyler chopped down the fallen tree, the hairs on the back of his neck stood up. Leaving the ax embedded in the tree, he listened. He was on full alert as he picked up a rustling noise deep in the woods.

While he scanned the area, he took notice of the stillness that surrounded him; not even a breeze was blowing. He waited and listened, but there was only silence.

He shrugged his shoulders; it was probably just a small animal scurrying about. The attack earlier had him overly paranoid. He couldn't go on full alert every time there was a rustle or snap in the woods.

As he lifted the ax once more, he heard the sound again. Something was definitely moving in the woods. It was too heavy to be a squirrel or other small animal. He peered into the woods waiting to see if the sound might have been a deer.

As an owl called out before taking flight, Tyler's neck hairs stood on end. Years of training, instinct and now paranoia told him something was out there. He picked up the ax before creeping into the woods.

A swarm of mosquitoes buzzed about this head. Fighting the urge to swat them away, he continued forward. He chose his footing wisely, avoiding any fallen branches or twigs and keeping each step silent. He paused in between steps, and he scanned the trees and brush around him.

No other woodland creatures were around. Did they know a predator was nearby? The lack of sound meant that whatever had caused the noise was waiting and watching. Most of the woodland creatures here would have dashed away in fright as soon as they caught a whiff of his scent.

It was too much of a coincidence with the attack on Josie and now another Rougarou. Shaking his head, he was getting ahead of himself. He couldn't afford to jump to conclusions. Maybe, a vampire followed Josie home. Then again, it could be a coyote wishing to test his luck.

He was letting his overactive imagination get ahead of him. Even though they dealt with the supernatural, it didn't mean it couldn't be something from the human world.

A sudden burst of movement to his left caught his attention. Before Tyler could react, one of the large oak trees reached out with gnarled branches and grabbed the creature lunging for Tyler. In one swift movement, the tree consumed the creature. Tyler walked over to the tree with extreme caution and observed the massive form trying to claw its way out from the confines of the tree.

He watched while the creature ceased its futile attempt at escape. Tyler took in the shape trapped inside the tree. It was a large wolf-like form. It looked as if the Rougarou did indeed wish to harm the two of them. They would have to keep their guard up.

***

Being prey was not on Josie's agenda, but the game had changed. She looked outside to watch as the darkness moved across the sky. As the sun set, the sky was ablaze with different shades of red. A chill rushed across Josie's body as she stared at the edge of the woods. Once again, she felt unseen eyes watching her every move.

Chapter 35

A mix of hip hop music with a jazzy tune to it pulsated through the dark club as Tina followed her best friend, Carrie, through the crowd of undulating bodies. Both girls were anxious to let their hair down and party.

Tina still couldn't believe that they were here. Neither of the girls told their parents that they would be in New Orleans for the weekend; if they knew they would persuade them to come home instead of taking some time for themselves. They hadn't expected college to be this difficult, and both needed a break. Even though New Orleans wasn't that far from Baton Rouge, neither girl had been to visit.

Tina was enthralled with the city upon arrival. As soon as they checked into the hotel, they discovered that the concierge could get you anything and everything you needed, of course, for a price.

The concierge freely recommended this place, Faux Pas, telling the girls to have fun. He even made a phone call that resulted in getting them VIP treatment.

Tina figured he would request special treatment later on, but, right now, she was glad he'd made the phone call. This place was completely off the hook. All around them was intense partying, and they had a difficult time making their way through the tangle of bodies on the dance floor.

As they made their way to the bar, a man reached out and grabbed Tina. She literally had to slap his hands off of her to free herself. As he removed his hand from her arm, "I only wanted to see if you wanted to dance, babe."

Shaking her head, she shuddered at the sight of the piercings on his face. As she looked at the various studs he proudly displayed, she wondered if there were more on his body. As if reading her mind, "We can find a back room if you'd like to see."

Shaking her head vehemently, "No, I came to have a good time with my friend."

Grunting, "You don't know what you are missing, babe."

Doubtful, she thought to herself as she looked at him once more. This guy was trouble.

Turning back around, she pushed through even more bodies to find her friend. Carrie handed her a drink as she made it to the bar, "What happened? I thought maybe you backed out."

"I got held up by someone wanting a dance."

Carrie's eyes danced with excitement as she looked over the dance floor, "Can you believe this place?"

As they went in search of the VIP room, Tina's admirer found them at the bar, "Are you sure you don't want a dance?"

"No."

Carrie pulled Tina towards the room, "Besides, we are meeting someone."

"If you say so, but it isn't safe for two beautiful women to be by themselves. It could be pretty dangerous out there."

As if sensing their discomfort, the bartender came over, "Your host is waiting for you." He nodded his head towards some doors behind the bar, "Just go right through these doors. The door you are looking for is on your right."

The two girls smiled at each other in delight. This was a dream come true, partying in a club with VIP privileges. As soon as they entered the dark hallway from the bar, they found themselves staring at the massive chest of an Adonis. He opened the door for the two girls, "Ladies, you both look smashing. Please make yourselves comfortable."

As they stepped past him and entered the dimly lit room, Tina could hardly believe her eyes. The luxurious room had several black leather couches strategically placed, along with candlelight and a plush fur rug on the floor. Splashes of red gave a punch of color to the dark room. Carrie let out a gasp, "Wow! Have you even seen anything like this?"

Tina walked over to the wall and reached out to touch it, "Carrie you have to feel this. It is an actual waterfall for the entire wall." The sound of the trickling helped give a mysterious aura to the room.

Several tall glass tables and a very long bar tended by a hot bartender completed the room. As if sensing her interest in him, he looked up and smiled. Just having him acknowledge her sent a chill of excitement coursing through her body.

Carrie whispered into Tina's ear, "So, do you think there will be a party here tonight?" Carrie looked around the empty room once more, "I mean we aren't the only ones here tonight are we? Where would the fun be in that?"

A voice from behind startled both girls, "Oh, don't you worry your pretty heads. There is a party tonight, and you are the guests of honor."

Carrie turned around quickly, catching her breath as she looked up at the man. The debonair man was tall with broad shoulders and lips made for kissing. As she stared into his silver eyes, she became mesmerized just by his gaze. Smiling up at the handsome man, she asked, "Seriously? But you don't even know us. If it hadn't been for the concierge, we wouldn't have known about this place."

Smiling down at the girls, "Oh, but Toby is a special friend of mine. I trust his impeccable taste always." Taking Carrie's hand in his, "Now, please allow me to introduce myself. My name is Evan, and I will be your host tonight."

Chapter 36

Keith Anderson gasped in horror as his master grinned wickedly, "My family, it is time for our hunt to begin."

Applause sounded out from the other members of the coven as they followed the master to the courtyard. Keith noticed that several of the blood slaves were also brought to the courtyard.

He shuddered in disgust at the wounds on the slaves. Welts and bite marks covered their bodies. One poor girl was so weak that she could barely stand. Someone drained her to the point of death. Most of these girls were brought here from Faux Pas. The bartender was one of the master's wights. The master paid him handsomely for the girls.

The master looked at the blood slaves as a sinister smile formed on his face, "Tonight, I will set you free. All of you will be given the chance to escape. If you safely make it off my property, your lives will be spared."

The guards began to remove the shackles that restrained each of the blood slaves. Once released, each slave took off in a different direction as they prayed for escape.

The master laughed out loud, "Run for your very life."

The master turned back to his coven and ordered, "You will give them five minutes before chasing after them, not a minute more. After all, it needs to appear that the chase is at least fair."

As the timer sounded, the members of the coven took off after their prey. Their speed held no comparison to that of the slaves. Screams filled the night air as the vampires easily hunted down their prey. The vampires fed on the slaves, this time draining each body of blood.

Keith watched in horror as the vampires preyed on the slaves with demented delight. At the sight in front of him, Keith knew that he must find someone who would help him stop this madness. He'd heard whispers of a rogue vampire killing their own kind. It was time he listened carefully to the rumors and sought her out.

Chapter 37

Brandon should have paid attention to his surroundings, instead of running through pickup lines. Being from here, he knew what the streets of New Orleans were like. But no, instead, he went over in his head the pickup lines his best friend, Gary, gave him to try out. The more Brandon repeated the lines, the dumber they sounded.

Maybe, if he had paid better attention to where he was going, he would have bypassed Pirate's Alley and stayed on the main pathway. He knew better than to come down the alley at this hour. At first, he just ignored the whoosh of cold wind that blew by him until he felt something sticky against his neck. He never even felt himself being thrown to the ground and nearly passed out from the sight of blood on his hand when he pulled it back.

He was surprised, and perhaps, a little turned on, to find a beautiful woman's face hovering above him. Until, he saw her teeth.

She purred into his ear, "Ah, cher, what is such a handsome man doing all by yourself? Nothing personal, mais oui?"

He shuddered as her tongue licked his neck. The coldness of her tongue shocked him. If only the coldness of her tongue helped to ease the pain from her razor sharp fangs.

He would never see his family or friends again. As his body grew cold, a howl pierced the night. He feared that maybe the devil's hounds were coming for him. As a black blur passed in front of his eyes, he wondered if this could be the angel of death looking down upon him.

As he slipped into unconsciousness, the vampire let out a blood-curdling scream as a horrible tearing sound came mere feet from him.

For a moment, he thought he saw another woman's face hovering over him, but he could no longer fight the darkness that called him. He was dying. Cold settled into his bones as his very life blood drained from the holes in his neck.

***

Josie looked down at the unconscious young man and let out an exasperated sigh. She licked the wounds on his neck to stop the bleeding and healed the bite marks. The fang marks closed in no time. As she tasted the coppery blood on her tongue, she fought off the hunger growing inside of her. "Come on kid stay with me."

She picked him up off the ground as she called Tyler. "I have another one that needs to get to the ER as soon as possible. I am afraid I may not have reached him in time."

Tyler met Josie behind the emergency room of the hospital. The young man had lost a lot of blood and needed a blood transfusion soon if they had any hope of saving him.

As Tyler walked into the emergency room, he shouted out, "I have an emergency. A young man was found unconscious near Jackson Square."

***

Dr. Thompson stepped out of Exam Room 2 when he heard the commotion. He wondered about this young officer LeBlanc. He was one of the only young officers with the New Orleans Police Department walking in with patients needing medical assistance and all very near death. Was he an "Angel of Mercy"? It wouldn't be the first time someone in their profession attempted to kill a person only to become a hero just in the nick of time. Wanting to see what this patient's medical problems were right away and curious to see if Officer LeBlanc did intentionally harm this young person, he called out, "Officer LeBlanc, bring him into Exam Room 4. It is available."

Just from looking at the young patient, Dr. Thompson saw that he was anemic and near death. "Nurse, let's disrobe him to find out where he is bleeding from. We also need to get lab work on him stat to find out what his levels are, and cross match his blood type. He needs a blood transfusion immediately in order to save his life." Dr. Thompson turned to Officer LeBlanc, "Was he hit by a car?"

Without hesitation, "It looked more like a mugging got out of hand, Dr. Thompson. I noticed some blood on his shirt and figured he was hit over the head."

Dr. Thompson stated, "Let's order a CT scan as soon as he is stabilized to make sure that there are no head injuries just in case." Looking over at Officer LeBlanc, "Thank you, we can handle it from here."

***

Tyler could tell that he was being dismissed by the pompous doctor. He would check on the young man later on to make sure that he was doing better. He also needed to see what he remembered about the attack. Since he was unconscious when Josie found him, she didn't know if he remembered anything about the attack. He hoped that he didn't.

Chapter 38

Flinging the paper away and pushing himself from the table abruptly, he caused the coffee to slosh over the brim of the cup as it rattled in the saucer. Katrina Chaisson flinched instinctively when she heard the noise. She waited in dreaded anticipation of what might come. Her husband was on the verge of erupting once again. His lips were tightly compressed, and his jaws were clenched. His nostrils flared out as he took deep breaths in and out. He had the whole community fooled with his practiced charm while she suffered in private from his mean-spirited nature.

Over the years, she'd learned how to adapt to his dark moods and placated him by playing up to his compulsive, self-opinionated personality. She had no idea what had upset him, but if she didn't defuse his mood quickly, she would be the one to pay. As always. She just needed to make him feel as if he had a sense of superiority over her. She needed to pacify his ego until he calmed down.

She poured him another cup of coffee and cleaned up the mess from the spilled cup. He looked up at her with a condescending smile; his flared nostrils hinting at the anger boiling inside of him, but he said nothing. The silence from him had her completely unnerved. She wasn't used to this side of him. She'd learned how to handle his explosive temper, but this composed man in front of her, she was uncertain of.

For just a moment, rage flitted across his face, and his mask of composure slipped. She prepared herself for him to unleash his temper. It caught her by complete surprise when he stood up and walked out of the kitchen. As he left, he said, "Don't wait up for me tonight. I am golfing this afternoon, and then a drink at the club."

Katrina found herself stunned by the easy dismissal. Lately, he'd used her as a punching bag more and more, but today he just simply walked away without even his perfunctory kiss. Did he find someone else to take out his aggressions on? She feared that he would come back home late tonight and punish her for any little thing he could find.

She stiffened her back and tried to find the courage to leave her husband today. If only she had someone to talk to, someone who would listen to her. Her husband was not who he appeared to be. No one noticed the monster living just under his skin. Lately, he had become more violent, and if she didn't do something soon, he would kill her. It was only a matter of time.

With his cool demeanor this morning, she feared tonight could be the night that he had something planned for her.

As if reading her mind, he turned at the door and stated, "Oh, my beloved wife, be warned that if you do run from me I will track you down."

Katrina stared into her husband's eyes and swore they shined gold for a moment.

Chapter 39

Josie jumped back to avoid the Rougarou's sharp claws. She bounced to her feet and prepared for the next attack. Looking down, she saw that the creature's claws had cut through her shirt. She shook her head at her own foolishness. The creature came very close to gutting her, closer than she cared to acknowledge. Acting quickly, she jumped out of its way as it lunged for her. Tyler caught the creature off guard in midflight.

Tyler flung it into a brick wall. Looking over at Josie, he gave her a quick reassuring smile before shifting into his Rougarou body. Josie caught sight of another creature just as it lunged for Tyler. She pushed him out of danger just as the creature's sharp claws ripped into her upper arm. She bit back the pain, but thankfully, vampires healed quickly. In the time that it took her wounds to heal, Tyler threw the newest Rougarou to the sidewalk, cracking its head wide open on the concrete. Josie cringed at the sight of the dark, almost black, blood pooling under its head. That could have easily been Tyler bleeding to death if she hadn't acted when she did.

Just as Tyler asked, "Where did he come from?" Josie round kicked another as it soared through the air in an effort to catch her off guard. She had to admit that they were more than determined to attack both her and Tyler. Unfortunately, the kick only dazed the beast. As it lunged for her once again, she hissed before kicking it square in the chest with the spike of her heel impaling the beast. With an ease she had become used to, she removed the dead beast from her shoe before turning back to Tyler.

She sensed what the next one planned and in one quick action flung her silver dagger straight at its heart. The creature let out an ear piercing howl of pain as the knife hit its mark. Out of nowhere, another one moved in to attack Tyler. He caught it in a headlock with his forearm pulled tight against its throat as his other hand gripped its head. Without even thinking, he broke the beast's neck. Josie watched its eyes roll back before falling to the ground. She looked into Tyler's eyes and cringed at the sight in front of her. She wished he healed as quickly as her, but it took time for him. Several gashes marred his cheeks and forehead. A large patch of blood seeped through his shirt from a gaping wound on the side of his chest. It was a difficult fight, but at least, they walked away with minor injuries.

***

Tyler ran a hand through his hair as he observed the bodies. He frowned down at the dead Rougarou's. They were smarter this time, knowing that they couldn't send just one to attack Josie. He didn't like that they hadn't given up on killing her either. If it hadn't been for him coming when he did, he feared that it would have been her instead of these brothers of his lying dead on the ground.

He let out a sigh before saying to Josie, "They are getting braver."

Averting her gaze from Tyler to the bodies, she said, "We can't leave these bodies here for someone to find."

Nodding his head in agreement, Tyler bent down to move the bodies deep into the bushes nearby. "They will be okay here. It won't be long before their leader sends someone looking for them."

Josie nodded her head in agreement. "Should we wait for them? Maybe, we can follow them back to their lair?"

Tyler shook his head. "We aren't prepared for battle now. We are both tired, and daylight will be here sooner than you realize."

Josie looked up at the sky. She hadn't realized how much time had passed.

Chapter 40

Josie woke the next night with an insatiable hunger. The previous night's events must have taken more out of her than she initially realized.

After a quick shower, she pulled on a pair of tattered jeans and worn tank top. Tonight, she decided to turn in her stiletto heels for a pair of battered boots. Someone was preying on the druggies and homeless, and for her plan to work, she needed to blend in. It may be her only chance to find out who was behind this. She suspected that it was vampires, but she was not certain. No bodies had been found, but the numbers on the streets had declined enough to catch her attention. She feared that these humans were taken for harvest. She'd heard rumors that some vampires abducted humans to use as blood slaves. If true, she vowed to put a stop to those committing this heinous offense.

She wasn't sure which offense was worse; being turned into a repulsive creature of the night without your consent or being held against your will only to be used as a source of food.

After tying her boots, Josie tucked her phone and weapons in her pockets. Tonight gave her a chance to try the new bullets Tyler had made. He upped the ultraviolet ratio in the center and added a new silencer to the gun. At first, the large gun felt strange in her hands, but after a few target rounds, she grew accustomed to it.   Her outfit tonight didn't give her too many hiding spaces. It was imperative that she looked like a destitute druggie. Thanks to her pale skin, she looked the part. To help complete the ensemble, she grabbed a bottle of alcohol, which contained a toxic dose of an ultraviolet liquid, holy water, and silver. Just being this close to the poisonous concoction in the bottle had Josie feeling weak. She carefully wrapped a paper bag around it, but kept the neck visible.

As an added measure to ensure she blended in with the dregs of society, she added a stagger to her walk. It helped that she added a lift to the inside of her left boot, so she didn't have to be conscientious about the way she walked.

If only she could go back in time and join the ranks of the ignorant. Most of these humans were lucky and lived in blissful denial of the true nature of this world. No, her innocence and her very soul were taken from her.

She often wondered if Tyler would be better off not having her in his life, but she couldn't survive this living hell without him in hers. For decades, she thought she was cursed to live a life of solitude. That was until she fell in love with Tyler. She often feared that she was putting him in the direct line of danger. If anything ever happened to him because of her, she could not live with herself. For this very reason, she never left behind any witnesses. No, it was better off to be invisible and lethal. It was necessary for her to lurk in the back alleys, staying on the margin of human existence. She haunted the night like a ghost, searching out her prey. Perhaps it was her destiny to kill these spawn of Satan. If only she could get one step closer to redeeming her sins by killing the vampires and other scum of the earth.

Up above, brief flashes of heat lightning lit up the dark, dismal sky. She looked up and prayed that she could kill every last evil vampire walking this earth.

She couldn't shake the feeling of doom that hung heavy in the air from recent events. As she made her way to the French Quarter, she had to fight the hunger taking over her body. She would soon find her food.

As Josie made her way down a dark alley, a noise caught her attention. She saw a group of vampires and wondered if they could be the ones she was looking for. The four of them crept through the steamy shadows.

As though sensing her nearby, they hissed, baring their fangs, and clawing the air with their hands as if crazed. These vampires must be looking for a fight because they came at her with full force, slashing at her with their ragged nails as they hissed.

As a vampire somersaulted over her, she fired. While the vampire vaporized in front of her, the other vampires were on guard and ready to attack. She back-flipped, firing midair as one charged at her. Her bullet found its mark, disintegrating another vampire with simplicity.

The two remaining vampires took on Josie as a team. As one caught her in the side with his long, ragged nails, she sent his partner back to hell. Ignoring the burning pain she prepared for the next attack. The last vampire hissed as it lunged for her throat. Fueled with fresh blood and the desire to send Josie back to hell, it attacked with a swiftness that Josie wasn't prepared for. As she tried to sidestep the attack, the vampire's face came in very close contact with her. She took aim on the last remaining vampire and finally ended his life.

As Josie surveyed her wounds, she found that they were already healing. This recent attack confirmed that the number of vampires was on the rise. No matter how many she killed, every week there were even more. These vampires tonight, thankfully, made easy targets.

While she made her way home, she paid special attention to the doorways, alleys, and rooftops just in case another vampire was waiting to attack. As she turned a corner, a wisteria vine hit her in the face. The fragrant smell reminded her of springtime growing up. Times that had been so happy, yet so very far away.

As she walked home, her boots clunked on the deserted cobblestone sidewalk, echoing in the silence. The moonlight cast eerie shadows as they danced around her like ghosts. Even at this hour, the air was heavy with humidity.

Suddenly, all of her senses were on alert. The hunter had become the hunted. The vampire who jumped in front of her had a sadistic look about him. From his snake and barbed wire tattoos, to his body piercings, he wanted attention. He gave her a bloodthirsty smile that told her he had no intentions of fighting fair.

The knowledge that she was hunting their own kind must have made its way to the other vampires. She might not leave witnesses behind, but she couldn't prevent them from talking telepathically.

The need for redemption coursing through her body gave her extra strength to fight this dark creature. She was condemned forever, only one step from hell, but she refused to turn into a creature as vile as this in front of her. When she tapped into his mind, she saw his dark intentions. This one had no desire to stop his cruel feeding.

She probed further and shuddered at what she saw. He may not be with the group of vampires she sought, but he was just as sadistic. He did not feed for need, but pure pleasure. This one had truly embraced the darkness.

She stretched her limbs as she waited for him to make his move. For once, she was glad Tyler insisted that she take dance lessons. They taught her how to make her body movements more flexible and agile.

As Josie read his mind, he closed the door shut with a loud bang. Then, he made his move. "Are you ready for a fight?" The vampire snarled out. With a bone-chilling laugh, he taunted, "Sending you to hell will be a pleasure. My master will be more than happy with that occurrence."

Josie waved her hand at him, summoning him to make a move. "If you think you can."

She wasn't prepared for the dagger, and the blade missed her body by an inch. He was faster than she calculated.

She dove into a handspring and landed on her feet. He anticipated her move, kicking her legs from under her feet as soon as she hit the ground. Fighting with this vampire was reminiscent of a dance. She gracefully moved her body to avoid the deathly dagger. As he blocked one of her moves, he sent her flying, causing her head to hit the pavement with a loud thud. Groggy, she rolled away from his next attack. As he made his move, she knocked him down to the ground. In one swift movement, she pinned him under her body, grinding his body into the ground with her knees.

This vampire fought well. When Josie saw a perfect opportunity, she plunged the silver dagger into his heart. The silver burned through his body as it made its treacherous path to its mark.

The vampire did not expect Josie's quick action and let out a guttural howl as it was sent back to hell. As his dust particles floated away into the night sky, she looked up in search of the dawn's pale tinge. She let out a soft curse as the first telltale signs washed away the darkness of night. With lightning speed, she rushed home.

At one time, she'd loved the sunrise, but now it made her cringe. It was just another item on her list of things she could no longer enjoy. Sighing, it was one of many, unfortunately.

The soft glow of the streetlights cast halos over the empty shops and cafes that made up New Orleans. Soon, the city workers would be out picking up the garbage that lined the streets before the city came to life once more.

If these humans were sensible, they would not walk around at night. Instead, the city remained unaware of the supernatural beings that walked amongst them. Even from here, she heard the traffic on the interstate. A few streets down, there was a car with a loud thumping car stereo as a siren wailed somewhere in the distance. She could even hear the whispered conversations in the surrounding apartments. To her left, a lady sobbed uncontrollably, and to her right, another moaned in sheer pleasure.

When she was first turned, the cacophony of sounds terrified her. Now, she had learned how to embrace her senses. It was these very senses that made her a lethal killer. Her superpowers were one thing about being a vampire that she did not find revolting.

Her stomach grumbled loudly, reminding her that she had not fed tonight. The hunger became unbearable as she made it closer to home. It became so intense that all she thought about was sinking her teeth into warm flesh as the coppery blood flowed down her throat.

She shivered as she recalled her first feeding. She could still taste the saltiness of her prey's terror. There were so many at first that did not deserve the lonely death of being fed on. Horrible images flashed through her mind as she recalled the deaths of those she'd fed on. It was a ravenous nightmare that she could never remove from her mind.

Josie swallowed back the bile that made its way up her throat as she recalled her past. Once again, she cursed the monster that made her. She cursed Joshua, as well. She had put all of her trust in him. She had been too gullible to see his true nature until it was too late.

So many times she screamed to heaven, begging for absolution. But knew deep down that was impossible.

She'd lost count of those she'd killed, mortal and immortal. That was her bane of existence in her own personal hell. On the positive side, there was Tyler and the love they shared.

As Josie rounded a corner, her ears perked up at the sound of footsteps behind her. Not slowing down since she needed to be home before sunrise, she listened harder. A tantalizing scent reached her nose as the footsteps came closer. It was the rich, coppery smell of blood, and her fangs elongated in anticipation of food.

She inhaled deeply and smelled the evil that lurked in this one's soul. Sunrise was around the horizon, but her hunger had become all consuming. Did she have time to feed off this individual before daybreak? Josie let her mind intrude on her potential prey's mind and found her answer. She could not allow this vile man to continue walking on this earth. He lured children into his home only to use them in depraved ways.

As the footsteps drew closer, Josie blended into the darkness of the night. Shadows enveloped her as she waited.

It was funny how until cursed she never even considered the meaning of life. She never contemplated the value of her life. Not once did she question whether or not there was truly a God. Now, she knew.

***

Tyler paced back and forth in the living room as he waited for Josie to make it home. She had pushed it lately with just how close to sunrise she made it back to the security of their house.

As soon as she entered the house, a sigh of relief escaped his mouth. He took in the very sight of her. He was pulled in by her dark eyes that were framed with long curling lashes, her exquisite, pale face, and kissable mouth. He couldn't wait to have those luscious lips under his and taste her again.

Desire filled him as he looked at her body. His skin tingled, and his blood rushed through his body as passion ignited deep inside of him.

"I was worried about you."

She rushed into his waiting arms. "I missed you," she whispered. Her voice carried with it a husky promise of pleasure. She looked up to him, and he felt the desire in her gaze. For a moment, he could only look down at her, transfixed by her beauty.

He couldn't wait to feel her softness underneath him. Feel that naughty tongue of hers teasing him. He was under her spell, completely in love with this woman. He wanted those luscious lips on his body, drowning him in her sweet love.

As if reading his mind, Josie moved against his body. She let out a soft moan, rich with excitement as his fingers became lost in her lustrous hair. He tasted the blood on her lips as he kissed her.

All he could think of was giving into the sinful pleasures she offered. He was dizzy with need as his pulse quickened. He was hers as she was his.

Chapter 41

From her high vantage point, Josie perched on the ledge and watched the dark alley behind the club where vampires tended to hang out. So far, nothing was going on except for a few rats searching around in the dumpster below her.

The other night she'd hoped to find out more regarding the unfortunate people disappearing, but that was a complete bust. She was certain that a master vampire ruled over a relatively large vampire family here. She had to find out before the humans got suspicious and came looking for answers.

A movement at the rear door of the club caught Josie's attention. She watched intently as a woman slinked out the door. She could tell the young lady was nervous. Her heart rate was high, and she was panting heavily. A dark sedan slowly pulled into the alley, not bothering to turn its lights on. The car stopped right in front of the young woman, and a man exited, looking around carefully before walking up to her.

Josie quietly moved to the back of the building to get the license plate of the car. She sent Tyler a text with the plate number so that he could research it.

Josie easily dropped from the roof to the ground, landing next to the man and the young woman. She covered the man's mouth with her hand and hoped the woman was too stunned to scream.

Josie raised her switchblade to the man's throat and addressed the both of them, "You scream, and it will be the last thing he does." The young woman barely nodded whereas the man let out a muffled hiss. Josie pressed the silver blade into the man's neck a little harder so that he felt the burn of the silver on his skin to know that she meant business.

The young woman reached out to Josie, trying to ease the knife on the vampire's throat. "Please don't hurt him. He meant no harm," she pleaded.

As Josie sniffed the air, she smelled that the human had a fresh bite somewhere on her body. The way the young woman acted told Josie that she had feelings for this man. "Are you two involved?"

Gripping her wrist, the girl tried to hide the recent feeding marks. "No one harmed me, and Abraham would never hurt me."

The vampire attempted to speak without the knife going deeper into his skin. "I just came to take my girlfriend home."

Josie asked the young woman, "Why sneak out the back door?"

"I work nights here at the club. I know what lurks in the shadows at night. I'm not gullible; not all vampires are like Abraham."

Josie slowly let the knife fall away from Abraham's neck. "Who is your master?"

Abraham turned to face Josie and explained, "I haven't seen my master for decades now. I am not like other vampires that live here. I do not need to kill humans to feed." Nodding to his girlfriend and he continued, "Belinda here is just one of the many girlfriends I've had over the years who willingly lets me feed off of her."

Belinda moved into her boyfriend's arms. "I have not told a soul about Abraham's existence," she promised.

Josie looked over the two lovers, failing to see what the woman found so fascinating about being with a vampire. Did she hope he would turn her so that she could stay young and beautiful forever? Josie almost laughed at that last thought. There was nothing beautiful about being a vampire. "Have you heard about a master vampire or other vampires possibly using humans as a blood bank?"

Abraham shook his head and replied, "No, I haven't heard anything about that."

Josie could kick herself; this was another wasted night. As she left the alley, she caught sight of someone who may be following her. She let out a soft curse for letting her guard down. As soon as her stalker realized he was spotted, he took off in a run.

She sighed as she began tracking him down. It was too early in the night to exert this much energy. The smell of the vampire dissipated fast in the humid night. She had no plan on losing this vampire, but with the number of humans around it was too difficult to kill him in public.

With a burst of inhuman speed, she cut through a dingy alley and pulled up short. The stench of decaying food from the dumpster hit her square in the face. Breathing shallow, she scanned the buildings, and the sound of a whimpering female caught her attention. It looked as if her stalker would get away, after all.

Walking in the direction of the noise, Josie called out, "Let her go."

A pair of vampires turned around, their red eyes eerily glowing in the night. The terrified female struggled against her captor's arms, shrieking for help. When one of her captors hissed and bared his fangs at Josie, the young woman's eyes rolled back right before she fainted. The poor woman was probably seduced by one of these young men with their pretty boy faces; unfortunately, she discovered that she had made the wrong choice.

Josie let out an exasperated sigh. She should have expected the woman to faint, but it just made her job harder.

One of the young vampires brought the unconscious woman's body close to him, baring her neck to his teeth. "Be gone woman! This is our food."

Josie just shook her head in disbelief. They believed she was here to steal their food. "That small thing doesn't have enough blood in her body for the two of you."

Josie carefully pulled her silver dagger out of her waistband, all the while paying close attention to the vampires. Suddenly, he tossed the young woman aside as they both came at her like unleashed dogs. Dodging the attack, Josie sliced one across the throat, turning him to dust instantly. The other vampire was better prepared and landed a roundhouse kick straight across her jaw.

The vampire hissed, "Not so brave now are you woman?" The vampire advanced, sporting a macabre grin.

Josie narrowed her eyes as she aimed her dagger at the vampire's heart. It was time to end this travesty of a fight. In one swift move, she sent the knife straight into his chest. A guttural hiss filled the night air as he dissipated into dust. Once Josie was sure that there were no more advancing vampires, she walked over to the unconscious woman. She checked her for any apparent injuries. Relieved to see there were no visible injuries, she gently woke up the young lady, erasing her memories before sending her on her way.

From the shadows, a vampire chuckled. Josie whirled around and grabbed the vampire by the neck, lifting him off the ground. Staring at her with pure malice in his eyes was a young boy, possibly seventeen. His fangs dripped with fresh blood as he sneered at her.

Josie squeezed his neck tighter as she probed his mind. The boy squirmed under her firm grasp. He rasped, "Let me go."

"I want to know about your master. You have exactly five seconds."

He hissed, "I don't know what you're talking about."

Josie squeezed harder. This young boy was newly turned, maybe a week or so. Josie cut open his shirt with her silver dagger and let the tip of the blade sizzle the boy's skin right above his heart. Maybe, she could scare the truth out of him.

The young vampire sneered at her, "You are nothing compared to my master. He is teaching us how to be the superior race. These humans are cattle to us."

Josie took the dagger and stabbed the young vampire in the heart. The body exploded into a pile of smoldering ash. She saw what was in this young vampire's heart and understood why his master chose him. His heart was black as night, even before he was turned. He was a psychopath in the making. It looked as if this particular master could also see a person's true aura.

Could it be his master vampire that she was searching for? The one who'd turned her into this creature of the night?

Chapter 42

Josie paid no attention to the wind that blew through the alley. She kept her attention focused on the couple in the alley, making no sudden movements or noise.

Keeping her gun ready to take the vampire out in one shot, she had watched it all night in the bar. He was sinfully good looking and smooth talking to the young women in the bar. The way he moved and watched people set off an internal alarm. Josie sensed that he'd found her even with his mind closed off. She quickly followed him as he hastily pulled a woman outside.

Even now as she tried to read his mind, she found he still had it blocked from her. He shifted a fraction before pulling the woman into his arms. She prepared to take aim, waiting to see what would transpire.

Instead of moving in to feed, the woman unbuttoned the man's shirt and pressed her lips to his bare chest. The man's head fell back in ecstasy. This woman was about to get a rude awakening. However, it would be better to witness a vampire burst into tiny dust particles rather than be drained dry. Besides, Josie would erase any memory of what transpired in the alleyway.

As Josie took aim, a noise behind her caught her attention. A familiar voice whispered in her ear, "That's not a good idea, Josie."

Josie spun around to find herself face to face with James. Glancing over her shoulder to make sure that the vampire hadn't fed on the woman yet, she whispered, "James, what are you doing here?"

She noticed that James was dressed for a night on the town. His dark shirt shimmered in the moonlight. He was no longer the man she knew from the carnival. He looked as if he'd stepped right off the pages of a magazine. Even his shoes looked out of place on him. They belonged on a boardroom executive pacing the floors rather than on James. "I have been looking for you, Josie."

Alarm bells went off in Josie's head. Was James betraying her? "You found me. Now, what is so important that you had to stop me?"

As James crossed his arms over his chest, she followed his eyes. His eyes transfixed on the couple in the alley. Disappointment filled Josie as she realized the distraction of James's arrival stopped her from killing the vampire before it fed on the woman. She watched as the woman held onto the man with a look of total rapture as he fed on her.

The way he held the woman, Josie could not get a clear shot without harming the woman also. Josie let out a muttered curse. "Do you see what you did? He will kill that woman!"

She hoped her words would have an impact on James but instead, he shook his head. "No, Josie, you are reading the scene wrong. He would never hurt her. They are in love."

She looked at James dumbfounded. This was the second vampire/human relationship she'd run across. "Since when do we make ourselves known this openly to humans?"

Josie studied the two down the alley with grim eyes. "Just what are you doing here, James," she asked.

"I don't want you to kill any of my family on your quest. We discussed this before, but I need to make sure that you understand not all is as it seems."

As Josie listened to James, she wondered why these people would be loyal to any vampire. Are they secretly hoping for a chance to live forever, to be free of illness and disease? She'd witnessed what ailments afflicted those she loved from a distance. Would they voluntarily trade their souls for immortality? Were they that foolish?

As the two friends stared at each other, an icy cold sensation ran down Josie's spine. Every instinct in her body went on red alert. She looked over at James and noticed that he sensed it too. Her eyes narrowed as she scanned the area. The scent that filled the air was one of blind hunger and death.

Josie threw James an extra gun she kept tucked by her ankle. The skin on the back of her neck crawled as her instincts took over. Her fingers itched to fire the trigger and send the vampire to the pits of hell where he truly belonged.

Josie listened carefully to pinpoint the exact location of the creature. When she picked up the vampire's voice, he was just a few streets over. Acting quickly, she and James took off at the same time.

They both froze when they watched the scene before them unfold.

"Where are you going pretty lady?"

The young girl never saw the man walk out of the shadows. She plowed right into him. His fingers gripped her arm hard; the chill of them instantly froze her to the very bone.

She said nothing, only looked up at him in complete fear. Just as he forced her head back, Josie moved in. "Leave her be."

The sound of her voice surprised the vampire. However, instead of confronting Josie and James, the vampire moved away from them with lightning speed, dragging the woman with him. Josie followed close behind when the vampire called out, "Unless you want me to rip her throat out, I suggest you stay the hell away."

Josie caught sight of James moving in behind the vampire, a smirk on his lips. The vampire tightened his grip on the woman's neck. "Let her go, and I will let you live," Josie taunted him.

The vampire shook his head and smiled. A maniacal smile, one full of threat and menace. "Oh, no, cher. I know exactly what will happen the instant I let this tasty little morsel go."

The vampire tensed as soon as it realized another vampire stood behind him. James warned, "That's going to happen, mon ami. You have the decision if you want to die a painful, slow death or quickly."

What happened next was too quick to process. As Josie moved in, the young woman's body went careening through the air. Acting quickly, Josie caught her before she hit the wall. Once again, Josie was glad to have someone else fighting with her.

***

James sat in the chair by the window brooding as he watched the sun set. He'd heard rumors that older, stronger vampires discovered they could tolerate increased amounts of sunlight, but he had his doubts.

He was turned over a century ago and would never be considered a weak vampire, but he could barely tolerate sunlight on his skin. Just the early morning's light left blisters on his skin that took hours to heal if he didn't get to shelter in time. From his conversation with Josie earlier, she couldn't take sunlight either.

He still couldn't believe that he'd killed another vampire. His mind told him that it had to be done, but another part of him had a hard time dealing with the fact he'd killed again. He left that life behind him. Now he, like Josie, found other ways to feed his hunger. Unlike her, he refused to kill. He'd learned there were those who willingly donated blood to their kind from a secret organization of humans that started many decades ago. To belong to this particular chattel was a true honor. The members were sworn to secrecy and, more importantly, were drug and disease free. To the humans, it sounded glamorous, but these chattels were only a blood bank for vampires with the hope that the members would eventually be turned.

James also suspected that those in this chattel were addicted to the bite of a vampire. When a vampire bit a human, the feeling was similar to that of a drug being introduced into their system. They became more addicted to the euphoria than the feeding.

Before James learned of this secret organization, he only fed for the amount of blood that he needed to survive. After each feeding, he erased the memory of his donor.

He agreed with Josie, though; something was going on. The vampire that he killed tonight had no control. Just the scent of blood turned him into a maniac. Newly turned vampires should be supervised until they had at least some sense of control.

Chapter 43

Carson McKnight looked at his surroundings once again and let out an exasperated sigh. This had to be the most boring assignment yet since he started working at the Department of Wildlife and Fisheries.

When Carson graduated high school, he was already enlisted in the US Army. His life had changed drastically a week before he was scheduled to depart for boot camp. As he climbed down his deer stand, the ladder snapped, sending him plummeting to the ground. As soon as he hit the ground, he heard the distinct crunch of bone and knew his injury was bad. It took two hours for his dad to come searching for him. There was a strict rule in the house for Sunday mornings; they had to be back home by seven in the morning since church was at ten, and no one could miss Mass with the family.

Carson broke his collar bone in the fall which ended his military career before it started. It took several months for him to heal, most of that time he spent sulking. Growing up, he wanted to make a career for himself in the military. What other job allowed him to play with guns all day long? Being from Louisiana and loving to hunt, he was a natural marksman. He not only enlisted in the US Army, but also signed up to be a sniper. The recruiter warned him that not everyone was accepted into the elite group, but Carson convinced him into going to the range to show him just what he could do. He impressed the recruiter enough for him to make a phone call. That one phone call sealed the deal for Carson to become a sniper.

After sulking around the house for several months, his dad had had enough and told him to get off his lazy behind. Fate stepped in that day by the name of Officer Benjamin Harris with the Department of Wildlife and Fisheries. On his way back from hunting, a young officer approached Carson. A cattle farmer had some of his baby calves mauled by a wild animal. By the look of it, whatever mauled the calves was fairly large.

Carson started talking with the young officer. On his way back home, he decided that was the job for him. That was five years ago, and since then this was his first lame ass detail. Of course, if he hadn't slept with his boss's sister, he might not be on this assignment.

As he swiped at another pesky mosquito, a smirk formed across his face. He had to admit that being with Sheila was worth this detail. Hell, who was he kidding? For another escapade with her, he would do this duty all over again. That girl was a wild ride and a half. Just thinking about everything they did, had him shifting uncomfortably in the boat seat.

As he reminisced, a sight up above caught his attention. Buzzards circled an area for one reason only; something dead was nearby.   Bored, Carson decided to investigate.

The smell hit him before he even noticed the carnage at the bank of the bayou. It surprised him that the alligators hadn't dragged it off yet.

As the boat rounded the bend of the bayou, the scene in front of him confirmed his suspicions. A large buck and the carcasses of a few smaller animals lay sprawled along the bank of the bayou. What happened here? Was the water polluted?

As he drew near the shore, he found a few more deer carcasses and a large carcass almost all the way in the water. Carson guided the boat along the bayou and secured it to a downed limb before making his way over to investigate.

Carson let out a soft curse as he took his cell phone out to call his boss. He dreaded making this call, especially knowing he was the last person Grant Voison wanted to talk to. Deciding it would be easier to post a picture rather than explain the sight in front of him, Carson sent his boss a picture before making the call.

"What do you want Carson?"

"Sir, something is out here on the bayou killing large animals and leaving the carcasses half eaten. I just sent you a picture of the damage."

"Hold on, it just came in." Carson heard his boss let out a muttered curse before speaking again. "What the hell is that? I have never seen an animal leave anything like that behind."

Most animals hunted only for what they could eat and never wasted meat. It was highly unusual for an animal to leave this much carnage behind unless it was rabid. "Send me your coordinates so that I can send you help. We should be there shortly," Voison said.

After sending his boss the coordinates, Carson examined the damage in front of him. His gut instinct told him that whatever animal did this, he was in the middle of its lair. That would be the only reason for so many carcasses in one area. Similar to a squirrel gathering nuts for winter, this animal gathered carcasses.

As Carson nudged a carcass with his boot, he caught a glimpse of something that did not belong. Carson rushed back to his boat for a pair of work gloves, not wanting to touch anything with his bare hands. He carefully moved the remains of dead animals, stumbling back in disbelief as he uncovered what he was searching for.

He quickly called his boss. "Sir, we need to send for the coroner and police, as well."

"What the hell for? We can handle a simple case of animal remains."

"Sir, there is a dead woman buried under the animal remains. Something tore her apart," Carson explained.

Voison took in a sharp breath. "Don't touch anything else. Take as many photos as you can before the boys in blue and the coroner get there. Once they are involved with the investigation, we will be cut loose. If this is an animal preying upon both humans and animals, we need to start searching for it ASAP before more people are killed. From the picture you sent me, I don't think this was an alligator. It would have brought the bodies underwater to ripen and not leave them out in the sun."

"Yes, sir."

"I will call in the dive team. We need to make sure there aren't any bodies underwater. Oh, and Carson, don't use your radio. If you need to make any notifications do it by cell phone. I don't want this to go out over the airwaves just in case someone is listening. We don't need the media or gawkers all over the area."

"Yes, sir."

***

Voison stepped out of the boat, allowing the humid air to settle over him before walking towards Carson. He smelled the impending rain that hung heavy in the air. They needed to secure as much evidence as possible before the storm hit. As he breathed in, another smell crept over him, the unmistakable smell of fear. He fought down the emotion, refusing to let terror overpower him. He couldn't let his men see that this image had shaken him to the very core.

Without saying anything, he walked in silence with Carson over to the carnage left behind by this deadly creature. He stared down at the mutilation in front of him. He'd seen his share of carnage, but with this, he felt his stomach recoil. As he looked over the scene, Carson asked, "Sir, what do you think ripped her apart like that? It almost looks as if a pack of wild dogs got ahold of her."

Chapter 44

The shrill of the ringing telephone woke Dupre from his slumber. He looked to see if the phone woke his wife, Heather. He watched as she let out a small sigh as she rolled over, burying herself deeper under the covers.

"Yeah," he whispered into the phone.

Newman's voice filled his ear, "Did I wake you?"

Grunting, Dupre looked over at the alarm clock and sighed, "No, I always make it a point to wake up at four a.m."

Dupre carefully got out of bed so he could have a conversation without waking Heather. Once in the kitchen, he asked, "Okay, what's up?"

"An officer with the Department of Wildlife and Fisheries found several mutilated animal carcasses yesterday in an alcove of the bayou. Later, he uncovered a woman's body under the animal carcasses. Upon further inspection, three more bodies were found. The coroner said a vampire didn't do this."

"What does he suspect?"

Newman let out a long sigh. "The bodies are eerily similar to some of the other victims' bodies found recently. Except this time, the vital organs were ripped out of the bodies unmercifully. The coroner called to let us know that the DNA came back early this morning showing some unusual characteristics."

Dupre let out a long sigh, "I am almost afraid to ask."

"Human DNA was found in the wounds, but a malformation showed up in the DNA readings. Dr. Ortego compared it to the DNA he had on file with the vampires, but it did not match. He also compared it to the zombie DNA, and there was no match for that, as well."

Dupre grunted, "Get to the point."

"Dr. Ortego stated that you knew some of the old timers on the bayou. He thought you could ask some of your contacts if they saw anything strange walking around lately."

"Just what do you mean by strange?"

Newman shared with Dupre, "The DNA breakdown was not only human but also canine as well."

Dupre let out a surprised laugh, "You have to be kidding me. So, what is he thinking? Could this be a werewolf?"

Newman hated to even utter what the coroner believed they were dealing with. Hell, he doesn't even believe it. He'd learned that Louisiana had its mythical creatures, but this was too unbelievable. It took him a while to wrap his head around the existence of vampires, but this was something altogether different. "Dr. Ortego believes that we may be looking at a Rougarou."

In the process of brewing coffee, Dupre spilled the entire pot of water all over the counter at that statement. At that moment, Heather walked in stifling a yawn, "What's going on?"

Dupre held his finger up to his lips as he asked Newman, "He can't be serious? The Rougarou is Cajun folklore."

He'd heard the term Rougarou before, of course. In voodoo, it meant someone cursed with an evil animal spirit. During the day, they appeared normal, but when the moon was full, they lost control of themselves. Some claimed that as part of the curse, the Rougarou could only satisfy his hunger with human blood. Others claimed it was a shape shifter.

"That's what I say, as well. Dr. Ortego then reminded me that zombies and vampires are real also."

Dupre threw his hands up in the air, "Okay, he has me there. I guess we need to start looking into this immediately?" Dupre ran his hands through his hair, feeling the beginnings of a headache.

***

As Dupre drove to the morgue, he recalled some of the stories locals told at some of the bars around town. Were these old-timers' stories about the Rougarou true? After all, when they fought the vampires, they ran into shape shifters. Hell, one of the guys still swore that while they fought the voodoo queen a wolf walked upright. At the time, Dupre thought the poor guy was revved up by what happened. He didn't put much stock in what he'd said, but, perhaps, he did indeed see something. Did one of the shape shifters manage to escape detection?

There was more going on than this possible killing by a Rougarou. Maybe someone killed Kevin Broussard over a story he was working on. They needed to take a closer look at his computer.

Some people whispered about strange happenings in the swamp late into the night. Hell, numerous people claimed to hear beating drums and chanting into the early hours of the morning. Some commented that it was downright eerie while others claimed it was kids partying.

Chapter 45

Ezrielle stepped out onto her porch and made herself comfortable on the old swing. She gathered her long hair into a makeshift bun as she listened to the sounds of the night. A slight breeze that caressed her body like a long lost lover blew in off the bayou. The spirits were restless of late. One of the spirits could not be calmed. Even though she had tried, this spirit refused to be tamed. His strong will was turning into a heavy burden for her.

It had been so easy to trick him into her world. She wrapped her lies around him with her soft words. She lulled him into her bed and then pulled him into her sordid world. Now, he sought revenge on those around him, but especially her. She knew he wished to exact sweet revenge on her if given the chance, but she planned on never letting that happen.

When he found out just how cold and dead her heart truly was, he left. He could not bear to have the hands of true evil touch him. He may try to run from this curse, but once a soul was turned away from God, there was no help for them. Ezrielle made sure no angels were nearby to send the soul to the light of God; instead, it slipped into the void of darkness.

She'd taught him well about pain. Only bitterness dwelled in his heart. Oh, he thought he could hide from her, but she knew at all times where he and all the others she turned were. Nothing happened in these bayous that she didn't know about.

***

He had the prey in his sights when images suddenly flashed through his mind. Anger boiled up deep inside of him as his prey scurried off. The cool wind blowing off the waters did little to quench the rage searing through his body. She was thinking of him once again. Damn that infernal voodoo woman. He often wondered if she knew that they were connected so intensely.

He used that information to his benefit. Somehow, he could read minds, far and near at times.

At first, Ezrielle twisted his thoughts until he figured out her true nature. If only he had realized her true intentions before it was too late.

The memories of her betrayal still had an icy grip on him. He tried to control his thoughts, but she still could invade his mind.

When they first met, she talked about how they were predestined to meet. He was attracted to Ezrielle as soon as he laid eyes on her. There was an all-consuming attraction between them, or so he believed. Now, he knew that she'd used him. Just like she used all men.

Letting out a ferocious snarl, he moved on to hunt for supper. It did him no good to think about her. Soon, he would destroy her and she would suffer for what she'd done to him. Others here may help him do what he yearned to do. She may have cursed his body and protected herself from him exacting revenge on her, but there were ways around that. He may not be able to kill his master, but another could.

Chapter 46

Dupre gently kissed Heather on the forehead before leaving. Letting out a soft yawn, she asked, "What's wrong?"

"Newman called. Another body was found."

Heather asked, "Is this one like the others?"

Dupre kissed Heather once more before answering, "I'm not sure. I miss the days of just simple vampires killing humans needlessly. We will find whatever did this."

Unable to stop, he kissed her again. "I do love you, Heather Dupre."

"And I love you too." Snuggling under the covers, she added, "Make sure you lock up. I'm going back to sleep."

***

As soon as Dupre saw the police cars ahead, he knew he was in the right place. Flashing red and blue lights lit up the early morning sky as a young officer busied himself by blocking off the entire area. Soon, traffic would back up as passersby slowed down or stopped, hoping to get a peek at what happened.

Dupre pulled off the road as far as possible before making his way to the young officer manning the crime scene. Newman signaled him with a wave of his flashlight.

Newman shook his head. "It's a bad one. It's worse than the bodies found by the bayou."

Dupre took in the scene. The body lay sprawled a few short feet from the road. Before lifting the sheet from the body, he took in a deep breath as he had learned from experience it would be bad. He could only stare at the mutilated body of a young teenage girl. As he flashed his flashlight over the body, he saw that whatever did this went straight for the jugular vein. A grimace formed on his face as he stared at her eyes once more. As he continued to look at the body, he felt his stomach lurch. "A vampire didn't do this; there is too much carnage. They would have drained the body of its blood."

Newman nodded his head in agreement. "I don't think this was the same creature that killed the bodies down by the bayou either. Whoever, or whatever, killed those victims wanted to keep the bodies hidden, but not this one. This is the same one that killed Kevin Broussard. It appears that this one kills just for the fun of it."

Dupre studied the wounds on the girl's neck again. "It looks like a large wolf or dog mauled this poor girl.

Have forensics put a rush on this. I recommend having them compare the DNA samples to confirm if this was the same creature or not."

"Did you want to be present for the autopsy?"

Just the thought of attending an autopsy caused Dupre to gag. "Not really, but I should be there."

Suddenly, a gunshot rang out in the not too far distance. Both men raced toward the direction of the noise while each whispered a silent prayer for their safety.

A man called out, "Detective, over here!"

Newman kept his gun ready in his hand as he called out, "What the hell happened?"

"Officer Adam DuPont was attacked, sir. He thought he saw movement down by the bend and went to check it out. He fired at whatever attacked him, but it still managed to take off."

"How bad is he hurt?"

"He's in pretty bad shape sir. Whatever pounced on him must have been fast and went straight for his neck. An ambulance has already been called."

As Newman and Dupre rushed over to the young officer, he struggled to sit up. Dupre pushed him back down. "We need to keep pressure on the wound, neg. The ambulance is coming."

Newman looked at the injured man, wincing at the deep cuts on the man's throat and chest. "Did you get a good look at what attacked you?"

The young officer nodded his head slowly as he struggled to speak, "It didn't seem real. At first I thought it was a man… but…" he continued to gasp for air, every breath a struggle.

"Take it easy," Dupre placated him. "We need to get that wound taken care of."

The young officer reached out and grabbed Dupre's arm, "Not a man…" Struggling for air he continued, "a dog…" He gasped one more time, "but it walked."

Dupre looked at Newman as this young officer just confirmed their worst fear. The men attempted to tend to the officer's wounds as best as they could until the ambulance arrived. Dupre feared the worst as the young man's breathing became even more labored. He called out to one of the officers, "Find out how long before the ambulance is here!"

"I already called sir. They are pulling up right now." As Dupre checked the officer's pulse, he called out, "You better get those first responders down here quick. His pulse is weak; he is going into shock."

Sirens broke the silence as the crime scene became a flurry of activity. The first responders arrived as well as the coroner and K9 Unit.

Newman calmed Dupre, "With any luck, they can track this creature down. A blood trail will make the task easier."

Newman met Officer Mark Gaudet at the K9 Unit van. "Officer DuPont is sure he hit whatever attacked him. Let's hope there is a blood trail for your dogs to follow."

"Do you have any idea what attacked him?"

"Well, now, I need you to keep an open mind on this, but he said it was a large dog that walked upright."

Officer Gaudet looked at the detective in complete disbelief. "Sir, I'm sorry but are you sure you heard him correctly?"

Dupre quickly interrupted, "Officer DuPont is lying over there in the grass, possibly dying from the attack. His throat and chest look as if a large wild animal mauled him. Regardless of what we believe did this, there is a dangerous creature wandering these woods."

Officer Gaudet gave his men directions, "I want everyone to stay in groups of three. Whatever was responsible for this had no problems attacking a human. We already have one body and an officer down, so I don't want anymore. Also, under no circumstances do I want you to let your dogs off their leash. They are one of us after all, and if they catch wind of whatever they are tracking, they could take off after it. Stay with them at all times."

As the medics loaded up Officer DuPont in the ambulance, they confirmed Dupre's suspicions. "We are heading to the hospital. He is in shock. There has been a great deal of blood lost. What the hell happened to him anyway?"

"We believe a wild animal, possibly a dog, attacked him, but we aren't sure at this point. The K9 unit is searching for whatever attacked him right now."

"The lacerations are deep. It must have been one hell of a large dog to do that much damage. It would be best if you found what attacked him so they can rule out rabies."

***

As the K9 unit headed towards the marshland, they were engulfed in a curtain of rolling fog. Each man in the search party tried not to think about their surroundings, or worse, what they could be searching for.

A young officer's voice quickly and unexpectedly broke the silence. "Stop!"

Everyone stopped in their tracks, looking around. Officer Gaudet shouted, "What's wrong," as he cocked the lever on his gun.

Pointing to a large oak tree not far from the water's edge the officer explained, "I saw movement there by the large oak tree."

All of the officers gazed into the fog. After a few minutes of surveying the area, Officer Gaudet suggested, "It must have been the moss blowing in the wind."

The officers ventured deeper into the woods when another officer shouted, "Moss, my ass. Something is moving out there. It is circling us."

The men pulled out their guns, keeping their eyes focused on their surroundings. Each man stared into the fog hoping to see what was lurking about. The dogs became uneasy and restless. "They caught a whiff of something they don't like."

A piercing howl echoed through the swamp, sending chills up and down each man's spine. The stark terror each man felt was like nothing they'd ever encountered before.

***

Visions suddenly plagued Ezrielle as she prepared for tonight's ritual. She saw one of her Rougarou lying on the ground; his fur matted with dried blood. He had not shifted into his complete human form, and his large nails clawed into his skin as he tried to put pressure on the gaping wound in his shoulder.

His yellow eyes stared into the sky as he called out for help. For a moment, she considered ignoring his pleas. After all, he refused to heed her warnings and acted out on his own.

Once again, he screamed out her name, pleading for her to come help him. As his pleas persisted, she let her vision wander. She saw the destruction he'd done once again. A body was lying on the ground, covered by a sheet, and another injured man was being tended to. This one was becoming too reckless with his kills. The world did not need to know about their presence. Her pets were for her and her alone.

As his pleas echoed through her mind once more, she knew she had no choice. She gathered what supplies she needed and headed out to tend to her injured child.

She made her way through the bayou, maneuvering the small pirogue through the dark waters with no sound. Several people on the banks went about their normal activities; yet, all seemed to ignore her very presence. She did not envy these minuscule people and their simple life. Her life was so much greater.

The fog began to grow thick as she eased the pirogue up to the bank. As she made her way through the marshland, she made out the shape of her injured Rougarou. Even from here, she saw the large gaping hole and the area with matted blood. His large yellow eyes watched her as she moved toward him.

The sound of barking dogs came to her. She must hurry and get him into the boat in order to tend to his injury. She could not let him be found like this; it would bring too many questions. His body was that of a large man covered with thick black fur, but his face was still in its most grotesque form, that of a large wolf. When his thick black lips drew back, a row of razor sharp elongated fangs became exposed. His long claw-like nails dug into the dark earth as the pain wracked his body.

The dogs sensed her presence and picked up speed in their pursuit. Their barks came closer as men called out, ordering them to slow down. She quickly loaded the injured Rougarou into the pirogue and pushed away from the bank. They moved deeper into the fog just as the dogs splashed into the water.

One of the men called out, "Can you make out anything?"

"No, the fog is too thick," came a frustrated answer.

"Let's move along the bank and see if we notice anything further up. They caught the scent of something."

As the men attempted to pull the K9 dogs away from the water, the dogs continued their fierce pulling. "They don't want to leave this section."

"Well, we can't allow them to swim out there. Order them back."

Low growls and angry curses pierced the air as Ezrielle slipped through the dark, murky water. Once in the middle of the bayou and safe from the dogs, Ezrielle tended to her Rougarou's wounds. The darkness and swirling fog surrounded her as she worked.

She continued to listen for any sound coming from the shore. Once the wounds were tended to, she moved through the water once again. She decided she must do something about his disobedience.

At the bank, she allowed her eyes to move over his face, noting that his yellow eyes were losing their brilliance. His muzzle grew warm as an infection moved in. Nature may take care of this one without her having to step in. Until then, it looked as if she would have another one to pay close attention to.

With morbid fascination, she watched her Rougarou changed from a thing of evil to his deceiving persona of a handsome, human being. She wondered how many here in this town knew of his true inner self? Did his wife wonder about his terrible temper tantrums and late nights?

Chapter 47

"What is your theory on all of this?" Newman asked as they made their way to the coroner's office later that afternoon.

As they walked through the doors, Dupre replied, "We may have an actual Rougarou running loose here in the parish. Even worse, we may have at least two if the doctor confirms my theory."

Newman ran his hands through his hair, "Jesus Christ. I didn't think moving to New Orleans would open my life to the supernatural."

"Yeah, well, I learned a long time ago that there is a lot more here than meets the eye."

"I know, but still I can't believe that there is some kind of half-human, half-wolf creature running loose out there," Newman explained.

"Well neg, you better get used to it." As soon as they entered the building, the strong odor of disinfectants reached Dupre's nose. "This is one place I haven't missed."

When Dr. Ortego met the two men outside the autopsy room, he said, "I don't have anything yet for you. I was about to start when I heard you talking."

Once inside the autopsy room, Dupre looked down at the body lying atop the cold, stainless steel table and said a quick prayer before the doctor began his ritual. The overhead lights made the wounds appear more grotesque.

"By the looks of it, a rather large dog attacked this person." Using his scalpel, the doctor pointed to one of the larger wounds. "It looks as if the creature managed to take out the throat in one bite. Whatever did this almost decapitated your victim. What bothers me though is the angle of the bite. It is almost as if something grabbed the victim by the hair and yanked the head back before zeroing in on the throat."

Newman asked, "How long do you think it will take for the saliva and hair samples?"

"It will take a few more hours. The ER doctor ordered a rabies test on the young officer since the animal was not found."

Before heading back to the police station, they stopped by the hospital to check on Officer DuPont. When Dupre opened the door to DuPont's room, he was greeted with semi-darkness. The blinds were closed, and the curtain was drawn. The steady beep of the heart monitor and the hum of the blood pressure cuff were the only sounds heard.

Before the men could step inside the room, a nurse called out from behind, causing both to jump. "No one is supposed to be in here."

Newman displayed his badge for the nurse to see. "I am Detective Newman with the New Orleans Police Department, and this is my partner, Detective Dupre. We stopped by to see how Officer DuPont was doing."

The nurse ushered them back out of the room. "Officer DuPont is still unconscious. The lacerations are rather deep, and honestly, his being unconscious is for the best. The doctor will be here soon to check on his progress. A rush was ordered for the results of the rabies testing."

As the nurse closed the door, an ear piercing scream sounded from the room. The nurse, not bothering with formality, pushed the two men out of her way as she rushed in to check on her patient.

As soon as she entered the room, she let out a blood-curdling scream. They rushed in to witness a scene from the worst nightmares. All that remained of Officer DuPont was mauled beyond belief. Dupre had caught the nurse before she fell to the ground from fainting.

Newman muttered out loud, "How in the hell did something get past us and the nurses?"

A breeze blew in from the open window as Dupre pointed to its discovery, "Something tells me whatever did this found a way in."

"Damn it! What a goddamn mess. We should have posted a twenty-four hour guard in here. I never thought the creature would want to finish what it started."

Dupre looked out the window and said, "We are on the third floor. Whatever did this created one hell of a feat."

Chapter 48

Twilight lingered up above the murky bayou waters, shrouding the entrance to a world known only to a few of the privileged. Eerie shadows danced over the area, merging with shimmers of flickering light from the blazing torches.

Ezrielle walked through this shadowed world, a world of her own making. This was where she could be herself without outside interference. This world was one of her own creation. A slight breeze blew across her face. Suddenly, everything around her moved in slow motion. Under the wind was a voice she had long forgotten. "Ezrielle…"

"Bianca is that you?" Ezrielle called out. Before Ezrielle's eyes, Bianca Honore appeared in a fine mist. "How can this be? You came back from the other side?"

Bianca let out a maniacal laugh. "Mais non, cher, not from the other side. I chose to remain earthbound. I have too much to do before leaving this world."

"But, I don't understand. I heard they destroyed your body and sent you back to hell."

A sinister smile formed on Bianca's face, "Those fools thought that they could kill my spirit. How wrong they were. I healed my spirit." Bianca watched as a look of disbelief moved across Ezrielle's face, "You, more than anyone, should know that just because the body dies does not mean that the soul moved on. My mind, soul, and gifts are healing, becoming stronger with each passing day. Soon, I will be ready to exact my revenge on those who tried to send me to hell. Soon, my army will be ready to fight for me once again."

Ezrielle shook at just the thought of what this woman planned to do. She died such a horrible and terrifying death. "You have no reason to fear me." Bianca told her, "I had hoped you would help me exact my revenge. With our powers combined, think of what we can do. Right now, I am simply a spirit lingering in these bayous. I don't have a body to lay claim to."

Ezrielle backed away from the apparition in front of her. She had no desire to allow her body to be taken over by this woman. Out of instinct, Ezrielle pressed her charm close to her neck with one hand as the other grasped her Gris Gris bag tightly.

A deep-throated howl pierced the night as a shiver of excitement rushed through Ezrielle's body. Her Rougarou had answered her call. In the glow of the full moon, hulking shadows moved amid the moss covered trees; their red eyes glowed like burning embers as they showed themselves.

Ezrielle called out to them once more, "Come. You have nothing to fear."

The apparition standing before her called out, "No, send them back. I have business to tend to with you, Ezrielle. If they come, they will not allow me to enter your body."

"I will not allow you to enter my body Bianca. My pets have come to me as I requested."

The hulking shadows moved from the trees, coming even closer to Bianca. "No. Send them away. They are not welcome here." Bianca pointed her fingers at the shadows, "I order you to stay back."

The shadowy figures paid the apparition no heed. Instead, they walked through her vaporous spirit and took their rightful place beside the woman who welcomed them.

Five more grotesque creatures walked upright, keeping their Rougarou appearance. Their hungry eyes stared out into the night as their master urged them to come closer. A sharp growl filled the silence as the apparition took form once again.

The largest of the creatures stepped forward, drawing back his lips and snarling. The large beast's muscled arms and long, sharp nails cut through the air as if trying to tear her spirit apart.

Chapter 49

Tonight, the bar was crowded with the usual yuppies. There were the up and coming stars of the community, along with the wannabes who hoped that being seen in here would help them climb the social ladder.

Grant was new to this scene, but he hoped to make some real connections. He was ready to make a name on his own. As soon as he saw the dark haired beauty wearing a low cut, yet very sleek, red dress, he knew he had to meet her. The tight dress accentuated her sultry womanly curves. She was almost as tall as him with her high heels on.

Even with the crowd as thick as it was, everyone noticed her as soon as she walked in the door. Grant watched as she crossed the room. The crowd parted to allow her complete ease to the bar.

He ran over a few pickup lines in his mind as he checked his hair in a nearby mirror. He had a fantastic body to go with the handsome face he saw in the reflection. He was always quite the ladies' man.

Once he had his pickup line selected, he moved in. His mind went blank when he walked up to her. Her beauty was astounding up close. When her silver eyes looked up at him, he was mesmerized. There was a darkness underneath the dazzling silver that drew him in even further. Frozen in place, he even forgot to breathe; he could only stare at her beauty.

She smiled up at him. "Would you like to buy me a drink?"

Grant wasn't sure what was happening. This wasn't going as he planned in his mind, yet he obediently bought her a drink. "Yeah."

"What's your name, cher?"

Taking a seat next to her he answered, "Grant."

"Well, Grant, would you like to get out of here?"

Grant didn't even blink at the statement. Men's dreams were made of this. He would never once turn down an invitation such as this from a beautiful woman.

He followed her outside the bar and down the alley. Outside, she had a limo and driver waiting for her arrival. The driver was a tall, lanky man who any other night would give Grant the creeps. Tonight, however, Grant paid him no attention. He kept his attention focused on the beautiful woman. Her whole body was too divine not to watch. As soon as they got in the car, she ran her hands up and down his chest. By this time, Grant was totally enthralled with her.

Her dress left nothing to the imagination, and when she moved he saw what was underneath the scant material.

As he looked into her eyes, they lured him in even more. It was as if he was looking into a crystal ball. Grant picked up her wrist and kissed the inside of it. He took no notice of the tattoo branded on her skin.

***

As the car drove away, the woman looked over at her eager companion with a grin and sparkling eyes. This had been so easy; he had no willpower at all.

Of course, that wouldn't stop her from feasting off of him. She ran her hands through his dark hair as she took his mouth in hers. As she kissed him, she tapped into his mind. He had information that she could use for her own good. She continued to kiss him as she probed his mind.

Slowing things down, she whispered in his ear, "Not yet, cher." They continued to kiss as he moved his hand up her dress, massaging her body while it traveled upward.

As the car entered the gates of her estate, she dismissed her date, "That's enough for now."

She led the young man inside by hand and let him upstairs. Her control over him was staggering. As she closed the door to her bedroom, he just stood there, waiting for her to make another move. He would be easy to turn.

Standing in front of him, she unzipped her dress, letting it drop to the floor in a heap. Her date continued to stare at her, mesmerized. Her long hair cascaded down her back. Her seductive body swayed sensuously with her graceful moves.

"Get undressed." Without question, he obeyed her every command. She walked over to the window and opened the curtains. Moonlight flooded into the room, caressing her skin. Next, she walked over to the tiny bar and fixed him a drink.

Handing him the drink, she pushed him down on the bed. She was just as fit and trim as the day she became immortal. Leaning down, she whispered in his ear, "Are you ready for me?"

"Yes, oh yes!"

She kissed him again on the lips before moving down his neck. Like a number of men before him, he would be one of her Rougarou. Very few men could resist her charms. This one would be obedient.

Some remained here on the property, and others she controlled. Those she sent back to their daily lives and called upon them when needed. It wouldn't be until the next full moon that this one realized what she'd done to him.

As she slipped on a white satin robe, she looked over at her new captive. It was time to begin the ritual and fully turn him. This house was only for show. Her real house was a little shanty cabin near the bayou. There, she could live deep in the swamplands in the world she created for herself. The people of New Orleans had no idea of her true identity or age.

At the bottom of the stairs, she passed her extensive library. She'd spent years accumulating books on the occult, legends, curses and anything mystical. The shelves of the bookcases kept secrets not meant for the mere eyes of mortals.

She stepped out into the night air with her new captive right at her heels.

***

He heard the beating of the drums from the confines of his lair. She must have found a new captive to add to her fold.

There was no doubt; he had seen the depths of hell. He'd committed horrible acts over the centuries all in the name of Ezrielle. Death followed him as the blood he spilled had painted the land.

Ezrielle clouded his vision, and he developed a blood lust. The truth was he'd gone too far for redemption.

His discovery of the lies and deceit came far too late. He'd done too many evil deeds.

He became a hunted creature futilely running from his master. He developed the skill to remain undetected, but for how long. Her powers were too strong, and he had no desire to spend his immortal life as prey.

If Ezrielle captured him, she would make him pay for his betrayal if he didn't get to her first. However, even in death, it would only be the beginning for his already tortured soul. Who was he kidding; every day of his miserable immortal life he lived in hell.

Revenge kept him going.

Chapter 50

Just as Josie prepared to leave, her phone rang. She was surprised to see that it was James calling. "James is there something you need?"

He was quiet for a minute before answering, "Watch your back tonight Josie."

"James, you should know more than anyone I am careful. What happened? Is there something I should know?"

"No, it's not that. I just have a feeling is all."

"What do you think is up?"

His voice carried an edge of fear. "I don't have any concrete evidence yet…"

Josie interrupted her friend. "James, do you think that I am walking into a trap tonight?"

As he talked, Josie could almost see his hands waving about. "Not that I have heard, but be careful."

"James, just what are you afraid of?" Josie asked.

He let out a sigh before answering, "I have been doing some research on my own. There are more vampires around New Orleans than usual, and the number is growing. Worse, some of these vampires aren't careful about what they do with the bodies. A lot less homeless and druggies are around the Quarter lately.”

“Have you heard why there are so many more vampires? Do you have any idea where they came from?”

“I haven’t been able to find out anything concrete, but I suspect that Joshua learned a lot from your master.”

“Like father, like son. I always say.”

Before Josie could ask James another question, he abruptly hung up. What was the phone call truly about? Was he trying to find out how much she knew? Did he find some information he wasn’t sure what to do with? She’d heard the fear in his voice, and that was something she’d never heard from James before.

***

This particular derelict neighborhood had long since been forgotten. It still looked as if the devastation of Hurricane Katrina took place just mere weeks ago. Most of the houses were one story brick buildings that the locals called shotgun houses.

There were a few two story duplex brick homes scattered around the area, but those were few and far between. All the abandoned houses were boarded up and waited to either be sold or demolished.

In one of these homes may be the vampire she was searching for, the one who could help her find her master.

Near one of the duplexes, she thought she saw movement in an upstairs window. Most of the homeless that lived here kept to the one story shotgun houses. Perhaps, this was her vampire in the second story of the duplex.

Josie made her way to the back of the house. The grass was over waist high and the in ground pool, a luxury in this neighborhood, was filled with stagnant water. Ignoring the stench from the pool water, she slipped in through the back door.

The interior of the house smelled worse than the outside. The kitchen was downright filthy. The only person who would dare to come into this place was someone desperately looking for a place to sleep or hide.

To the left of the kitchen was a room with a door ajar. In the small bedroom was a makeshift bed with a body lying on it. The boy had to be no older than sixteen and bite marks covered his neck and arms. Whoever fed on him had been sharing. Looking at the young corpse, she felt revulsion for the creatures that did this to him. All that remained of the boy was a callow husk.

A movement behind her caught her attention. The vampire stood in the doorway; his mouth smeared with fresh blood and his fangs stained by all the blood he drank to keep his unholy existence. The vampire's skin had the appearance of white marble with green and blue veins visible under the skin. This vampire in front of her wanted to keep with the goth look by wearing tight black leather pants and a black silk shirt.

As they stood there facing each other, waiting to see who made the first move, his eyes turned red. He hissed at her as he made his move. Josie pointed her weapon at him and fired; the silver arrow made its mark, pinning him to the wall. His skin sizzled from the wound.

"You bitch," he hissed. The vampire reached up and tried to free the arrow from his shoulder.

"Tell me where your master is."

The vampire just laughed at her. "Go to hell."

Josie picked up her gun as she took aim once more. "You first." She fired again, hitting the creature in the chest. A scream escaped his mouth as he hissed. Josie made sure not to kill him just yet. She wanted to cause him as much pain as possible right now. She needed to find out the answers first.

The vampire hissed out, "Just who the hell are you?"

"That isn't any concern of yours."

The creature looked down at the bullet hole in his chest. He was in extreme pain as the silver burned him severely. She smiled at him, "By now the holy water encased in the bullet should be spreading throughout your body."

"Why do you want to kill me?"

Josie scowled at him, "You killed that young man there for nothing more than his blood."

"I need his blood to survive. You are the same way. Why would you want to kill me for doing what we both do to survive? Besides, he's no one important. He won't even be missed. He lived out here on the streets. He's a nobody." Josie rolled her eyes as the vampire continued to rationalize what he did.

"These humans are not your food source. You don't have to hunt them down for your survival. There are other ways to feed."

Unable to listen to any more of his insipid whining, Josie fired two bullets into his heart. He vaporized in front of her. She had hoped he would give up the location of the master, but instead, he whined.

Josie sent Tyler a text to let him know that the police department needed to remove a body.

Chapter 51

Josie was still in disbelief over the invitation she'd received while Tyler was wary. The request came from a vampire who had a coven at an antebellum sugar plantation an hour up the Mississippi in a small town called Vacherie.

She swore that her master lived not far from there, but then again, the surroundings had changed over the century. She might have set her hopes too high, and this was merely another coven of vampires. She was anxious to find out which vampire ran the plantation.

This could very well be a trap. She wasn't sure why he'd requested to see her, but more importantly, how he knew about her?

As she drove up to the plantation, she took in its extensive and impressive property. Whoever owned this place was extremely wealthy. As if anticipating her arrival, the black iron gates opened without her having to make a request. She drove slowly down the main road canopied by massive oaks for what had to be a good mile and kept on the lookout for an ambush.

The plantation house caught her by complete surprise. The pristine white stucco glistened in the moonlight. Doric columns graced the front porch, and the black shutters appeared not to have aged over the years.

This was the sort of plantation they fought for in the Civil War. She wondered just how it had survived all these years without any signs of neglect. It had to be that a very old vampire lived here.

As she walked up the cobblestone sidewalk to the front door, she still kept a sharp lookout for signs of an ambush. If this vampire were anything like Joshua, he could have shape shifters serving him.

Before Josie had the chance to knock, a hulk of a man dressed in black Dockers and a black button up shirt opened the door. From his clothes to his appearance, this one looked menacing.

As he looked down at Josie, he kept his face expressionless. Josie paid close attention to him in case this was a wight. A wight was a corpse brought back to life to serve his master who controlled his soul to ensure his obedience. Did this master learn some of the voodoo tricks Bianca used? If this creature were, in fact, a wight, then that meant the master here was an old vampire. A young vampire would not know all the spells to use. Even Joshua had only started to learn the old spells and incantations.

The servant led Josie to the back of the plantation. Josie peeked down the hall and saw a small kitchen that appeared to be the only room in the plantation that showed neglect. It would fit with the fact that a vampire lived here.

The garden was breathtaking; she could envision herself enjoying it at night. Instead of this plantation home overlooking the bayous of Louisiana, it backed up to a heavily wooded area. There was a change in the air out here. Josie was almost certain that this vampire had shape shifters working under his control.

A man in his early forties walked up to Josie, "Welcome to my home." The man astonished Josie. She had pictured him to be much older, but instead, he was a very distinguished younger looking man, although small in stature. He barely stood six feet tall and weighed no more than one hundred forty pounds.

The way he carried himself oozed old southern charm and money. From the tips of his shoes to his Armani suit, he screamed money. In the moonlight, Josie made out a small amount of gray peppering his black hair. His skin appeared almost pasty white in the moonlight, which helped to age him. There was a translucency to his skin that only happened to older vampires when their skin eventually began to deteriorate over the centuries. Vampires did not age the same as humans, but the aging process was still there – just much slower.

He took Josie's hand in his, brought it up to his lips and kissed her hand. "Mon cher, thank you for coming to see me. Allow me to introduce myself. I am Alexander Remington, and this is my family home, Remington

Manor. My family and I have lived here since the early 1800's."

"It is a beautiful plantation."

Josie noticed that the man's eyes scanned the area as if he too was watching and waiting. Motioning to one of his servants, "Would you care for a drink?"

Josie looked to see where he had motioned and bit back a gasp. There at the bar sat a human who was having blood syphoned from it. It took everything Josie had not to end this. Too many were present for her to fight alone, and if she wanted answers, she needed to bide her time. In the corner of the courtyard, another sight startled Josie. Several men and women were on display so that vampires could open a vein and fill a cocktail glass. As a vampire finished filling their glass, another vampire sealed off the wound. Josie had a feeling that these humans were drugged so they wouldn't have a clue as to what took place around them.

Her hands itched to draw her sidearm and start shooting even if that meant inevitable death. Two wights carried more humans outside for the vampires to feed on. The group swarmed the fresh blood. The wights continued onto the bodies left behind, taking them away like discarded trash.

As if reading Josie's mind, Alexander explained, "Don't worry, mon cher. They will take them back inside, tend to them, feed them well, and allow their blood supply to be replenished before sending them back home. They will not even remember being here. They are in a trance for a few hours."

Josie looked at him doubtfully. His words were as empty as his soul. "Let us get down to business. I have some matters to tend to later. A beautiful young woman is dying to join our coven."

Josie shuddered as he laughed at his own joke. "I am surprised that you found someone willing to die for eternal youth. I thought you would just take it upon yourself to turn a human without asking questions."

Alexander tsk'ed at Josie's comments. "I do not allow my children to turn humans without obtaining permission from myself first and then the intended's permission. However, the coven that you are searching for has no scruples about whom they turn nor do they care about whom they feed on. They are rogue vampires who must be stopped before our existence is known to the entire world."

"I agree that this vampire must be stopped. I have yet to find a good lead that will take me to where this particular coven hides. They reside on a plantation in or near New Orleans, but the exact location is unknown. It has been such a long time since I was turned that I no longer remember where he lived. Joshua and I left soon after I was turned, and I never returned. Joshua visited our master a few times, but he never asked if I cared to join him. I believe he knew that I despised the man for turning me against my will."

Alexander enlightened Josie. "We may have some useful information for you."

Josie looked at Alexander and asked, "And what is the price for this information?"

"Ah, and that is a very important question. 'What do I want in return?' I do wish for this master vampire to be put out of business, but I also have a favor to ask of you, as well. This master vampire knows where a particular voodoo priestess resides, and I want to know her location. I want this woman expunged from this plane of existence and returned to hell. For you see, this particular voodoo priestess revels in turning men into Rougarou for her own devious pleasures and must be stopped. What is worse, rumors are that she is turning vampires into some very unpleasant creatures as well."

Tyler had already told Josie how a woman lured him to the swamps and cursed him for eternity. He was searching for her as well. "Surely, this woman would have died years ago," Josie said.

Alexander shook his head. "Mais non. For you see, she made a pact with the Dukes of Hell for her powers.

They granted her not only powers, but also immortality.”

“Do you have the name of the voodoo priestess?”

“No, unfortunately I do not. We have been unable to find her home. She may have cast a spell over her land that prevents it from being detected.”

“I shall ask Tyler to continue canvassing the marshlands and swamps in case anything looks familiar.”

Alexander nodded his head in agreement. “I wish him luck. I have asked others turned by her if they recalled where she lived, and, to date, none have found her. Most of the Rougarou she keeps under her control.”

“You may be right. My master knew her and requested a coven of Rougarou for himself and Joshua. When Joshua gave Tyler to me, I set him free unbeknownst to Joshua, mind you. However, Joshua still had several Rougarou under his control at the time of his own demise. I don’t know what became of them after Joshua’s death.”

Alexander shared some more with Josie. “A few Rougarou were too strong willed for her to keep under her control. However, just like I have my wights, she has several Rougarou under her complete control. You must beware; by day, they can live a normal life around humans, but come a full moon, they are hers once more."

Josie announced to Alexander, "I want it understood from the beginning that I will not spill innocent blood."

A cruel smile formed on Alexander's face that had Josie fearing she'd just agreed to work with the Devil. "You don't have to worry about killing any innocents. I will forewarn you, though; that I do believe this particular vampire is very old, older than me. The secrets he must know have to be overwhelming. It would be almost barbaric to kill him."

"No, he must die. Though, I promise you that his death will be swift."

Chapter 52

Josie made good time as she drove to Harrington, Louisiana. The purr of the car's engine helped relax her as she shifted gears.

She'd heard rumors of an alligator hatchery in St. Tammany Parish, near the Tchefuncte River. It was a popular visiting place of a vampire who may be able to answer some questions.

From what she'd discovered, the hatchery and farm were on a nice sized piece of property. It was owned by a local, Harvey Boudreaux. It appeared Mr. Boudreaux ran a reputable business during the day, but, at night, he participated in an abhorrent side-business. He ran cockfights on his property that several vampires frequented.

As Josie pulled up to the alligator ranch, she had no doubts that she was in the right place. Even at well past twilight, the place was lit up better than a football stadium.

As she made her way past the gate, a very large man in overalls stood guard with a shotgun. The guard's face scrunched up as he asked, "Password."

"Tante Marie sent me."

The guard moved aside so that Josie could enter. Josie continued to scan the area as she found a parking spot. There must be well over one hundred cars parked here tonight. Josie questioned if the hatchery's daytime business ever saw so many customers at one time.

There was a main house, a hatchery, a nursery, and a small souvenir shop where customers could purchase wallets, belts, and boots. It also had a stadium seating area that enabled tourist groups to sit safely away from the alligators during the performance.

Farther back from the main area stood an old brown barn. Judging from the noises coming from there, the cock fights were taking place. Josie just observed the area for a moment. A pier with several boats tied off to it was near the barn. The cock fight had been set up where you could come here by water or land, meaning the barn would be extremely crowded. Tucked in the shadows, Josie made out about ten men armed with guns. The crowds must get pretty rowdy for such ammunition.

Tonight, she'd dressed in tight black leather pants and a spandex halter top. She kept her guns tucked safely in her high heeled boots.

She swatted at a mosquito that buzzed annoyingly by her ears. She should have known with the alligator ranch being this close to the water the mosquitoes would be out in full force.

Josie passed by the corral for holding alligators and shivered at the nearness of the beasts. There was nothing cuddly or lovable about these reptiles; yet, people came from far and near to gawk at them. Not her, though, she would much rather see them from a distance, a very far off distance.

She had not come prepared for a crowd this size. While Tyler patrolled the woods, she prayed that he was safe.

A voice from behind her called out, "Cher, do you care to place a bet for tonight?"

A large mulatto man with a shaved head, a goatee and wearing a dark shark skin suit took Josie by surprise. She hadn't even heard the man walk up behind her. In the moonlight, the large diamond he wore winked at her as she tried to ascertain if he was a creature of the night. Josie shook her head. "I just came to observe. I have never seen a cock fight."

"Not too many women are interested in watching these types of fights."

Josie smiled up at him, "What can I say – I'm not your typical woman."

As Josie found a spot near the ring, she noticed several men walking around with coolers selling beer. This Mr. Boudreaux appeared to be quite the business entrepreneur. He probably would have it on cable as a pay per view event if he could. Judging by the size of this crowd, plenty of people would order the fight. She did not understand why anyone wanted to watch something this barbaric and inhumane.

All around her was a cacophony of noises; men were laughing, arguing or just downright bullshitting. Her plan remained simple; she needed to determine if vampires frequented these fights and find out about the coven they belonged to. She was anxious to find out if this would lead her to her master.

However, she also wanted Harvey Boudreaux arrested and put out of business for good. But if that happened, she may lose her chance to obtain the information she desperately needed.

The men here felt courteous tonight, moving out of the way to allow her a front row spot to watch the fight, which was the last place she wanted to be. A movement to Josie's right caught her attention. A man in his mid-fifties walked into the room with a Black Jack vine walking stick. Even more interesting than the actual walking stick was the quartz stone resting on top. It resembled a prism, catching the light and mesmerizing anyone that stared into it. His appearance screamed regality among the ruffians in the barn.

Another man handed him a bullhorn. "Gentlemen," and as if sensing Josie's presence, his eyes honed in on her, "And lady, our first round is about to begin!"

As the fighting roosters were brought out, a shiver ran through Josie. Several of the roosters had knifelike items on their tiny bodies, more than likely to give them an unfair advantage over their opponent.

The men in the room had delighted smiles on their faces as they anxiously waited for the fights to begin. These men only saw one color - green. Well, except for the vampires. They came to see the blood, as well.

Her stomach churned at the sight in front of her. As two of the roosters were let out of their cages, they instinctively circled each other. The crowd cheered as the roosters pecked at each other in an attempt to draw blood or worse, to kill their opponent. These men were greedy bastards. This wasn't something to be cheered or bet on, but outlawed. The men here were warped as they cheered on this barbaric fight.

With feathers pulled and bleeding, one of the black roosters made a move that sent the knife secured to his tiny body directly in his opponent's body. Cheers erupted an entire decibel level. The opposing rooster fell to the ground as the black rooster continued to attack its fallen opponent.

A man removed the defeated rooster as a new opponent was brought in to fight the winner.

It only took a few minutes for round two to be completed. The same rooster won once again. If this kept up, it would be a quick evening, but no one seemed to complain.

The man took the bullhorn handed to him. "Once again, we have to wonder who will be the winner. Know one thing, one will die and one will live. I don't know the outcome, and neither do you. Let the fight begin."

Without drawing any attention, Josie meandered through the crowd in search of another vampire watching the fight. As she made her way through the crowd, she sighed in disappointment. This appeared to be another false lead.

On the way back to her car, she noticed a man slipping into the back of the hatchery. Curious as to why anyone wanted to go there this late at night, she followed. It was pitch black in the building, but her night vision quickly adjusted to her surroundings. Boxes and junk were piled almost up to the open rafters.

A distinctive smell emanated from the building and became stronger the closer she moved to the boxes. Josie looked up to see that the ceiling was open rafters. She jumped to a rafter with ease.

The closer she moved to the back of the building, the worse the smell became. There was a heady mixture of rotting meat, fecal matter, and decay. Even from up here, Josie heard the faint breath of a human.

Keeping to the shadows, she moved closer to where the smell emanated.

"Hurry up Joe. Those bloodsuckers will be here soon to get this next shipment. I have no plans on being their food tonight."

Josie's breath caught in her throat at the sight beneath her. There were four stalls with two humans in each. It appeared that they had been held captive here for a while now.

Before she could move closer, two vampires walked into the barn. Josie crossed her fingers and hoped they were the only ones sent to retrieve the humans. If not, pandemonium would ensue when she attacked.

Josie quickly mapped out a plan in her mind. Both vampires had to be killed, but she could only kill one of the humans if she wanted to find out the mastermind.

Needing the element of surprise, Josie threw her dagger into the first vampire's heart while she took aim with her gun and fired at the other.

Unfortunately, this vampire was quicker than she anticipated. She hit him close to the heart, but it wasn't a direct hit. The gunshot sent him sprawling to the ground. As he attempted to stand up, Josie leapt from her hiding spot and aimed once more, killing him instantly.

The two humans attempted to flee the scene. Josie took aim and shot one in the kneecap, sending him sprawling to the ground. The second human moved in to attack Josie as she took aim and hit him squarely in the chest.

Josie secured the human before peeking outside to make sure no one was coming to check on their progress. The last thing they needed was company. She sent a message to Tyler, informing him that she needed help. Not only did she have to free the captives, but she needed to erase their memories of what happened to them. Once released from the cages, Tyler could help lead them to safety.   The pitiful human being she'd captured, though, she had special plans for.

After all, she was hungry. It had been a long night, and she needed to eat.

Josie walked over to the whimpering human. "Who are these humans being delivered to?"

He snarled up at Josie, "You messed with the wrong person vamp. These guys don't play around."

Josie took the heel of her boot and twisted it into the gaping bullet wound. "I don't want you to lose all that precious blood you know. I have worked up quite an appetite."

"Do what you will. When they get through with you, you will wish you were dead. But death is too good for the likes of you."

Josie hissed at the man and bared her fangs. He dragged his body further away from her. "You may as well kill me because I have no plans on telling you anything. I am as good as dead, thanks to you. These vampires will come looking for their meals when they are not delivered. They will want payment for them being let go."

"I will ask you once more – where were these humans being delivered?"

Leering at her, he snarled out, "Vamp, do you honestly think they would tell us anything? We are only the delivery men. I wait for the vampires to pick up their packages and drop off the money."

Josie gripped him by the neck and lifted him off the ground. She squeezed his throat as rage built up inside of her. "You mean to tell me that you kidnap these poor humans and sell them to vampires as if they are cattle?"

He snidely commented, "What do you care? You are just like the others, feeding off of humans." Shrugging his shoulders, he added, "My boss saw a way to make some quick money. Those living out on the streets are easy pickings for us. Most of them are so drunk that they don't even know what is happening to them."

Josie hissed at him once more. "And you think that is okay?"

"Pauve ti bête, I didn't have a choice. Besides, they will die out there on the streets. The way I see it, we are just speeding up the process."

"How many here in New Orleans do you supply food to?"

"Maybe a couple dozen vampires. Hell, for all I know, it could be more than that; there is always a flux in numbers." Sneering at her he added, "We send supplies to other areas, as well. Shipments are sent to New York, Los Angeles, and Las Vegas."

"Why do you send these poor people to other cities?"

"The people here have a distinct taste to their blood that vampires crave. Maybe, it is all the good Cajun cooking, who knows. Maybe, the victims' blood in other cities is too tainted. All I know is that the money is good, and my boss tries to accommodate his customers' needs."

Josie hissed out, "I want to know who the master is?"

A humorless grin stretched across his face, but no words passed through them for a moment. Instead, he just glared at Josie. "Go to hell vamp. I have no intention of giving you any information that could help you."

Angered by his comments, Josie threw the man across the room. He hit the other side of the building with a loud thud. Josie had hoped he would give her more information to stop these monsters.

The only other valuable piece of information she'd learned tonight was that this particular coven had several politicians along with other influential men and women in the community in their pockets. A cold chill crept down her spine as she thought about the people lining their pockets from these barbaric vampires.

Josie needed to put aside her emotions before dealing with this particular coven. She must be methodical and careful with vampires that are as powerful and as well connected as these may indeed be.

***

Ezrielle watched as the vampire and her Rougarou lover made their way home. This pair was turning into a regular vigilante team, one that could cause her problems if she weren't careful. She had not made her presence known to the Rougarou since he wanted revenge for his curse. When she'd turned this one, she thought she'd made a wise decision selling him and several of his brothers to the vampire. Back then, the money was too tempting, but now she regretted that decision.

As she neared their house, she laughed at their pitiful attempt to protect the property. They actually thought some second rate spells and juju done by an infant to the practice of voodoo could stop her. No, they must conjure up something far better if they wanted to keep the likes of her out; however, for the time being she would let them think they were well protected.

Chapter 53

Josie pulled up a chair next to Tyler at the kitchen table. "I think I have some viable information to use. There is a man named William Jensen who lives near Pirate Alley. It won't take much for him to turn on those he works for."

Tyler looked up at Josie with skepticism. "Do you think you can trust this information?"

Josie hoped so. She wanted to find out where everyone in this particular coven resided, not just in New Orleans but throughout the world. "I want to find out how willing he is to talk to me."

Tyler's face darkened as he contemplated what Josie told him. "I am sure it comes with a price. Don't get too excited about this. It may be a trap."

Josie squeezed his hand as her eyes filled with anger. She had steel determination in stopping these vampires. "Don't worry. I don't have any plans of walking into a trap."

"I just worry that whoever fed you this particular bit of information may believe he found a way to eliminate you. We both know some out there want you banished from this world."

Josie replied, "This man is a recruiter for the coven. He finds them food and potential recruits."

Tyler looked Josie directly in the eyes. "I am going with you tonight. There is no way I am letting you go there without me."

"Don't you want to take a power nap before leaving? You worked all day."

Tyler shook his head, "I will be fine." Taking her hand in his he said, "Dr. Ortego believes he is close to understanding the genetics of vampirism. He has run test after test lately. He swears he is close to a breakthrough on the unique qualities in vampire blood."

"We need to keep a close eye on him. If the other vampires find out about his research, they may kidnap him for their own purposes."

***

As Josie and Tyler made their way to the rundown apartment near Pirate Alley, she wondered what may be in store for them there. Josie dropped with ease on the man's balcony from the roof.

What she saw took her by complete surprise. She thought a recruiter for a prestigious vampire coven would be more appealing. This man was a slob with stringy, unkempt black hair. If his "tighty whities" were ever indeed white, it had been a long time ago. He was pathetically thin, way past the malnourished stage, and yet, he had an agility to his stance that had her wondering his true strength.

As if sensing her presence, he turned his bloodshot eyes toward the balcony. Josie had slipped into the darkness before he saw her. From where Josie stood, she had a perfect view into his bedroom. On the bed was what she could be looking for, a laptop. She eyed the laptop like a prized jewel. She had a gut instinct that this laptop held lots of unanswered questions for her.

Out of nowhere, a female vampire appeared in front of the bedroom window snarling at Josie, ready to pounce. With a hiss that increased her primal, feral appearance, she soared through the air at Josie.

Without hesitation, Josie sent a bullet straight into the vamp's chest. The man moved into action, bolting for the front door. He jumped back at the appearance of Tyler, "What do you want?"

"We have some questions to ask you."

Pulling out a gun, he aimed it directly at Tyler. "Forget it man. I would be better off dead rather than talking to you."

Josie didn't even think about the consequences; she fired a bullet in the chest of her possible informant.

"Let's look for some clues. The first place I plan on looking is the laptop on the bed."

Tyler looked around the apartment as she waited for the computer to power up. Once she booted the laptop, she looked through some of the files. She found one particular file that interested her. It was a spreadsheet with various locations and numbers. This could be a list of dates and amounts of money.

Tyler walked up behind her, looking over her shoulder, "I didn't see too much in the rest of the apartment."

"Well, it looks as if our guy kept a spreadsheet of dates and amounts of money he received. Once we get back to the house, I will continue looking over the information. He has a ton of emails. I don't think he ever cleaned up his computer; that is a good thing for us."

Chapter 54

No matter how many times Josie walked through the French Quarter, its sheer size still amazed her. The bar was tucked in a dark corner, and from the outside, it looked deserted. Even a well-trained cop would walk right past the entrance in search of louder bars with drunks stumbling in and out of the establishments.

The interior of the bar took Josie by surprise. The exterior may be worn down, but not the interior. Stepping into this bar was reminiscent to stepping back in time. The walls were painted a rich gold and lavish red velvet curtains draped the windows. An antique gold gilded mirror hung over the bar, and even the furniture had to be from the Victorian era.

Even more surprising was the bar was packed with customers. Josie couldn't seem to find an actual living human among the group. This would explain the dark interior; most of the patrons didn't need the extra lighting.

As the band started to play, Josie made her way up to the bar. At least here she fit in. Even the bar was standing room only. One look at the bartender explained why. With his disheveled, dirty blond hair, green eyes and bulging muscles, this man would attract the ladies. His brooding nature, tight jeans, and muscle shirt made him look even more ruggedly handsome.

As Josie waited for her drink, she took in her surroundings. This place was quite nice, a place where she and Tyler could come to relax, that was if they allowed Tyler's kind in here. Josie doubted that these vampires would welcome a Rougarou in here. Most vampires considered themselves to be the superior species and the Rougarou as a cursed watch dog.

Josie found herself drawn to the band's music. They played a contemporary jazz number with a touch of rock. The bartender handed her the house wine, a Merlot mixed with a heavy helping of AB+, and asked, "Is there anything else I can get for you?"

Giving him a seductive smile she answered, "A friend of mine told me to come visit this place when I needed a little something special to pick me up."

Josie slid him the hundred dollar bill as he looked her over. "Did this friend give you a name to ask for?"

Josie purred out, "I was told Roman would know how to cure what ails me."

Smiling back at Josie he answered, "He may indeed." The bartender nodded towards the door in the back, "Over there."

Right behind the band was a door that Josie somehow missed when she first came in, but, then again, it could be easily missed unless pointed out to you. A woman walked out from behind the hidden door. Her long chestnut hair was pulled tight into a high ponytail, and her black leather skirt gave a whole new meaning to mini. However, more intriguing was that her eyes were as purple as the shirt she wore. Josie wondered if this was the same woman who'd walked into the police station a while back. She aimed the camera hidden in her purse and took a few snapshots for Tyler to view. If he hadn't mentioned her eyes, Josie might not have even bothered with her.

Josie was given a better chance to obtain a picture when a man swept her into his arms for a dance. Uninhibited on the dance floor, she moved seductively up against her dance partner.

If this is the woman Tyler saw at the police station, then it couldn't be a coincidence she was here. Perhaps, a little surveillance work needed to be done on this particular bar and this woman. Forgetting about the back room, Josie left the bar. She didn't want to take a chance that the mystery woman would alert anyone of her presence. While Josie wasn't sure if the woman knew of Josie and her mission, it made her uncomfortable that she had left the police station at the mere sight of Tyler. With it being so crowded, Josie had a feeling that the bartender didn't pay attention to what had happened to her. The place was packed by the time she left.

While inside the bar, a light rain had fallen. The streets had more than a few good-sized puddles.

The night air was cooler than usual from the unexpected rain shower. To a vampire, seventy-five degrees had a definite chill to it. For a weekday night, quite a few people were milling about in the French Quarter. A few of the street musicians still played hoping to earn a few more dollars before heading home.

A shadow up on a rooftop caught Josie's attention. The hairs on the back of her neck rose as she scanned the area for a sign of who could be following her. Knowing that someone was following her, she took the long way home.

By the time Josie made it home, fatigue had consumed her body. Tyler pulled her into his warm embrace where she fell into a deep sleep almost immediately.

As Josie slept, she felt the presence of another enter her mind. Someone was rummaging around her very thoughts and memories. Josie tried to wake up, but it was difficult; it seemed almost as if someone had her in a trance. Josie forced whoever was in her mind out, and she slammed the door shut.

Now that her mind was rid of the sudden intrusion, she sat upright in bed. Tyler had left her a note on the pillow. "Off to work. Love you."

Whoever had intruded on her thoughts had to be nearby. Josie peered out the windows, avoiding the direct sunlight as much as possible.

She hoped whoever had intruded her mind had not gathered any useful information. She did not like the idea of an unknown enemy having an advantage over her.

As Josie waited for Tyler to come home, her cell phone rang. She almost ignored the blocked call, but curiosity got the best of her, and she answered, "Hello."

"If you want answers to the questions you are asking, meet me at the River Walk at midnight."

Josie asked, "Who is this? How did you get this number?"

"That is not important, cher. I have the answers you seek, but you must hurry before it is too late."

The caller sounded like a woman trying to talk husky, but she couldn't be sure. "How will I recognize you?"

"You will just know," laughter filled the air before the phone was disconnected.

***

Josie heard Tyler open the front door and motioned for him to come beside her. "What's going on," he asked.

"I'm not sure. I just had a strange phone call saying they could give me information that I need. But they want to meet at the River Walk tonight."

Tyler looked at Josie, concern filling his eyes as he asked, "You don't plan on going, do you?"

"My gut tells me not to, but this may be my only chance to get the answers we need." Josie kissed him before continuing, "Besides, I believe it was a woman trying to disguise her voice. The voice sounded too high pitched to be a man."

Tyler pulled Josie close to his body. "Let me shower and change. I will go with you."

Josie shook her head, "No, you had a rough day. I can tell from the way you are carrying yourself that you need to rest. Keep your phone handy just in case I need help."

***

As Josie arrived at the River Walk, she was surprised to find the area almost devoid of life. Generally quite a few people, especially tourists, frequented this area. Midnight in New Orleans could be considered early; yet the area was empty except for a lone woman sitting on a park bench near the water. As if sensing

Josie's presence, the woman turned and looked directly at her.

Even from this distance, Josie made out her purple eyes. This was the woman from the bar and the same one Tyler saw at the police station. "Thank you for agreeing to meet me."

The woman appeared to be nervous and on edge. She kept playing with the large amulet around her neck; twisting the long gold chain around her finger over and over before letting it go only to repeat the cycle once again. The amulet was the same deep shade of purple as her eyes and appeared to be encased around an object.

Josie looked around, still wondering why she was nervous. Sensing Josie's apprehension the woman said, "I didn't call you here to harm you."

Josie confessed to the mysterious woman, "That's good to know. Exactly why did you call me?"

The woman looked around once more. "I must warn you that all is not what it seems. There is some powerful voodoo following you and your boyfriend. You must be very careful. Black magic is at work here."

"Is that why you called me? To warn me?"

The young woman shook her head, "No, there is much more that we need to discuss." She looked Josie in the eyes. "I have heard about you."

Josie suddenly became very aware of the world around her, "And how did you find out about me?"

"Not much happens in this city that I don't know about. Dark forces are at work here. Some of these forces are too dangerous for the likes of you, cher."

"I will be okay. I have Tyler to help me."

"You and your boyfriend are out of your league dealing with these dark forces. There is more to this world than Rougarou and vampires. There is a whole world to fear. A world of demons, fallen angels, and spirits who treat this world as their playground."

The mystery woman looked deeply into Josie's eyes as she continued, "There is one here who wants your mate."

"You saw him the other day at the police station; why didn't you talk to him there?"

"The Rougarou can be controlled by the voodoo witch so they cannot be trusted. She cannot know about my presence yet."

Josie looked at the woman, "So, you do know who controls the Rougarou? I believe she knows who my master is. She has power over some of the Rougarou.

Tyler mentioned that at one time he was under her control. He didn't like it, but he couldn't remember how he got there."

"No, he won't. She is powerful. She more than likely erased his mind of certain memories. Her powers came from the Dukes of Hell themselves."

Josie looked at her with uncertainty. "The Dukes of Hell?"

"You have much to learn about this world. The Dukes of Hell are the ones who created immortality."

The mystery woman handed Josie two Gris Gris bags, "It is imperative that the two of you keep these bags around your necks at all times."

Josie looked inside of them. There was a purple amethyst similar to the one on the woman's necklace along with an alligator's tooth and an arrowhead. "This bag keeps the evil spirits away. The alligator's tooth wards off evil sorcery. Amethyst is known to promote healing, help with spirituality and protect you from evil spirits. The arrowhead is to help keep you safe from hexes."   Looking around, the woman said, "I must go now. I have been here long enough. Take care, cher, and be careful just who you trust."

After the woman left, Josie returned home. When Josie made it home, she found Antoinette LaRue sitting on her front porch. Antoinette walked over and hugged Josie tightly. "Cher, I had a strong feeling that I needed to come see you."

"You are always welcome in this house, Antoinette." Josie opened the front door, "Come in, and I will pour you a strong cup of coffee."

Antoinette noticed the Gris Gris bag around Josie's neck, and her face clouded over as she continued to study it. "A very strong practitioner of voodoo gave you this. Was the one I gave you not enough?"

Waiting for an explanation, Antoinette stared at her friend. "A woman gave it to me. Let's go inside, and I will tell you everything I know."

As Josie made the coffee, she handed Antoinette the Gris Gris bag for closer inspection. "Whoever made this is very intuitive. This is a powerful and yet fascinating, talisman," Antoinette admitted.

Tyler walked in as Josie finished brewing the coffee, "Good morning, Antoinette. What brought you by so early this morning?"

Josie handed Tyler the Gris Gris bag the mystery lady made for him as well. "You and I were given some Gris Gris bags to wear."

Antoinette advised Tyler, "This is not just any Gris Gris bag. These talismans are powerful Gris Gris created by someone who knows their stuff."

Tyler looked at the bag Josie handed him, "Who gave you these?"

Josie replied, "Your mystery lady. We met in the park last night. She shared some very interesting information."

Tyler asked, "Do you think we can trust her?"

Josie shrugged her shoulders before answering, "I am still not sure. Lately, the only two people I trust are you and Antoinette. She never even told me her name."

Antoinette asked, "What did this mystery woman look like?"

 "She appeared to be in her early twenties with the most unusual eyes; they were the prettiest purple, but when I looked deep into her eyes, there was something more in there. I can't explain it, though."

Antoinette listened intently to everything Josie and Tyler told her. "Let me ask around and see if anyone knows about this woman. Someone has to know of her."

After Antoinette had left, all Josie wanted was to fall into a deep sleep for a few hours. She had barely closed her eyes before an image of James floated through her mind; he was calling out for her. An array of emotions pummeled her mind as she tried to make sense of the dream.

Horrid images of James being tortured and his screams reverberated through her mind. Josie bolted upright as tears filled her eyes. She tried to calm her emotions while attempting to dial James's cell. She kept chanting in her mind, "Please be all right; please be all right." As the phone continued to ring, dread settled deep into Josie.

Why would someone seek out James? He and his coven had remained low-key ever since their arrival. Josie called Tyler, "I fear that something bad has happened to James. I had a vision of him calling out for help."

"Text me his address, and I will go check on him."

Josie reminded him, "I am not sure how his coven will accept you."

"I will be careful, don't worry."

Josie paced the floor as she waited to hear from Tyler. It had to be a nightmare. James had never reached out to her before. She didn't even know that he knew how to use telepathy. Most vampires didn't realize that they had these powers.

***

Tyler pulled up to James's house and was surprised. Most of the people living here were well off and influential. The area was filled with antebellum homes that oozed wealth. The houses were not only historic but elegant, not exactly the place you would expect to find a coven of vampires residing.

Tyler got out of his car and took in his surroundings. There was an unsettling stillness about the area, not even a dog barked in the distance. Something in the air had his nerves on edge as if evil lurked nearby. The place was just too quiet.

Tyler sniffed the air. He smelled not only the pollen from the numerous flowers and plants from the many gardens in the area, but also another copious smell just underneath the normal scents. It was that of death.

Just from the sound of Josie's voice earlier, he knew she had seen horrid images that she would rather forget.

Tyler knocked on the front door and waited. He strained his ears as he waited to hear someone coming to answer the door. They couldn't all be asleep.

Tyler peered inside the window, and his gut dropped. It appeared as if a struggle had taken place inside. Walking around back, he noticed that someone had left the back door cracked open. He had never met a trusting vampire in his life. He didn't see one of them leaving the door unlocked, much less open.

Slipping inside, he closed the door. The smell of death, decay, and ash permeated the air inside. A massacre had occurred here.

As he moved deeper inside of the house, he made out blood splatter on the walls and furniture. The bodies of the vampires may have dissipated into the air, but by the amount of blood left on the walls, there was definitely an attack. When he looked closer, he saw the tiny particles of ash floating in the air. The massacre happened recently.

Tyler moved into the bedroom and grimaced at the sight. On the bed was a large man, his body vivisected and dismembered. Whoever did this wanted this person to feel the tortures done to their body.

In the next room was another body. The young woman's face was beaten so badly that her jaw had been broken and hung from her face.

Tyler slipped on a pair of gloves as he moved deeper into the house. Before calling this in, he wanted to search the crime scene for clues as to who did this. He could not let Josie inside of this house. Whoever did this turned this place into not just a crime scene but a slaughterhouse.

The deeper into the house Tyler moved, the more horrific the scenes became. These murders were overkill. In one room, a young woman lay on the floor with her face upward. Whoever did this plucked her eyes out and just discarded them on the floor. Another man's face had been bashed in and his throat slit from ear to ear.

Another young girl's body was covered in bite marks as if several vampires had fed on her at the same time.

Bile made its way up from Tyler's stomach to his throat. A primal feeling of revenge settled over him as he witnessed horrific murder after murder. Adjacent to the feeling of revenge was fear. This same torture could happen to his beloved Josie. This person had no scruples about killing.

As he called in the crime scene, a mixture of feelings ran through his body. All at once, he had a profound feeling of hatred. He had to control his feelings if he wanted to find the person responsible.

Next, he called Josie, "I didn't find James inside the house. I am so sorry, but whoever did this tortured the humans that lived here. The attack was brutal."

"Send me pictures, please, Tyler, so I can see what we are dealing with."

"No, you don't want to see this. You don't want these images in your mind, Josie."

She asked him, "What can I do?"

He tried to soothe her, "I managed to find a few laptops here in the house. I will bring them to you."

Josie sighed, "When you get here, I will go over everything with a fine tooth comb. I can't believe this happened to them."

"I don't understand why this happened. The attack was done for pure torture."

***

Josie mourned the loss of not only James but all those who'd died in that house. Anger and guilt consumed her over the killings. Did James accidentally stumble upon some information for her? Did another coven consider James's coven some sort of threat?

As soon as Tyler came back home, she pored over the laptops he brought. Tyler asked, "Do you think this was a preemptive action to instill fear in you? Perhaps, someone is afraid you or James was close on their trail and attacked."

"I don't know. James hadn't mentioned anything about discovering any information. I honestly didn't think he was interested in helping me. He seemed content to live his life without ruffling any feathers."

Tyler ran his hands through his hair as he contemplated what Josie told him. "You need to be careful how you approach finding out more information from here on out. If they feel that you are on their trail, they will destroy you."

Chapter 55

From the information Josie retrieved from James's laptop, he had indeed stumbled upon some useful information. James was staking out a vampire who hung out near the Zoological Gardens and preyed on the young women who spent time there.

Tonight, Josie planned on hunting him while he searched for prey. More than likely, he wouldn't even notice her. According to James's notes, the vampire stayed too engrossed in the hunt to notice what happened around him.

Tyler warned Josie, "Do not kill this one. If you kill him, his employers will come after you. They will want revenge for his death. If James's notes are accurate, then this particular vampire is important to them."

"I agree. It appears he is one of the vampires capturing young women to be used as blood slaves. However, if I kill him, then it will bring his coven out of hiding."

"It is too dangerous. Perhaps, you can persuade him to share a little more information with you."

"I thought about that. There is also a name that James was researching, Jacque Olivier."

Tyler looked up at Josie, "Joshua changed his last name to Olivier several decades back. He said that it was to pay homage to his master."

"I knew Joshua's surname was Savoie, but I never questioned as to why he changed it. With Joshua, I learned it was better not to ask. He looked up to our master. I truly believe our master was the only person Joshua ever cared for, besides himself."

Tyler announced to Josie, "It looks as if James may have been on to something here. I typed in Jacque Olivier's name and look what came up."

Josie walked up behind Tyler, and a shudder moved through her body. She could barely breathe as she stared at the grainy picture on the screen, "That is the man who turned me. I am sure of it."

The photograph was taken in the late 1890's. Jacque Olivier stood with four other well-dressed business men. Tyler brought up another photo of the same man again, but it was a turn of the century photo. He had a goatee, but there was no mistaking his eyes. Once again, he stood with another man dressed in business attire. This time, however, they stood proudly in front of a hotel. "It appears that Jacque Olivier kept the same name over the years. From what I can ascertain, he is a wealthy member of society in New Orleans."

As Josie read over the research Tyler found on Jacque Olivier, it appeared he stayed involved in various charities and social functions around town. Tyler shared with Josie, "I found some information about Jacque Olivier all the way to the mid-1700's. He has yet to change his name."

Josie and Tyler found various images of Jacque Olivier that spanned the centuries. "We are dealing with an extremely old vampire. Joshua told me that he was the first vampire that our master had turned, and I was the second. The master was selective in whom he turned; yet, I can't help but wonder if he kept to the same practice over the years."

"Jacque Olivier is probably worth billions now. I found several shell corporations that linked back to him."

"Now if only we knew where he lived. I gathered research that showed he moved out of Joshua's family plantation; a woman now owns the plantation."

"Do you know who owns it?"

Josie shook her head, "No, but there must be some information."

"In the morning, I will go to the Clerk of Court. They should have something on the current owner. Someone has to pay the property taxes."

Josie kept researching Jacque Olivier. "Jacque Olivier funded the mayor's last campaign. He was also a huge benefactor in rebuilding New Orleans after Katrina."

Tyler surmised, "So, on the surface, Jacque Olivier comes across as a golden-hearted entrepreneur."

"If we dig deeper, I bet we discover that he is evil through and through."

Tyler's stomach dropped as he pulled up another photo, "This doesn't look good."

Josie looked at the picture and cringed. "Do you think Senator David Landry knows who he is standing next to?"

Instead of answering Josie, Tyler kept staring at the photo. Something about Senator David Landry looked familiar to Tyler; only, he couldn't put a finger on it. "Maybe, Jacque Olivier lined the pockets of politicians and people in power for many years."

Josie nodded her head in agreement, "This particular vampire will have the strength and resources that I cannot even fathom."

A knock at the door caught both Tyler and Josie by surprise. Tyler instructed Josie, "Stay here."

"Like hell."

The mysterious woman smiled at the couple. When Josie opened the door for her, she said, "Somehow I am not surprised to see you here."

"You must know someone with some strong voodoo powers. I was not expecting to counter a spell." After making herself at home, she looked over at Josie, "I am sorry to hear about your friend."

Josie let out a gasp, "How did you know?"

"I knew James. His was a gentle coven, but he asked questions about another group he shouldn't have. Some things are better left alone."

Josie looked at the mystery woman, startled. "But, the only thing James mentioned to me was that a group of mortals freely gave their blood to the vampires."

"That may be, but you should well know, not everything is as it appears."

Tyler asked, "Are you telling me that James stumbled on something that got him, and his entire coven killed?"

"Mais oui. James was a very dear friend, and I came to help you. I have my own resources here in New Orleans."

Josie replied, "I appreciate the help, but you never did tell me who you are."

The mystery woman shook her head, "That is not important. It is best that you don't know my name. Just know that I want to help you find who did this to James."

***

Josie found out from their mystery woman that the vampire she was searching for hung out near Loyola University. She told Josie that this particular vampire was vain and used his good looks to lure women to their demise.

As Josie surveyed the area, she saw a young lady that fit the vampire's type. She wore a tight little T-shirt that barely reached her midriff and snug jeans. Instead of paying attention to her surroundings, the young girl listened intently to whatever music played through her earphones. Even if Josie called out to warn her, she doubted the young girl would hear anything.

There were very few people nearby tonight, which meant that there wouldn't be any witnesses to worry about. As a young girl walked down the street, Josie wondered how long before her vampire made his appearance. If he were a creature of habit, he would make a move soon.

She wanted to stop this particular creature. If what she'd discovered was true, he had preyed on college students for a while now. As soon as the man stepped out of the shadows, Josie knew that she'd found her vampire. The pale skin didn't give him away, but the way he carried himself did. With a strikingly handsome face, he dressed like a predator, all in black.

Josie watched as he sniffed the air to make sure he liked the way his potential prey smelled. As the young woman passed him, a wicked grin formed on his face. He caught the scent of his prey.

The young woman was so engrossed in her music that she never even paid attention to the man walking up behind her. The hunter was so intent on his meal that he didn't notice Josie following him.

With lightning speed, the vampire grabbed the young woman, removed her earphones and whispered in her ear, "You caught my interest, cher. I have not decided if you would make a better meal or perhaps a pet."

Sensing Josie nearby, he tightened his grip on the young woman by drawing her close to his body. In his present position, Josie could not get a good shot of his heart.

If Josie had any hopes of saving this young woman and finding out any pertinent information, she needed to act quickly. She took aim at his shoulder and fired. The vampire grimaced in pain as the silver bullet made its way through his shoulder. He dropped the girl as he gripped his arm.

Josie reached for the young woman and moved her out of the way. She took aim once more, this time firing a bullet into his left knee. He dropped to the ground with a groan escaping his lips. "What do you want with me woman?"

Josie asked him, "Who are you supplying these girls to?"

He laughed. "You may as well kill me now. If I tell you, I am as good as dead anyhow."

Josie fired again. This time into the vampire's right knee. "I will keep firing bullets into your pitiful body until you tell me what I need to know."

The vampire hissed at Josie, "Go to hell, vamp."

Josie laughed at the comment. "I am already there, and so are you." With that remark, Josie sent another bullet into the vampire's stomach. He let out a guttural scream as the pain enveloped him.

He hissed out, "I work for Jacque Olivier."

"Tell me something I don't know. I want to know where his coven is."

Sneering at her he said, "Do you think I know that? Vamp, he keeps himself secluded from others. He is a loner who hires out for his dirty work."

"What about his coven?"

"If he has a coven, I haven't heard about it. There are rumors that he turned only a select few, but I have never seen him with anyone other than his bodyguards."

Josie hissed out, "So, you were selling these poor women as food?"

"He saw a need and filled it. I wish I had been smart enough to do it on my own. Hell, the man is practically sitting on a gold mine."

"Where do you bring the women?"

The vampire hissed out, "I have told you enough."

When Josie fired once more, this bullet grazed the vampire's face. "Where are these women being held?"

"You are the one who freed my previous captives aren't you? You cost me dearly. I should kill you now for the pain they put me through."

"Yes, I am the one who freed those poor women. Now tell me, where is the new location? If not, what they put you through will be nothing compared to what I will do to you."

As Josie took aim, the vampire hissed out, "There is a warehouse on the river that we use now." As he gave Josie the location, she sent the information to Tyler. They needed a plan before moving in. This place would be heavily guarded.

Once Josie had the information she needed from this particular vampire, she fired a bullet into his heart, sending him back to the hell he so richly deserved.

The young woman looked at Josie with tears in her eyes, "Please don't hurt me."

Josie held out her hand and looked into her eyes, "I have no intention of hurting you. Come on, I will walk you home."

By the time Josie delivered the young girl to her house, Josie had wiped her memory clean of tonight's activities.

As Josie made her way home, she studied her surroundings. She had been in this area of New Orleans only a few times. The row of houses was too close together to allow any privacy for vampires to feed without fear of detection.

A woman's scream from one of the houses caught her attention. It was a small muffled cry, but enough to warrant inspection. For a moment, Josie feared that this may be a trap. However, if a woman was in distress, she would never forgive herself for not checking it out.

Josie kept to the shadows, listening for any noises that may be coming from the house. Hearing another muffled scream, Josie cautiously entered the house. The house was too dark. No lights were on. She kept her guard up; only a vampire kept it this dark. A human would at least leave a small lamp on somewhere in the house for light.

The smell of death was heavy in the air. As Josie looked into the living room, she saw what she feared the most. An elderly lady sat in a rocking chair, dead. As Josie walked over to the body for a closer inspection, she saw the two fang marks on the woman's neck.

Two vampires stepped out of the shadows. One of the vampires stood well over six feet tall with long hair that was pulled back, and he was dressed in black. The other vampire was barely six feet tall with various tattoos covering his bald head. Both looked ready for a fight.

They hissed at Josie, exposing their fangs. From behind Josie, a noise caught her attention. The two vampires suddenly appeared jumpy as a man in his early fifties walked into the room. Josie had seen this man at several of the bars she visited, but she couldn't put a name to the face. He wore his usual shark skin suit, but tonight, there was something harsh and uncaring about him.

He ordered the two vampires, "Back down."

The two vampires crossed their arms over their chest, but kept an intense gaze on Josie, waiting to attack without hesitation. These two must be his bodyguards.

"You have been asking questions that are of no concern to you. My employer sent me with a warning

– go back to killing the humans that deserve to die, but leave our kind alone."

"How do you know me?"

He let out a laugh that sent chills up and down Josie's spine. "I have my ways, mon cher. Nothing happens in this city that we don't know about."

"If you know me, then you know that I won't stop looking for the information I need."

"That is what I figured. We cannot let you continue with this quest." With a nod of his head, the two vampires moved in. Josie threw a silver dagger into the first one's chest with complete ease.

The second one pounced and Josie aimed her gun, sending a silver bullet into his chest. With great speed and dexterity, the vampire in charge made a move for the door. He sneered at Josie, with his hand on the door, "You honestly think you can stop me and my kind. We are some of the most powerful vampires here in New Orleans."

Josie couldn't believe the arrogance of this vampire. He actually believed that she would allow him to walk out of this house. Josie took out another silver dagger and aimed it directly at his heart. As the blade sank deep into his chest, the vampire's face morphed into his true being. His fangs elongated as his eyes turn black. He grabbed for the dagger as if he could stop it from making its way deep into his chest. He hissed out, "You will pay for this."

Josie sneered down at the dying vampire. "But, it won't be you who seeks out revenge, now will it?"

The vampire dropped to his knees before exploding into a pile of ash.

***

While Tyler paced, Josie gave him a recount of what happened. "I don't like this one bit. Don't let your guard down, ever." Sweeping her into his arms, he added, "I need you too much in my life to lose you."

"You are my very life Tyler. Do not worry, I am careful. I treat even the shadows as possible attackers."

Chapter 56

Josie sat quietly at a table near the back of the bar. She sipped the concoction the bartender gave her; however, she was not in the mood for alcohol tonight. She kept her head down as people passed by. Tonight, she dressed in an oversized sweatshirt and jeans. The hood of the sweatshirt helped hide her hair and eyes from the others in the bar.

She didn't want to be recognized. She kept a watchful eye on the man at the bar. He had his raven black hair pulled into a low ponytail. The hairstyle emphasized his steel gray eyes and handsome facial features. As usual, he wore all black, down to his dress shoes. A young girl, barely eighteen, kept him company.

The young girl hung onto the man's every word, smiling ecstatically at his jokes. Yes, this girl was definitely in the prime of her youth and exactly what he liked.

He kept a fake smile plastered on his face the entire night that disgusted Josie. This vampire manipulated this young girl.

Josie looked at her watch once more and winced. It was only one a.m. She hoped that he wrapped this up soon and headed out. She was ready to put this masquerade to an end.

Just as she thought they would never leave, the couple stood up. Josie waited until they had walked out the door before she followed them. As they walked down the street, Josie slipped into the alley near the bar and jumped to the roof. It would be easier to follow them from up above to keep from being seen.

The man led the young girl into an alleyway and whispered, "I need just a taste of you, cher."

No sooner had they turned down the alley, than his eyes reddened and sharp fangs extended. The young girl gasped in shock as she tried to back away from him. He pulled her closer, moving to sink his fangs into her neck.

He tilted her head to the side as she tried to push him away. Josie dropped quietly from the roof and landed behind the vampire.

As if expecting her arrival, he smirked, "I was wondering when you would show up."

Josie, not bothering to answer, aimed her gun at the vampire. He shook his head, "I wouldn't kill me just yet. I have answers that you are searching for. You have been following me for a while now. I left enough bread crumbs so that you would seek me out."

Josie asked, "And why would you seek me out?"

The vampire let the young girl go. "Leave me. You will remember none of this."

The vampire's actions surprised Josie. She hadn't expected him to let his prey go so easily. She surveyed the area to make sure that this wasn't a trap. He assured Josie, "Don't worry, we are alone." He looked at Josie intently. "We are the same, cursed by our existence."

***

As Josie made her way down Julia Street still in disbelief of what had just happened, a sense of apprehension washed over her. The streets were quiet and empty; the only sound echoing through the night were her footsteps. Yet, she couldn't shake the feeling that she was being followed.

It was barely three o'clock in the morning; very few people were out in this section of New Orleans. Still, she swore someone watched her every move. She felt their eyes on her back.

In the darkness of the night, she surveyed her surroundings. On a park bench just a few feet from her, a homeless man slept. Even from here, she smelled his filthy clothes and the alcohol heavy on his breath.

Up above her, she heard the rustling of the leaves. Since there was no breeze to speak of, it caught her attention. Suddenly, a thin vampire dropped from the tree. Without thinking, Josie threw a silver dagger into the vampire's heart.

Unexpectedly, the homeless man jumped up, ready to attack. With a quick flick of her wrist, Josie sent a dagger into his heart.

Another vampire hiding in the trees panicked. It realized that they were now the prey, no longer the predators and took off. Josie aimed her gun and shot the creature in the back, sending the vampire sprawling to the ground.

In an attempt to fight Josie, the creature attacked the air with its long nails. Josie laughed at its futile attempts. She aimed her gun once more and sent a silver bullet straight into the vampire's chest.

She must be close to the truth, a truth that someone did not want her knowing. She was still unsure about trusting Keith, but he may be her only chance of surviving this.

Chapter 57

A cold shadow passed over Antoinette. For no apparent reason, it became extremely difficult for her to catch her breath. It was as though someone had placed their hand over her mouth, trying to smother her.

Josie called out, "Antoinette, are you there?"

Antoinette looked at the phone in her hands as she took a deep breath against the waves of darkness trying to overpower her. "I'm sorry. My mind wandered for a moment."

Josie felt the change in Antoinette's emotions, "For a moment, I thought we were cut off."

"No, but it felt as if someone walked over my grave. I better go for now."

"Antoinette, are you sure you are okay? I never meant to bring any danger into your life."

Antoinette let out a deep sigh. "Josie, you didn't bring danger in my life. I believe that whatever is happening just may be my destiny."

With that, Antoinette said goodbye and hung up the phone. Leaning back against the couch, she looked outside and saw the storm brewing. It was an omen; trouble was soon to come. Suddenly, a premonition hit Antoinette. She found herself standing in front of an antebellum home, one much older than those she visited. There were trapped souls wandering the grounds. Something evil kept these poor spirits earthbound. There were too many to count. The sadness that followed them was almost overpowering. Whoever lived there was of the darkest evil.

Antoinette tried to find out more, but something blocked her. Without warning, Antoinette felt herself being transported to another location. She was in front of Josie's house, but a dark shape lurked near the bayou.

Someone, or something, was watching the house that had a profound connection to the house. She felt the hatred for anyone living in the house emanating from this person.

She must warn Tyler and Josie. Antoinette needed to place a few more protection spells around the house and her dear friends.

Feeling suffocated inside her tiny little home, Antoinette walked out onto her back porch. As she looked out over the water, her mind lingered on what the spirits tried to tell her. They warned her about an impending danger, but there was something more.

Ever since Josie and Tyler moved into the house, she'd felt something evil lurking about.

The wind blowing off the bayou carried with it the scent of rain. Her heart sped up at the thought of the impending showers. A good thunderstorm would help calm her. As a child, she loved a rainstorm; the more turbulent it was, the better.

The earth seemed to come alive after a downpour. It reminded her of a house getting a good spiritual cleansing.

***

The new moon cast its glow on the land, aiding his way to her house. As he neared the quaint little house, he was pleased to see that it sat all alone, surrounded by tall trees dripping with low hanging moss that stirred in the night's breeze.

Exhilaration flowed through him as he caught her scent. Tonight, she would be the one to quench his cursed hunger. Her sweet flesh would feed his bloodlust. No, she would not escape him tonight; his hunger was too strong.

His breath quickened as he listened for her movement. His yellow eyes glowed against the darkness of the night. The need for blood tormented him without mercy tonight. She had alerted him to her presence earlier.

A movement near the house caught his attention. He stepped behind a tree and waited. He kept his eyes steady and saw only a cat lurking about. Perhaps she had already gone to bed.

As if the cat sensed something evil lurked in the darkness, it hissed, arching its back as it stared toward the trees.

The back door opened. He watched in earnest as she stepped outside. He moved quietly as his sinister plan took shape. She walked gracefully down to the bayou, and before she could scream, he pounced. As he stared down at her body, excitement grew inside of him.

He smelled her terror. The tantalizing odor of fear sent blood rushing through his veins. The moonlight bathed her face so that he saw her stark terror staring back at him.

As she drew a breath to scream, he lashed out and slashed open her chest. Paralyzed in fear, she stared up at him trying to make sense of what couldn't be happening to her. Her screams sounded like pitiful moans whispering in the stillness of the night. His hot breath was foul on her body.

Her flesh would satisfy his latest envie, a taste he never grew tired of. Unable to wait any longer, he lunged, sinking his teeth deep into her throat. Her hot sweet blood gushed into his mouth.

As he made his way home, past nearby houses with people sleeping, a smirk formed on his face. These people sleeping innocently in their homes had no idea that evil just passed within their midst.

***

Tyler heard the call come in over the police scanner. At first, he thought he'd heard the dispatcher wrong; a young woman was mauled to death by a wild animal. When Detective Newman was called to the scene, his worst fears were confirmed.

How did something get to Antoinette? Her house and property had protection spells cast.

Tyler turned the car around as an overpowering urge to protect Josie washed over him. He needed to tell her face to face.

***

As Josie walked down the street, a gut wrenching pain wracked her body. The pain became almost unbearable. Suddenly, the pain disappeared and was replaced by a feeling of loss, one that she couldn't explain.

Josie tried to close her mind to the images that flashed through her mind. Anger quickly replaced the sorrow that overcame her. She called out, "You better get ready you son of a bitch. I will make you pay for this.

Mark my words, I will find you and when I do, your time on earth is done."

***

Detective Newman looked down at the blood-soaked woman and said a Novena for her departed soul. She was so badly torn apart, she no longer looked human.

The responding officer walked over to Newman and said, "I have never seen anything like this before. Her throat has literally been ripped out."

With Newman's voice full of sorrow, "I have."

The young officer looked over at him, "Do you think this was the same thing that left behind the other bodies?"

"Dr. Ortego has to make the final determination, but yeah, I do."

"Just what kind of crazy, mixed up world do we live in?"

Newman ran his hands through his hair as he contemplated the question. "We are not dealing with a rabid dog, but something much worse. I am no longer sure what is real and not."

The young officer nodded his head in agreement. "It is as if all the horror movies filmed have come to life here."

Chapter 58

He fell to the shower floor, allowing the coolness of the tile to seep into his heated body. Exhaustion consumed him; he was ready for the transformation to be finalized. He forced himself to remain still as the pain of the transformation wracked his body.

Once he returned to human form, he turned on the water and showered. There would be consequences for what he did, but he must draw the vamp out. Killing the voodoo woman would cause the vamp to seek retribution.

Now, he must make plans. His anger continued to burn at the mere thought of this vamp. She was ruining all that they'd worked so hard for. Up until she became nosey, no one even suspected that he ran a blood slave market.

As it stood, Detective Newman questioned the wild animal attacks. A rogue Rougarou needed to be tended to. He had a suspicion of who it was. If correct in his assumptions, Ezrielle would pay him dearly for ridding her of the problem.

In the master bedroom, he heard his wife wake. The silly woman never once suspected he had a true dark side. On the nights that his body cried out in hunger for the taste of fresh blood and flesh, he drugged her.

She was so afraid of his every move that she dared not disobey him.

Over the years, he considered showing her the full extent of his secrets, but the foolish woman could not be trusted. He saw her eyes flutter open when he returned home from satisfying his jaded appetites, but she knew better than to question his whereabouts. She never once acknowledged witnessing him returning in the early morning hours. Questioning him would only bring down his wrath.

Chapter 59

Josie's hands gripped the steering wheel of the Audi R8 tighter as the headlights cut a narrow path through the Louisiana night. She stepped harder on the gas, wanting to be done with what she had set out to do. All the twists in the road seemed endless in the darkness.

As she walked through the morgue, the smell of death enveloped her. Tyler had arranged for her to view Antoinette's body without anyone asking questions. She and Tyler befriended a vampire who worked in the morgue at night. Between him and another vampire who worked at the funeral home, they had an unlimited supply of blood to feed on.   Working in the morgue, he found out which bodies were disease free, and he let his friend know. They had a nice, profitable side business going on. Josie saw no harm in what they did. The humans were already dead; no one was killed for their blood. Besides, the blood would be discarded during embalming.

It surprised her that Dr. Ortego set it all up, but he swore he wanted to help. Dr. Ortego was determined to find out what made vampire blood so special; he was searching for a cure. His wife's cancer was progressing at a slower rate now and Josie feared he was feeding her vampire blood to slow down the progress until he could complete his research. Josie and numerous others begged him not to turn his wife. If he truly loved her, he wouldn't inflict this life sentence on her. Immortality had a hefty price to pay.

As she stared down at her friend's body, the grief became unbearable. Antoinette's head barely hung on to her body. Significant damage was done to her poor body. She had not expected this extent of raw hatred to be taken out on her friend. What used to be the flesh of Antoinette's neck was ragged and torn. The killer was in a frenzy to kill her. He didn't care to take his time.

Josie's brow furrowed as her pinched face continued to observe Antoinette's mangled body. All that remained of her friend was this husk of a body lying on the cold steel table in eternal sleep. It should have been her that the Rougarou killed; she was what he wanted. Why did it have to hunt down Antoinette? She never meant anyone any harm.

Josie was so wrapped up in her emotions she never heard the human enter. She knew right away who he was; she'd watched him a lot lately.

***

Newman looked down at his watch and groaned. It was past midnight, and he was still working on the latest murder case. Newman had no proof, but this killing had a personal feeling to it, very personal.

Earlier, Dr. Ortego sent him a text message that he had the DNA results, but he wouldn't be happy. Dupre went home to spend some time with his wife, but Newman couldn't put the autopsy report out of his mind. With the confirmation that another Rougarou hunted in the streets of New Orleans, he wanted to compare the latest victim's injuries to the others.

As soon as he walked into the autopsy room, he stopped dead in his tracks. Standing over the body was a vamp. Newman could tell she was mourning over this individual. There was a grim expression on her almost lifeless face. The raven black hair made her pale skin translucent under the harsh morgue lights. He called out, "What the hell are you doing here?"

She confessed to him, "I came to say goodbye to a friend, Detective Newman."

Newman found it surprising this woman knew his name. "You have me at a disadvantage. You seem to know who I am, but I have no idea who you are."

The woman shook her head, "My name is of no importance to you."

"I am not so sure about that. I could haul you in for contaminating evidence. How did you know the body was here?"

She smiled weakly at him, "I have my own sources here in the city."

Newman was in no mood to play games, "What do your sources say about this murder then?"

"Antoinette was getting too close to a particular individual." Letting out a sigh, she looked over at him, "I believe there is a human trafficking ring run by vampires here in New Orleans. I suspect the person in charge of this particular ring has several influential politicians and businessmen in their hip pocket."

Newman looked surprised. "I haven't heard a whisper of any such ring."

"Why do you think that is? They have been very careful in keeping their agenda hidden. Trust me, we have released a few of their blood slaves but have been unable to stop them. As soon as we release the blood slaves, they just capture more."

Newman tried to get her help. "If you have an informant, it would be nice of you to share, especially if it helped to solve the murder of your friend." In a threatening demeanor, he added, "Trust me, the last thing you want is an obstruction charge hanging over you."

She just laughed, "You can do your own detective work. You are good, so I am sure you will get the information you need." Shaking her head in disapproval, she added, "You should know that I don't scare easy. Making veiled threats will do you no good."

Newman threw the autopsy report over to her. She caught it in midair with a questioning look on her face. "This is the autopsy report on your friend. You saw what this creature did to your friend, but perhaps, you should read it." She stared at him with an icy glare. "Maybe after reading what happened to her, you will tell me who in the hell you are and why you are here looking at my murder victim?"

She didn't even flinch at the anger thrown her way, "I don't know what…"

"Do not even bother to try and bullshit me. I want answers, and I want them now."

She looked at him with contempt in her eyes, contempt for him or what happened to her friend; Newman wasn't sure. "Trust me; you are better off not knowing all the answers right now. Soon, I will answer your questions. The time isn't right. Too many innocent people have died already, and I refuse to have your blood on my hands as well."

Newman watched this vampire in front of him. She was not what he expected a vampire to be. Vampires were supposed to be cold, heartless, bloodsucking creatures from hell, but this one seemed to care about innocent people dying.

Chapter 60

The Louisiana night surrounded Josie like a wet
blanket. She planned to use tonight for surveillance,
but she warned the others to be prepared for
anything.

The old plantation was imposing in the moonlight. It
was built in the late 1800's, but Keith warned her that
it had been retrofitted with the latest technology.

The plantation consisted of almost one hundred acres
of land. Fortress like gates, armed guards, and the
perimeters were heavily monitored by vile little
creatures called homunculi. The creatures were good
for only one thing, taking orders. To kill them, you had
to incinerate the little bastards. If you cut off their
head, they continued fighting; the removal of an
appendage did not work either.

Without warning, a vision of Antoinette's death
flashed through her mind. She saw the large shape of
a Rougarou feasting off of her friend. She watched in
horror as he ripped her body apart. Josie felt the pain
as the creature's long, sharp teeth sank into
Antoinette's body. She heard the creature growl in
satisfaction as his hunger was sated. Repulsed by the
vision, she forced the image from her mind.

Josie pushed the pain of her friend's death deep down inside of her. She must turn that pain into anger if she wanted to stop the evil from taking over this place.

That was when she saw him. Why was he here? Was he one of the influential people the master had in his pocket? When she saw him shift into a Rougarou, she immediately knew he was the one who killed Antoinette. This went far deeper than any of them had ever suspected.

She took a picture of Senator Thomas Chaisson leaving the house and then changing into Rougarou form. Thank goodness, she had lightning speed and could do it before it was too late.

After sending the picture to Tyler and Newman, she called Detective Newman. "I have a lead for you, but you should check your text messages first."

"Hold on a moment, it just came in." Josie heard Newman's sharp intake of breath, "Holy shit, is that who I think it is?"

"That is exactly who it is. If he is involved, then there is no telling how many others are involved as well."

Chapter 61

Newman looked across the bayou once more. He still found it strange how this investigation had played out. The department had teamed up with a vampire to help bring down a ring of vampires abducting humans who were used as blood slaves. Then there was also a rogue Rougarou with his own agenda.

The coven's walls were crumbling, but so far, none of the members wanted to lose their power. Tonight, Newman led one team to seek out the Rougarou while Josie and her team's mission was to stop the vampire and his coven. If this went well, both teams would be successful.

Leaning back against his SUV, Newman called out to the police officers, "All right, we are getting ready to move in. I want each of you to remember that what you are about to see will have you questioning your beliefs. We have no idea what we are truly up against. We have seen what the creature has left behind, and we know that those deaths appeared to be caused by a rabid dog. It is believed a Rougarou did these killings. However, since no one has seen one of these mythical creatures, we need to be prepared. You heard what Office Tyler LeBlanc had to say about these Rougarou, but let's not forget to use common sense as well."

Newman still wasn't sure how Officer LeBlanc knew as much as he did, but he had an exceptional police record, so at this time he wasn't ready to question his research. Something about Officer LeBlanc's demeanor had Newman questioning whether the young officer had more than a little experience with the Rougarou. His grandmother would consider LeBlanc an old soul. Something about the man, despite his present age, made him appear older than he was.

As the police officers prepared to move in, Newman continued with his speech, "We have been warned that a voodoo priestess controls these Rougarou, if not all then most. Just because the person may appear to be a woman in front of you, please remember that evil can indeed come in the form of a male or female. You cannot doubt yourself when facing the 'enemy'."

One of the young officers stepped forward and asked, "Sir, are you telling us that you believe we are about to fight a Rougarou? Those were fairy tales most of us were told as kids to get us to behave."

Newman nodded his head, "As a matter of fact, I do believe that we are up against a Rougarou."

Another of the officers stepped forward, "Well, sir, have you noticed the moon?"

"I know it is a full moon, but we have a job to do. Just aim and shoot. If they are coming at you, take no chances and at least maim the creature."

"And what are we hunting down these creatures with?"

Newman announced to the group, "Each of you have been issued special guns and silver bullets. You each have a Gris Gris bag and a crucifix. Keep your rosary handy at all times."

"My Grand'Mere talked about the Rougarou when I was little, but I never believed the stories."

Newman suggested to him, "Well, we are about to find out if this is a fairy tale or a nightmare. Just remember that whatever it is we are up against needs to be taken out any way possible."

"Sir, did you need any of us to patrol the bayou by boat?"

Newman nodded his head, "I will need some volunteers to man the boats. We also need some of you to patrol the banks, as well. Remember to stay in a group and under no circumstances should you separate."

One of the men called out, "We could only round up about four boats, sir. Most of the boats are being used for the vampire coven."

Several of the men grumbled about the lack of boats. "We will be okay with what we have. Our fight will take place in the marshlands rather than on the water."

Newman addressed the men, "We are going in by foot. The last thing we need is the sound of an engine alerting anyone of our presence."

One of the younger officers mumbled, "It sure would be nice if we knew what to expect. I don't like that all we have to go on is myth and legend."

Newman warned the men, "According to Officer LeBlanc, these Rougarou are almost indestructible in their altered state. They are more susceptible to death when in human form. However, I don't see that happening tonight for sure. The silver bullets were designed to kill these creatures, but they have not been tested. Do not worry about wasting any ammunition, blow this creature to hell."

 "If this thing could be killed easier when he is in his human form, why don't we wait until daylight?"

Newman shook his head, "According to LeBlanc, that is a myth. The really old Rougarou can shape shift at their convenience."

Another officer retorted, "Plus, if he is in human form, we have no way in hell of knowing who the Rougarou is."

Newman reminded the men, "You must be careful. Remember with this being a full moon, this creature's hunger is in full force. He is out hunting." Newman looked at the officers surrounding him and continued, "And I know none of you want to be this creature's next meal. Keep in mind that his night vision is better than ours. After all, he escaped us before in the dark."

One of the men asked, "Will these Gris Gris bags work? Didn't he already kill one voodoo priestess?"

Newman ran his hands through his hair. He heard the fear in some of the officers' voices. "To be honest with you, we don't know anything for certain. Yes, Antoinette, wore a powerful Gris Gris bag when she died. Somehow, the creature managed to break through the protection spells she had around her place. No one is sure how it managed that. There are rumors that the Rougarou is a man cursed by a voodoo priestess here in New Orleans. That means this particular voodoo priestess is extremely powerful. She would certainly know how to counter protection spells and Gris Gris bags."

A low lying fog crept over the marshland, curling around the trees like snakes. The men tried their best to ignore the dampness seeping into their clothes. The cloying touch added to their uneasiness as they gazed into the humid darkness. They were looking for an evil that until now only existed in their nightmares.

Suddenly, an owl screeched up above causing each person's heart to lodge in their throats. The young officer next to Newman complained, "This is not how I envisioned my career on the police force."

As Newman swatted at a mosquito, he replied, "Trust me son, this is not how any of us pictured our career."

One of the older officers added, "The one thing we should have remembered was some damn mosquito repellant. These blood suckers are out in full force tonight. Searching for some Rougarou is bad enough, but now, we have to deal with these damn things, as well."

Another officer commented, "Repellant would be our downfall. The scent tends to carry out here in the swamp. If this creature is anything like a wolf, it will catch the scent easily."

The older officer scoffed, "At least the mosquitoes would be tolerable."

As a snake slithered by, an officer barked, "Mosquitos aren't the only things out tonight." Up ahead they heard a snake slide into the water. Just the thought of running into a lethal cottonmouth sent a shiver of fear down Newman's spine. "The swamp is full of snakes."

Dragging his shirt sleeve across his face, Newman countered, "I don't know how these people survive living in the swamps with their shotgun houses and no air conditioning. It is so muggy out here that even at night it is hard to breathe!"

One of the men snapped, "When you are raised that way, you get used to it. For most of us here, it is a way of life. Some have no choice; they are too poor to live anywhere else. Hell, man, some of the older folks just consider themselves lucky to have a roof over their head."

A noise up ahead caught Newman's attention. He whispered out, "Look! Something tells me that isn't a regular swamp dweller we are looking at." Up ahead, they could see what appeared to be a large animal with thick brown hair covering its entire body. Newman could barely believe his eyes. The creature was walking on its hind legs. Its face was part-man and part-wolf, as well. Its yellow eyes glowed in the darkness of the night.

Newman grabbed his gun and aimed. He fired all six rounds into the creature moving towards them. One of the officers shouted out, "I know I heard the impact, but the thing is still coming toward us."

Newman ordered, "Everyone take aim and fire."

One of the men called out, "If this doesn't stop him, we are all goners."

Without warning, the large beast threw back its massive head and howled into the wind. Suddenly, it charged at them. "I don't understand how the hell this creature can still move with all the ammunition we fired into it. It doesn't even appear to slow it down."

Newman simply replied, "We aren't dealing with a normal creature, but it is slowing down."

***

As the bullets slammed into his body, he cried out, "Ezrielle, help me."

Blood flowed down his body, but still, he pushed on. He would kill these men who dared to follow him. He fell to the ground as the strength drained from his body. Was this how his life would end? He still had so much he wanted to do. Why wasn't Ezrielle coming for him? He always treated her better than any of her other Rougarou. Had he not been her most faithful lover?

***

As they made their way to the vampire coven, Josie felt the negative energy surround her. She forced her body to relax and concentrated on the task at hand. She needed to center that anger into stopping this creature for good. The closer they were to the plantation, the nature, and the scenery took on an ominous appearance. Even the vegetation around here seemed to hold secrets.

With each step they took towards the old plantation home, danger surrounded them. Evil lived in the very air they breathed. Tonight, they would battle an ancient evil, one that would refuse to leave this earth. No, this evil was determined to fill the earth with hate and discontent.

Jacque Olivier was an evil man. His black soul had embraced the darkness for far too long. He would be incredibly strong on this plane. Josie hoped that God was on her side tonight. She would need the strength of God's light if she wanted to defeat this evil adversary.

She looked over to Tyler and was glad that he had insisted on being with her tonight, instead of with the other cops. He had briefed them beforehand on everything they would need to know when fighting the Rougarou. With him by her side, there was no way they could lose. Josie announced to Tyler, "I want to finish this, tonight."

Tyler reminded her, "Even if we do stop this one human trafficking ring, there will always be another."

"That may be, but I can't bear knowing that this man may still walk this earth. He must be stopped before his powers strengthen even more." Josie looked at Tyler with coldness in her eyes, "Thank you for coming with me. You must remember to kill every creature that you see. You must kill them mercilessly, or they will kill you."

Tyler took her in his arms and kissed her, "Don't worry, my love. I have no qualms about killing these creatures."

"I just worry that if they sense you it will put them on high alert."

Tyler shifted into a more predatory form; his long nails and fangs emerged, "I will be okay, but you must be careful, as well. They know you are after their master by now."

Josie adjusted the sword strapped to her back as they continued on. Dressed in black, they were well equipped for the task at hand. They had several clips of ammo and sheaths with swords. This journey started as a vendetta against her master, but now, it had become so much more.

Without warning, a vampire dropped to the ground from a tree. The vampire peered at Josie with hatred showing in his eyes. In one quick move, she swiped the vampire's legs from under him and in a flash drew a silver sword she had concealed across the creature's throat. With cold calmness, Josie watched as the vampire burst into dust.

A pleased grin formed across Josie's face as she prepared for the next battle. She looked over at Tyler and stated, "That was satisfying. I am ready to see what else they try to throw our way."

Tyler peered into the darkness and shared with her, "I don't think the other attacks will be quite that easy."

Tyler worried about the danger that was to come. Josie and Tyler both sniffed the air. Josie confirmed, "Vampires are definitely present, but there is something else also."

Tyler nodded his head in agreement, "I smell humans, some are near death, but there is something else that I haven't smelled in a long time. It is homunculi. It appears that your master is indeed in allegiance with the voodoo witch who turned me."

Josie cupped Tyler's face in her hands, "If she is there I promise you that I will do my best to destroy her." Josie sniffed the air again. "Rougarou are also present, so maybe your scent will not throw them off."

The plantation was once impressive in its grandeur. However, the evil living inside destroyed its beauty. The Rougarou, patrolling the grounds, caught their scent and came charging on all fours. Without hesitation, they fired two rounds at each Rougarou. The creatures had expected the attack and avoided the bullets, sending dirt and grass into the air. The next two shots found their mark, killing the Rougarou. As they died, they transformed from Rougarou to dead men.

As they made their way to the front entrance, three more Rougarou attacked. In mere seconds, they were taken out. The shotgun blasts sent pieces of fur over the grounds.

As they readied themselves for another attack, they slowly walked up the steps. Tyler whispered, "Remember that a mere gunshot will not kill the homunculi."

Josie took out her small crossbow. "The arrows are treated so be careful. Once they hit their mark, the homunculi will start to burn from the inside out."

Tyler took his small crossbow out, "It is too bad that we didn't get to test this first, but this should kill the annoying little bastards."

Josie sniffed the air before moving in and held out her hand. "Wait, Tyler, we need to head upstairs first."

Tyler scaled up the building using his sharp claw-like nails. Josie quickly leapt to the second floor balcony. They slipped in through one of the balcony doors and found themselves in an elegantly furnished room. Josie drew out her gun and readied it when she sensed someone in the room. A large vampire burst through a closet. He stood well over six feet tall with bulging muscles and his coal black eyes shining red. The creature in front of her looked more like a raging psychotic beast than a vampire. As it charged them, Tyler fired his gun with expert precision. This particular vampire was difficult to kill. It had taken four bullets before it returned to hell. As they made their way through the second floor, God must have been on their side. Each shot was true to its aim, hitting each vampire directly in the heart.

One of the vampires moved down the hall with gymnastic moves, avoiding each of the bullets. Tired of playing with it, Josie took out her small crossbow and tried the arrow on this creature. Within seconds, the creature was hissing in pain as it burned from the inside out. While the creature hissed, Tyler fired a silver bullet into its heart.

As Josie entered a room to the right, a vamp dropped down from the ceiling, landing on Josie. Josie struggled to free her small silver dagger from her waistband. Tyler moved in, lifted the creature off of Josie and tore her head from her body in one fluid movement. As Tyler tossed the vamp's head, Josie stabbed the dagger into her heart.

Suddenly, another vampire flew past them much like a predatory bird, colliding into Tyler. As Tyler fought off the vampire attacking him, another lunged at Josie with its talons out. Josie aimed a round of silver bullets into the vampire before turning to the other attacking Tyler.

The two looked as if they could be martial artists performing a show instead of attacking each other.

The vampire fighting Tyler had just as much grace and power as he. As soon as Josie had a clear shot, she fired a bullet into the vampire, sending him back to the hell he belonged in.

When Josie entered the next room, she was surprised by the conditions. In the center of the room was a large cage with ten humans held captive. From the looks of the place and prisoners, they had been kept in abject conditions. Gathering from the filth on their bodies and grease in their hair, they weren't allowed to bathe in a long time. What remained of their clothes was so dirty that they were void of color. The room was full of dirty dishes and cups. The cage had one cot and one filthy blanket. Josie was surprised that the prisoners hadn't died of disease before now.

One of the younger girls held out her hand, "Please, do not hurt us."

Josie shook her head, "We are not here to hurt you. Before we can set you free, though, we must make sure that the rest of the vampires are killed."

One of the women stood up, "They are probably in the ballroom. Several of the prisoners were brought down earlier for a 'snack.'"

As Tyler and Josie made their way downstairs, a man stepped out from the shadows. It was the man she had despised for over a century. Amusement glittered in his eyes as he stared hard at Josie, "I see that you are still a dark vision of loveliness, mon cher."

With a smirk on his face, "All those years ago, I thought you were just what my Joshua needed." Stepping even closer to the stairs, he asked, "Why must you punish us so? After all, I did so much for you. Didn't I give you a better life?"

Josie hissed at her master. "A better life! You think you gave me a better life?"

"My child, I gave you immortality."

Josie hissed under her breath at his arrogance, "You gave my soul to the devil himself."

As Josie made her way over to him, a vampire bodyguard stepped in front of him with great speed. With one clean blow, Josie removed the vampire's head. Next, she took the blade of the sword and plunged it into his heart twisting it with a vengeance. The dead vampire's body burst into ash.

Keeping her sword pointed at her master, she moved slowly toward him. He laughed, "My child, did Joshua teach you nothing? You cannot kill me. I will live forever."

With a snap of his fingers, the homunculi came toward them. The ghastly little beasts charged them with a speed she didn't think they could possess. They took out their arrows and fired at the vile creatures. One by one, they dropped to the floor, all the while squealing like pigs.

The master vampire looked over at Josie, "I see that you have done your research. I assume that your friend here," nodding towards Tyler, "told you about the voodoo priestess who cursed him and her other minions. She is the one who gave me the homunculi along with other creatures, including the Rougarou guarding the area."

Josie replied, "I knew that you sought her out for your own Rougarou."

"Oh, my child, there is still so much that you don't know." Looking at Josie he said, "I see that you are much like me and prefer the dangerous type. We are not that different." He gave her a wicked smile before continuing, "Soon the final battle will begin. If I were you, I would stop this foolishness of yours and come back into the folds of your family." Spreading his arms wide, he said, "I am sure that your brothers and sisters will welcome you back."

The surrounding vampires moved closer, hissing with their fangs elongated. "This will be the final battle Master."

Josie and Tyler both aimed their guns, the clips fully loaded. They wouldn't have time to reload. It would be a battle of speed and efficiency. Josie said a quick prayer that God would truly be on their side. Tyler would go after her master while Josie worked on sending the others back to hell.

God must have been on their side as one by one Josie sent the vampires back to hell. The smell of ash was heavy in the air. As each of the master's children was sent back to the fiery pits of hell, Tyler took aim and sent an arrow into his heart. His cries of anguish and pain echoed through the plantation. The sound coming from the master vampire sent shivers down Tyler's spine.

After the fight was over Josie looked back at the plantation as they left. Tyler pulled her in his arms and told her, "It's over my love. Your master is no longer. He finally met someone who was stronger than him, and yet, in the end, it turned out to be a child he made."

Josie looked up at Tyler, "Let's go home. I am ready to put this mess behind me." Kissing him, "Thank you for helping me to kill my own master. I promise to help you do the same."

Sweeping her into his arms, "You are what is important to me, Josie. We will get our chance."

Epilogue

Gabriella watched as Josie and Tyler made their way home. She was certain now that she had made a wise decision to enlist their help in the quest of Good versus Evil. The battle lines were clearly drawn, and Satan had welcomed even more demons into his fold.

Gabriella squeezed Antoinette's hand, "I told you not to worry; your friends would be okay."

Antoinette had tears in her eyes at the sight of Josie and Tyler, "I was just so afraid that they would both die tonight."

***

As Josie made her way up to the front porch, she gasped when she saw Antoinette's spirit, and the mystery woman were waiting for their return. Antoinette floated over to her friends, wrapping them in her warmth, "I was so worried about you two." Antoinette turned towards Gabriella, "I would like to introduce you to Gabriella."

Gabriella stepped forward, "I have a proposition for the both of you, but first, let me tell you a little bit about myself. I am one of the Powers. With regards to the Celestial Hierarchy of Angels, we tend to hold one of the most dangerous tasks, maintaining the border between Heaven and Earth. We are constantly on guard for demonic attacks. We have been appointed by God to fight against the evil spirits and to defeat any wicked plans."

"We also ensure that when souls leave the mortal world they reach heaven safely; demons are always on the lookout to steal as many souls from us as possible. Unfortunately, we have several fallen who have joined the ranks of Satan."

Josie looked at her in amazement, "That was why you knew so much."

Gabriella nodded her head in agreement, "I have been watching the both of you now for a while. I have been given approval to offer you a chance to redeem your souls if you help us in our quest."

Josie looked over at Tyler, with excitement in her eyes. She had always feared that God considered her a lost soul and turned his back on her. Now, she knew that He was all forgiving and was giving her a chance to redeem herself. He took her hand in his and squeezed it, "What do we need to do to help you?"

"There will be a meeting soon that you must attend. It is imperative for your souls to be saved that you do not give in to temptation and cross over to the dark side. Once Satan and his minions know you joined our ranks, the temptation will be great." Gabriella turned to Tyler, "This will be especially hard for you I am afraid. Ezrielle still walks this earth, and she is but a slave to the Dukes of Hell. Her powers are growing. As of yet, we have been unable to defeat her. Tonight, a severe blow was made to her; several of her Rougarou and followers were killed, but with great ease, she can make more."

Josie asked, "Why has it been so hard to locate her?"

Gabriella admitted to her, "We know about the entrance to her world; unfortunately, she cast a spell surrounding her grounds to keep it hidden. Her evil is spreading. The surrounding area of the swamp is dying, and that makes it easier for us to pinpoint where she is. Time is of the essence now; we believe she is on the verge of opening the gates of hell. When that happens, it will be a hard battle to win."

Suddenly, Antoinette jumped up and ran to the perimeters of the woods. She called out into the darkness, "Rougarou, I know that you are watching. No more will I allow you to terrorize my friends." In one swift movement, she hovered over the creature, "I fear you not."

Antoinette called up her powers, summoning the creatures in the trees, "This one means harm on your master. End his life now!"

***

The Rougarou watched as creatures emerged from the oak trees, their long, taloned arms reaching for him.

As he took off into the darkness of the night, they swooped out to drag him into the tree where he was swallowed whole. Antoinette walked over to the tree and gently caressed it, "You must remember to protect these grounds even after I am gone. Their lives depend on it." The trees gently bowed to their master as they lay in wait for the next presence of danger.